Securing the Bag and His Heart

By Kyeate

Connect with Kyeate

Facebook: Kyeate DaAuthor, Kyeate Holt, Kyewritez & Thingz

Instagram: KyeWritez

Twitter: Adjustnmykrown

Novanna

The ride back was silent, which it was something that I liked after being someone that I wasn't for half the night. At times, I like to get my thoughts together and push them into the back of my head so that I can prepare myself for the guilt trip the following morning.

"Thank you for accompanying me tonight, I added an extra bonus because I'm sure my colleagues bore you to death," Big Money said as he leaned over and placed his hand on my thigh. I shot him a half smile.

"It's ok, it wasn't that bad," I lied.

The truth was it was every bit of bad. These motherfuckers, all they did was sit up and talk about a tax bracket that I probably would never see and why Agent Orange was doing an awesome job running the country. When the car came to a stop, I couldn't get out the car fast enough. The air was perfect on this spring night, and I took my time walking upstairs to my apartment that I shared with my roommate Kelly. I prayed that she wasn't up because I would have to sit through another one of her lectures. I met Kelly freshman year on campus. We were what you called fresh meat here at Vanderbilt University. We both looked out of place, so we clicked instantly. Kelly was in her junior year now, and me well, I dropped out our sophomore year. We stayed close to campus in an apartment. It was just better that way since the cost of living was crazy.

Reaching the apartment door, I placed my ear to the door to see if I could hear the television or any noise. This was dumb as hell I was a grown ass woman and hated to come home because I hated being lectured about what I did for money. Oh, I'm Novanna Collier, but a lot of people call me Nova, and when I dropped out of college, it was because I couldn't afford the tuition and my mother's checks weren't covering my expenses. See, my mother still sent checks thinking she was paying for my college, but honestly, I was just putting them in the bank with the rest of my money. I made fast money by accompanying the men that couldn't get dates or just simply wanted to have a nice-looking woman to talk to.

I guess you can call it an escort. I rarely and I put emphasis on rarely, slept with the men that I went out with, but sometimes the opportunity presents itself, and if the money were right, I wouldn't turn it down.

Placing my key in the lock, I unlocked the door and slowly entered the apartment. Thank God from the looks of it Kelly was in her room sleep. I tiptoed to my bedroom trying not to make a sound. Once inside, I closed the door and plopped down on my bed letting out a huge sigh. I looked up at the ceiling at the painted Nova, the pink and the purple hues gave me peace. There was a light tap at my door, and I knew that it was Kelly. I didn't want to answer, but she would enter anyway.

"Yes, Kelly?" I yelled. The door opened, and Kelly peeked her head in.

"I just wanted to make sure you made it in, that's all. Your mother called the house phone also. I wrote the number down and left it on the fridge," Kelly said. Sitting up on my elbows, I looked over at the door.

"Thanks." I smiled. Kelly nodded and closed the door.

Easing up off the bed, I started to undress so that I could shower and get comfortable. I was a night owl, so sleep was the furthest from my mind. I pulled my dreads up in a high ponytail on my head. My locs were everything and my favorite part of me.

I guess you can say I was easy on the eyes and that made my job easier. Poor me, I didn't know what I was mixed with but shout out to my pops whoever he may be. My skin was the color of warm honey in the hot summer sun. My locs fell to the middle of my back, and I wore them brown and honey blonde. I had a set of green eyes the color of sage that would make you stop and stare. My lips were small but full in size; even Kylie Jenner would be jealous. I worked out faithfully to maintain my pear shape body. My small waist and wide hips to match this ass I had gave me and these men life. I looked in the mirror at my naked body satisfied and jumped in the shower to wash Nova off and get back to being Novanna.

After my shower, I grabbed my laptop and sat in the middle of my bed to let loose. This was what I lived for, writing. When I was little, I would write out complete stories in journals. Over the years as I grew,

I collected so many journals. Now being older, I placed everything on my laptop. I wanted to share my work with the world. I loved reading and writing, especially Urban Lit. I got lost in those types of worlds. I picked up where I left off and wrote until I looked at the clock and it was damn near four a.m. Shutting the laptop, I finally closed my eyes to get some sleep.

* * *

"Nova! Nova!" I heard Kelly calling my name. I opened one eye, and Kelly stood over my bed looking at me.

"What girl?" I moaned.

"It's your mother again," she whispered, handing me over the phone. I shot up and grabbed the phone. I looked at the clock and peeped the time so that I could come up with some sort of excuse to move this conversation on out the way. I placed the phone up to my face.

"Hello," I said in the phone.

"Novanna Collier, I know you not still sleeping, don't you have class today?" she asked.

My mother was old-fashioned sort of speak, and she was all about education. One thing I hated about her was that she had been slaving for the Hamsteads half her damn life. The Hamsteads were a wealthy ass family. They were like the Obamas of the south. My mother would get mad because I always say she slaved for black folks, but she always would say it was so much more to what she did.

“Ma, class was postponed, so I’m catching some extra shut-eye because I was up late working on a paper,” I said, letting the lie roll right off my tongue.

“Well, baby the real reason I called was because well, I have an issue, and I didn’t want to bother you with it when it first happened, but now I think I should tell you. The house burned down, and we lost everything,” she cried. My mouth flew open, and my stomach started to turn.

“Mama, where are you staying I’m coming home. I can help you.” I started speaking fast.

"No chile, I'm ok. Malcolm and Elizabeth have been kind enough to let me stay in their guest house for as long as I like," she stated. I rolled my eyes.

"Mama it's bad enough you're the help, now you want to live there. It's nothing to get you an apartment," I said.

"Look, this weekend I want you to come stay with me. Franklin isn't that far, and I miss your face. I swear since you went off to college I see less and less of you. Nova, you're only like thirty minutes away, and it feels like you in a different state," she complained.

"Ok, mama. I promise I will come out Friday," I told her so that I could hurry up and get off the phone. I could hear clapping in the background, so I knew she was happy.

"Yes, can't wait to see you. Well, I'll let you catch up on your sleep and talk to you later. Love you," she said.

"I love you too, mama," I said and hung up the phone.

Grabbing my robe from the back of the door, I threw it on and walked into the kitchen to see Kelly feeding her face. Kelly looked up as I walked in. See, Kelly was my girl. She was bougie as hell and sometimes I thought she was a white girl trapped in a black girl's body. Don't get shit twisted though; Kelly had her moments. I leaned on the counter and sighed.

"What is it?" Kelly asked without even looking up from her food.

"I'm going to stay with my ma for the weekend. The house caught on fire, and she's just now telling me she's been staying in the Hamsteads guest house," I said while I toyed with one of my locs.

Kelly stopped eating and looked up. "Maybe that's a good thing. You could use a break from your *JOB*," she said, putting emphasis on the word job. Rolling my eyes, I placed my hands on my hips and tilted my head

"Look around Kelly, look at how we are living, but we are supposed to be struggling college students. Your little job contributes but let's not get beside ourselves here because I'm bringing in the majority. Why is it a big deal what I do? Why does it bother you so much?" I asked.

Kelly dropped her spoon on the plate and bit her lip. I knew she was mad now. "Why you always got to bring up the fact that you are doing the most. Excuse me for actually going to college and not being able to work as many hours because my education is a priority. I just be worried about you while you're out. You don't know them men and motherfuckers are crazy, Nova," she said.

Now I felt bad because all she ever did was worry about me. This was normal for us. This same argument happened almost every time that I went out and came back in. You would think she stopped bringing it up.

"Have you ever thought about if you decide to date someone serious? The consequences that may occur, you may not sleep with most of the men, but you're still labeled as a prostitute, Nova. And I'm not saying that to be mean. I'm just being real," Kelly spoke as she walked over to the sink and washed her dish out. The silence was awkward because I didn't have a comeback.

"I guess I'll cross that bridge when and if I get to it," I said.

Muzaini

It was early as hell, and the sun was creeping through the tall glass windows as I crept in also trying not to wake Cru. A nigga was bout to shower and head straight to the office. I wanted no parts of Cru's ass this morning. Cru was always on some arguing shit no matter how many times I told her I didn't care for that negative shit. Every day I would say I was going to end it with her, but I never did.

I'm Muzaini Muhammad, one thing you gone learn about me is that I'm that nigga. When people see me, they instantly think I'm another drug dealing no good nigga. Never judge a book by its cover, I owned Muza Entertainment. The hottest company in the game, I was the Diddy of the south. Under my company, you could find the hottest rap and R&B artists, rock the hottest in male and female gear, drink the best Cognac put out by a nigga, or you could eat at any one of my franchise restaurants.

At twenty-eight years old, I was set for life. It took time and dedication to get where I got. Of course, I knew the streets never forgot where I came from. If it weren't for my aunt and uncle taking me in when my mama died, I would've been a lost cause. My Uncle Malcolm was a breaded nigga, and he got my head in the business.

I walked down the hall to the bathroom furthest from the bedroom. Standing in the mirror, I removed my jewelry placing it on the counter and lined it up to perfection. I rubbed my face, reminding myself to have the barber come to the office today to line me up. Removing my clothes, I hopped in the shower.

Last night had got real, and I was staying my ass out the clubs for a minute. Being on the scene was a part of my job, so that was another reason why I kept Cru around also. She looked good on my arm, but we all know that everything that looks good wasn't good.

"Where the fuck you been all night, Muza!" I heard Cru yelling.

And there she is. I closed my eyes and placed my head under the showerhead and let the water run over me. The glass door of the shower opened, and I turned around.

"Cru get the fuck out and let me finish showering. I'll deal with your ass when I feel like it," I told her. Cru smacked her lips

"Where they doing that at? Deal with me when you feel like it? Muzaini, I swear I can't stand your black ass!" she yelled as she stomped out of the bathroom.

Now I was about to hurry my ass up and get the hell up out of here. Turning the shower off, I stepped out and wrapped a towel around my waist. Wiping the mirror, I took in my looks. A nigga was decent, I made my pecks jump, some shit that drove the ladies crazy. I ran my hand over my waves; I rocked a low-cut fade. Taking in my looks, I resembled my father a lot, brown skin, stood 6'3 and a nigga worked out, so I was cut. At 200 pounds, I was solid brick with no tattoos I respected my body, to each his own, so I had nothing against those who liked it. My teeth were perfect, pearly whites. I had a diamond-crusted set of pullouts that I wore on occasion. The only thing about me was a nigga always wore shades. People would joke about it, but that was my way of reading people. I could read people well, so when out and amongst a group of people, I used that to cover my eyes. Cru would always say my eyes were my best quality, but I didn't think so. They were just hazel.

Turning the lights off, I headed down the hall to the bedroom. Walking into my personal closet, I press the button so that the rack could move to my business attire. Reaching up, I grabbed a button down from my Muza collection and a pair of Gucci slacks. I could feel Cru's eyes on me, I didn't even know where she was at in the room, but I knew she was watching me.

After dressing and sliding my feet in my loafers, I came out of the closet and Cru was sitting there pouting, Cru was beautiful her dark chocolate skin made a nigga weak in the knees. She had the body of an African goddess and long legs that belonged on somebody's runway. She wore her hair down to her ass, and something about that shit turned me on.

"So, you gone act like you didn't stay out all night and ignore my calls?" she asked in a calm voice. Spraying on my cologne, I grabbed my keys.

"Look, Cru. I was out with some new artists celebrating, a nigga has to focus on how people move, I can't be answering no phone calls every five minutes checking in because you want to sit up on the phone and talk. Right now, I'm going to close this deal. Hopefully, I was able to convince them enough last night, but you got to chill with the nagging because you and I both know that lately we ain't been on the best of terms. Tomorrow I'm going out to my aunt and uncles and staying the weekend, so you need to take that time to get yourself together and get used to the space because I'm not feeling this, us right now," I said, trying to sound logical as possible.

See Cru had it bad with taking things she heard and hearing what she wanted to hear, meaning she did what the fuck she wanted. I could break up with her ass five times, and she still would pop up talking about I didn't mean that shit. I was officially tired.

"Nall you don't mean that, Muza." She stood and made her way over to me reaching for me. I held my hand up to stop her from touching me.

"I meant every word, Cru. Don't piss me off," I said. Grabbing my keys, I left her there looking stupid.

I hit the lock on my 2017 Porsche Panamera and headed to my office. Life for me was great. I had everything I wanted and needed. Well, everything except a family. I was starting to get up there in age and of course settling down was knocking on my door. Hell, a nigga wanted some kids. See that's another reason I couldn't kick it with Cru any longer because the things I wanted she didn't want. She just wanted to spend a nigga's money and sit around having lunch with her friends and shit taking trips like she was auditioning for a season of *Love & Hip Hop*. Cru always mentioned how she couldn't stand kids. Even though I never pushed the topic, I always peeped that shit when she mentioned it. There ain't no way I would settle with someone that I didn't share common interests or likes with. That would just be setting myself up for failure. I pulled into the parking lot of my building and gave the keys to valet as I walked in like the man I am.

"Good morning, Mr. Muhammad!" my front desk worker greeted me. I hit her with a head nod as I made my way to the elevators.

Stepping on the elevators, I pulled my phone out and pulled up my emails. I was expecting one that I really needed. Seeing the email pop up, I opened it and was satisfied with what I read. Stepping off the elevator, I walked straight to the conference room to sign another artist to Muza Entertainment.

Nova

Today I opted for some retail therapy. My bank account was sitting pretty, and since I barely touched it, I decided to spend that shit for once. It was a nice 68 degrees here in Nashville, and I had just got my baby washed. One thing I loved was my Range. It was a 2016 but so what. Now mama would shit bricks if she saw me driving this; the only thing was I didn't pay for this shit. This was a gift from the owner of one of the Range Rover dealerships here in the city. I guess you can call it an even swap of services— paperwork and everything in my name and paid for. So, I cherished this baby. Parking my truck, I grabbed my bag and threw my shades on hopping out the car. I had my locs in two ponytails at the top and the back down. I was wearing a Tommy Hilfiger crop top and a pair of cut up jeans that were hugging to me like glue. I skipped across the street carefully and entered Green Hills Mall. The first store I hit up was Louis Vuitton, followed by Nordstrom and Sephora. I normally wasn't a label whore, but everything was making me feel like I didn't have a care in the world.

Walking over to Starbucks, I grabbed a seat and checked my messages. I had two clients that I had to reschedule telling them it was a family emergency. I needed to grab my mother something because once she found out about me not being in school anymore nor having a plan to go back, she was gone send my ass back to my maker.

I looked up deciding which store I should go in next, but my antennas went up, and I saw the finest nigga that I had ever seen in my life. Not only that but the way he carried himself smelled like money. I grabbed my bags and decided to follow him. Keeping my eye on him, it felt like it was just him and me in the mall. The mystery man walked into the Burberry store. I walked over and started looking at some items, making sure to keep my eyes on him.

“Mr. Muhammad how are you doing today sir?” the white girl greeted him.

Hmm, Mr. Muhammad, I thought.

“May I help you, ma’am?” I already knew what the snooty heffa was doing by coming to me, but I wanted her to know don’t play with me.

“Yes, actually can I get two of these neon clutches, one in blue and the other in green? I’ll also take the pink neon leather tote,” I asked.

“No problem, I’ll get those for you,” Snooty Booty said and walked off.

I walked up to the counter where the delectable Mr. Muhammad was standing while the lady gift-wrapped something for him. Finally, he turned around, and I shot him a million-dollar smile. This nigga nodded and turned back around.

“Ma’am, will that be cash or credit?” Snooty Booty asked. I reached into my bag and pulled out my card.

“Put it on my ticket.” Mr. Muhammad said not even looking at the items I had. *So he wanted to play big money.*

“Oh, no. I can’t do that, I don’t even know you, and I got my ticket covered,” I told him, handing my card to Snooty Booty. That’s when he turned around and faced me, and I got a good look at his face.

“Do you know who I am?” he asked. Even his voice was sexy.

“Am I supposed to?” I asked. He looked at me from head to toe, taking me all in. The lustful look in his eyes and the way he licked his lips let me know he liked what he saw. He chuckled slightly.

“Well, since you don’t know, then I won’t tell you. But just take this as a gift from me, the name is Muzaini and yours?” he asked.

“Novanna but everyone calls me Nova, and I guess thank you for the gifts, even though I’m capable of paying for my own things,” I told him.

He shook his head and handed the lady his card. Once he signed his receipt, he grabbed his bags and walked out of the store. I stood there still shocked. This nigga didn’t ask for a number or nothing.

“Girl, you don’t know who that is, he like the Diddy of the south. When you go home, Google Muzaini Muhammad or Muza Entertainment,” Snooty Booty said. I nodded my head and grabbed my bags still processing the shit that just happened.

Nova

Friday was finally here, and I was already dreading heading to Franklin. Don't get me wrong I wanted to see my mother, but it's hard for me to be around my mother and lie to her. My mother could read you in a minute. Keeping my schooling from her was going to be a task. Lord forbid she finds out exactly what I was doing for money. I was sitting in the living room waiting on my Uber because I couldn't drive my Range to see my mother. Surfing the internet on my laptop, I was looking up that fine piece of chocolate that I saw yesterday in the mall. Typing in Muzaini Muhammad my mouth fucking dropped, and my pussy started gushing. This nigga net worth was $820 million motherfucking dollars.

"Why you look like you just saw a ghost?" Kelly said as she made her way over to the couch where I was sitting. She glanced at the computer and looked at me.

"Why are you looking up Muza?" she asked. Now I felt dumb as hell if Kelly's no life having ass knew this nigga.

"So, you know who this nigga is?" I asked.

"Um yeah, and he's from here. It's shocking that out of all the big timers you accompany you haven't run into him," Kelly said.

"Ugh, I see this chick is all in his space so he must be taken," I said, taking a look at him and some dark skin chick. One of the pics said the girl name was Cru.

"So, he's your next victim?" Kelly asked with a hint of salt in her voice.

"Victim, oh you're funny. Actually, this is the guy that purchase those Burberry bags for me yesterday. You know the one you were quick to say thank you for. This man is going to be so much more if I ever see him again," I said with confidence. My phone dinged, and I grabbed it. It was my Uber, and it was waiting.

"I'll see you Sunday when I get back," I said, grabbing my things and heading out the door.

Muzaini

"Man Unc, a nigga had to cut Cru's ass off. Just my luck when I get back home, her ass is gone be waiting on a nigga like shit ain't happened." I sat in the backyard with my Uncle Malcolm sipping on some Muzanac, which was my Cognac.

"I can't tell you how to run your life Muza, but maybe you need to give these industry chicks a break and get you a regular girl," my uncle said.

"A regular girl, Unc I make too much money to be dating a regular girl. How do I know if she's just with a nigga for his money or what I'm able to do for her?" I asked.

"Muza, when you find the right one all that won't even matter. Stop being so damn friendly all the time, play hard to get sometimes," he said and chuckled. I laughed and shook my head.

"It's funny you say that. I just bought this damn girl that I didn't even know some bags yesterday in Burberry. Shit, she looks like she had her own damn money, but she was beautiful, Unc. She looked a little young, but I could tell she wasn't my normal liking. Damn, why did I leave so fast?" I said mad at myself.

We continued to talk, and my uncle's worker came out carrying a tray, placing the tray on the table between us.

"Thank you, Mona Lise, has your daughter made it here yet?" my uncle asked as he looked up over his glasses, and if I wasn't mistaken, the way he looked at Ms. Mona was not how you look at a worker. He had to be tapping that, but I wasn't about to say shit that wasn't my business.

"She actually called and said she was in the neighborhood, so I'm about to head out front and wait. That's why I went ahead and brought your food out, sir," she said.

Mona Lise was a nice-looking woman I could tell she was a fox back in her day. She put me in the mind of Pam Greer except she was shorter. She had been working for my uncle and aunt since I was a kid. I watched as she quickly turned on her heels and walked back in the house.

"Unc, have you ever cheated on auntie?" I asked. Unc started coughing and patting his chest.

"Boy, what the hell made you ask that?" he asked. I sat forward in my chair.

"I just want to know because you and auntie just don't seem to have a lot of problems, I mean if you do, y'all hide that shit good," I said.

"Me and Elizabeth have ups and downs like any other marriage, but that's between us and nobody else. Why put our problems or business on front street? For one, we are a well-respected family, so we can't be out there showing our asses giving folks shit to talk about. Don't let Elizabeth's boogie ass fool you either. She's still from South Nashville," Unc said, which caused me to laugh so damn loud because I couldn't picture my auntie even driving through South Nashville.

Finishing off the last of my drink, I placed the glass on the table and caught a glimpse of Ms. Mona and some chick who had to be her daughter. Whoever her daughter was I could tell from here her body was banging. My phone rang, and I looked down at the number, and it was business, so I excused myself to take the call.

Nova

When I pulled up to the Hamsteads' house, I was in awe. Now I had been to their old house which was still big as shit, but this bad boy was like five times bigger. When we pulled into the driveway, I saw my mother standing on the front porch with the biggest smile on her face. She stood there with her hand clasps together. Once the car came to a complete stop, I thanked my driver and grabbed my bag.

"Oh Nova, look at my baby," mama said as she walked down the steps towards me.

"Hey mama," I said and stepped into her embrace.

"Come on, let's get you settled. I can't wait to show you off." Mama said, grabbing my hand and pulling me towards the house. As we made our way in the house, I looked up at the ceilings, which was so angelic with white marble. We walked down a long hallway and through a door, which leads to the side of the house. I assume this was the way to mama's guest house. When we stepped out the door, and I saw the guest house, I couldn't believe this shit.

"I see why you so comfortable staying here, is this a guest house for one or the Brady Bunch?" I asked. This shit was big as hell.

"They are very good people, and they look out for family. I have worked here for damn near half of my life, and I deserve it. I don't mind, and I wish you get that slave mentality shit out of your head, Nova," mama said as she showed me to my room.

"This is where you will be sleeping, or you can sleep with me upstairs in my bed like old times." She smiled while giving me a nudge.

Looking at mama, you wouldn't think that she had just lost everything she had. She remained humble and kept a smile on her face. I admired that one thing about her.

"I want to introduce you to Malcolm and Mrs. Elizabeth, so you can place your things down and come on," she said.

"Umm, do I have to? I really don't want to see them right now?" I whined.

“Girl, if you don’t bring your ass. Them people are family, and it will be rude for you to be laying up in their house and not speaking,” mama said. She walked over to the door and stood there with her arms crossed waiting on me. Giving in, I made my way towards mama and followed her.

I was dressed in a blue jean button up dress that hugged my hips and showed these pretty legs, and I wore a pair of brown wedge heels. It was nothing major, but I was comfortable. I had my locs pulled up in a high bun on my head.

“Oh, I forgot to tell you that Malcolm I mean Mr. Hamstead’s nephew is also staying here the weekend. Stay away from him, Nova.” mama said. I laughed. We walked up a huge pair of stairs that lead to the back patio area, and I heard the laughter of men. I couldn’t see because mama had her big ass in the way.

“Mr. Hamstead, I would like to introduce you to my daughter Nova. Nova this is Mr. Hamstead,” she said, stepping out the way. I tried to open my mouth to speak but was choked up looking at Mr. Muhammad sitting right next to Mr. Hamstead.

"How are you doing, sir?" I said, taking in all of Mr. Hamstead. He was nice looking for his age. I could tell he was a playa back in his day. His skin was the color of almonds, and he was bald with a small beard that had speckles of gray in it. I noticed the way he looked at me with a lingering eye.

"Where are my manners, Nova this is my nephew, Muza," he said, introducing me to the man that had been on my mind since the very first time I saw him. Hearing mama voice in the back of my head saying leave this man alone, I nodded my head before I could say anything he spoke.

"We sort of already met," he said with a smile licking his lips. I rolled my eyes because I could see now his mind was on one thing only. Well, I guess you could say I sound hypocritical because with him the only thing on my mind was the money.

Muza

I could see Ms. Mona making her way towards us, and I couldn't make out the face of who I figured was her daughter because she was walking behind her, but to my surprise, as they grew closer and Ms. Mona moved out the way, it was shorty from the mall. Damn, she was bad, and to know that she was going to be here the whole weekend with myself, a nigga was fighting with whether to work my magic or let her be.

After the introductions, she stood there with this look on her face that I couldn't read. I watched her mom grab her and took her off to the kitchen. I don't know what that was all about.

"Why did Ms. Mona pull shorty away like that? That's the chick I bought that shit for yesterday. I ain't know that was Ms. Mona's daughter." I leaned over and told my Unc who also had a perplexed look on his face. Lifting his glass, he took a long swig of his drink.

"Ms. Mona doesn't want you to sink your claws into her daughter that's why," he mumbled.

"Ain't nobody finna sink no claws in nobody," I lied. I had plans, and I knew then I would have to catch shorty alone.

After chopping it up with my uncle, I decided to head to my room and chill out until dinner. Walking through the house, I had my head down and looking at emails on my phone. I heard a voice coming from the TV room, so I stopped to peek inside.

"Kelly, I wish you stop hounding me about that. I pushed all my appointments back, and I'm just going to tell my ma that I'm going for creative writing. It ain't like she going to ask for transcripts or anything. Then I'm going to lie and tell her I received a scholarship, so she doesn't have to mail any more money. I feel bad for keep taking her money, and I ain't even stepped foot in school. Look, I'm not about to keep going back and forth with you. I'll see you when I get back on Sunday," Nova said as she wrapped up her conversation. I eased away from the door and headed up to my room. I wonder what was up with shorty.

Flopping down on the bed, I unbuttoned my shirt and leaned back. I thought back to the message I sent my security detail making sure to keep Cru off my property. I knew she had to be having a fit and good thing I got my number changed because she would've been blowing a nigga up. Sometimes drastic measures had to be taken so she could see a nigga wasn't playing.

Mona Lise

I was a nervous wreck from the time my daughter arrived and even now. As I maneuvered my way around the kitchen to prepare tonight's supper, my stomach was turning monkey flips. This was the first time since Nova was younger that I had brought Nova to the Hamsteads home, and I wasn't sure if my secret would come out or not.

"Mona Lise, can you prepare an extra dinner setting for tonight? I have an extra guest that will be attending dinner tonight," Mrs. Elizabeth asked.

"Yes ma'am, I sure will," I replied.

"I'm dying to meet your lovely daughter. Where is she?" she asked.

“She stepped out to take a look at the grounds, probably trying to find her a writing sanctuary,” I bragged. Nova had a love for writing and any chance she got you could find her placing her thoughts on paper.

As soon as that sentence left my mouth, Nova came walking into the kitchen. She looked to be bothered, and I gave her a faint smile and nodded towards Mrs. Hamstead.

“Here she is. Nova, baby, this is Mrs. Hamstead,” I introduced the two.

Mrs. Hamstead placed her hand up to her mouth and let out a small gasp. I felt my hands start to sweat and little beads trickle down the side of my face.

“Oh, Mona Lise, she is exquisite. Have you seen Malcolm’s great-grandmother, the resemblance is uncanny?” Mrs. Hamstead said as she walked over to Nova. Nova smiled, and I could tell she was freaked out.

“They say everyone has a twin, but no I have never seen her,” I said, letting out a nervous chuckle.

“How are you doing, ma’am?” Nova asked.

"I'm doing great. I'm surprised my nephew hasn't sunk his claws in you yet. Muzaini happens to be a ladies man. I pray one day he grows up and gives me some little babies. Have you had the pleasure of meeting him yet?" she asked Nova.

"Slightly, nothing major," Nova spoke.

I didn't know where this convo was going and I didn't like it, especially since I told Nova to stay away from him.

"Nova is focused on her studies. She has no time to be entertaining anyone," I said as I took the dishes to the dining room to set the table.

Nova

I couldn't believe my mother was acting so damn uptight. I don't know what Mrs. Hamstead was hinting at, but shit, I need to get in good with her. She may be my way to Muzaini.

"I don't know why my mother acts like I'm still a child," I told Mrs. Hamstead.

“I assume that’s how mothers act. I never had the honor of having kids, but I did raise my nephew. Malcolm claimed he never wanted children, but when we married, and I took in my nephew, he was so awesome with him. I will never tell you to not listen to your mother, but I can see you with my nephew,” Mrs. Hamstead said while nudging me and cheesing.

Little did she know I could see myself with him too. The thought of me even being Mrs. Muzaini Muhammad made me wet. We walked out of the kitchen and headed to the living room area where we continued to talk.

Malcolm

Sometimes in life, things are better left alone, but when they hit you in the face, you have no choice but to question things. I made my way to my office and unlocked my desk drawer. Rambling through the things inside, I pulled out a small book and opened it. Taking a long look at what I needed to see, I placed it in my pocket closing the drawer and locking it back. Making my way to the kitchen, I noticed Elizabeth and

Nova sitting in the living room wrapped up in conversation. That made my job even better. Entering the kitchen, I stood there and watched as Mona Lise moved around comfortably doing what she does. I cleared my throat gaining her attention. Mona Lise turned around, and the look on her face let me know she knew exactly why I was here.

"Mr. Hamstead, you scared me," she had the nerve to say. I walked closer to her.

"Don't try to be all Mr. Hamstead now. You're talking to Malcolm right now, and I think you got some explaining to do, Mona Lise," I said through gritted teeth and pulled the book from my pocket turning it to the page and shoving it in her face.

"Do you know who this is?" I asked. Mona shook her head no and closed her eyes.

"This is my great-grandmother, I find it really odd how your daughter looks like her, and if her age serves me correctly, you better pray that ain't my child," I told her.

"Nova isn't your child," she said. The way she said it, I didn't believe shit she said.

"Mona Lise don't toy with me. Who is that girl's father?" I asked in a more serious tone. "Haven't I always looked out for you most of your life. We have an understanding, or so I thought. Have you kept a child from me?" I asked.

The voices from the living room got closer, and I scooted away from Mona, but I kept an eye on her. She looked defeated yet relieved. She wasn't giving me an answer with her voice, but I could tell by her body language that Nova was indeed my child.

"Ma, Ms. Elizabeth and I are about to go upstairs she wants to show me the pink room whatever that is," Nova said. She looked at me and then at her mother.

"Ok, Nova. Dinner will be served in about an hour," Mona Lise told her. Nova left the kitchen.

"You know it's a damn shame that you won't tell me the truth, but you better tell me something before Elizabeth starts snooping around," I whispered.

"It's nothing to tell you, Malcolm. Once Nova leaves here, she won't be back. I have done just fine raising her for what all of twenty-three years. Let her be," Mona fixed her mouth to say.

"Let her be? Woman is you crazy? You can't just tell me I have a daughter then be like let her be. Dammit, Mona. What the fuck was you thinking?" I asked. I placed my hands on top of my head and took a deep breath. It was time for me to dismiss myself because I couldn't deal with this shit right now.

Mona Lise

I knew bringing Nova here was going to cause a problem. Dammit. Malcolm has always been my heart. I was supposed to be the one sitting up in this big ass house weeping all the benefits. He was my first love and the man I wanted to marry. When we were young, we were inseparable. That was until his mother threw Elizabeth in the mix. Being considered the help, Malcolm never treated me as such. Even after he married Elizabeth, he made sure I stayed nearby keeping me at his beck and call. Nova hated the fact that I loved to work for them, but the truth was I was very much in love with this man, even if I had to have my love rationed out in portions. Nova was conceived, and I kept it a secret. Malcolm always would tell Elizabeth how he didn't want children, so when I became pregnant. I ran off and made like I had gotten pregnant by someone else.

I knew Malcolm was angry, and I knew that Elizabeth was bound to put that shit together, especially since she already had mentioned

Malcolm's great-grandmother. Fuck, oh well. Maybe she will divorce his ass, and then I can have him all to myself.

It was time for dinner, and everyone was making their way to the dining room. I watched as Malcolm kept his eye on Nova and what the hell was Elizabeth doing sitting Nova next to Muzaini. The doorbell rang, and I excused myself to answer the door. Opening the door, there stood a dark skin girl that I had never seen before.

"How may I help you?" I asked.

"I'm a dinner guest, can you let Elizabeth know I'm here," she said as she stepped inside.

"Wait right here," I told her.

"What the hell are you doing here, Cru?" I heard Muzaini's deep baritone voice come from behind me.

"Well, I'm here for dinner. Don't you miss me?" the girl asked.

"Excuse me," I said, removing myself from the room.

Muza

"First of all, who the hell invited you, what don't you get about a nigga not wanting you?" I asked through gritted teeth.

"You always say that you don't want me, but we both know how we do. Muza, we are good for each other, and I know you don't want to throw all that away," she said.

I let out a sigh and turned when I saw Nova entered the room. She wasn't even paying attention, but I was paying attention to her. *Damn, she was fine. I pray to God this doesn't backfire what I'm about to do.* I turned to Nova.

"Baby, come here," I said as I was walking towards her. She wore a confused look on her face. I leaned towards her like I was about to kiss her on her cheek.

"Please play along, or I will tell your mother the truth about your little college situation," I whispered and planted a kiss on her cheek. She pulled away and looked over my shoulder.

"What is she doing here, Muza? I thought you said you were done with her," she said. I smiled and placed my arms around Nova's waist.

"Baby, I was just trying to figure out myself why she was invited to a family affair, especially since I made it clear that we are no longer together," I said.

The look on Cru's face was priceless. For once in her life, she was lost for words. Nova's perfume was tickling my nose, and as I pulled her close to me, I knew she had to feel my dick on brick because she looked at me, but she wasn't smiling.

"What is going on? We are ready to eat." My auntie came waltzing into the foyer. She looked shocked, and I hurried to speak before our cover was blown.

"I was just trying to find out who invited Cru to dinner because we are no longer together, and it's highly disrespectful to my woman," I said and winked at my aunt. Auntie placed her hand to her chest.

"Well, I'm partly to blame because Cru made it seem like you guys had to discuss a contract, so I invited her, but the last thing I want to do is disrespect Nova, so Cru you need to leave," auntie said.

"This is so wrong Muza, and you know it. I promise you will be back," Cru said.

"Not if I have anything to do with it," Nova shocked me and said.

Cru rolled her eyes, turned on her Giuseppe heels, and stormed out of the house. My auntie stood there looking at us with a confused look on her face.

"Now, I'm all for this union, but damn when did it happen?" she asked.

"It didn't happen. I just needed Cru to see that I ain't want her ass no more," I admitted to my aunt. She shook her head.

"Well, y'all come on. It's time to eat," she said as she walked back to the dining area, and I turned to Nova.

“Thanks for that, but you do know now that we kind of got to act like a couple,” I said, lifting a brow waiting on a response. Nova turned her nose up.

“What you mean, act like we a couple? How you know I ain’t got a man?” she asked.

“One, I’m a very important person, and I can’t tell her that we together and you’re never on my arm. I could care less if you had a man. It ain’t like I like you anyways,” I lied.

“And I don’t like your ass either, so it’s going to cost you,” she said.

“Cost me, do you remember I know about your little lie you’re keeping from your ma? I could just go in there, tell her, and crush her little heart right now. However, if you’re with me, you won’t have no worries. I will make it worth it, and then you might want a nigga for real,” I said cockily. She didn’t have a comeback.

Nova

I couldn't believe this shit. Here it was this man was basically asking me to pretend to be his girl. Shid, I knew after a little time with me, I would have him eating out the palm of my hands, and he's gone want to wife a bitch for real. This shit was becoming easier by the minute. I could take this and push my writing also. I was all about securing the bag, and this most definitely would be it. But, what if I end up securing his heart as well?

"Yeah, I got you," I answered.

"Cool, why are you not in school anyway?" he asked.

"Money issues," I said and kept it at that.

"Baby girl, money issues? You were just in the mall blowing a bag. You dress in labels, I caught all that so how is it you're not able to pay for your schooling?" he asked, making me feel like shit. There was no way I was going to tell him about my side hustle. I just pray that I could keep that shit under wraps.

"Ok, honestly, I'm just not interested in school. My love is for writing, and I just want to write books that people will remember me by or relate to. My mother would never understand that shit. She'd rather slave here, no offense to your folks, and send me them nothing ass checks," I told him.

"No offense taken, but maybe the best thing for you to do is sit down and talk to her about your feelings and school. I can pull some strings, and maybe you can show her that you're doing well without school. What is it that you do?" he asked. I had to think quickly.

"I do hair," I lied.

"Oh ok, well let's get in here and eat before they come out here bitching. We will discuss this some more later," he said.

I nodded my head and followed him into the dining area where we enjoyed a nice dinner my mother had prepared. The mood at the table was awkward, and I couldn't put my finger on it, but I wasn't worried about shit but Muza. I couldn't wait to tell Kelly this shit.

Kelly

My feet were sore as fuck, and I had one more table left before I was able to clock out for the night. I sat in the corner eyeing the man that was taking his precious time finishing his meal. He was easy on the eyes, so I was also staring for pleasure. I guess he felt that I was staring because he looked up and our eyes met. I tried to hurry up and look away. When I felt he wasn't looking anymore, I turned my head slightly only to catch him looking at me. He smiled and fingered for me to come over there. I stood up, wiped my hands on my uniform, and headed over to his table.

"May I help you?" I asked.

"Sit down," he said, pointing to the empty spot in front of him. I don't know why but I did as I was told and sat in front of him.

"Are you waiting for me to finish up because you were staring at a nigga pretty hard?" he asked. I felt so embarrassed my hands were clammy as shit, and I wiped them on my apron.

“No rush, but you are my last table,” I answered.

He nodded his head and took a sip of his Coke finishing it off. The way he licked his lips when he placed the glass down made me quiver. I wasn’t new to being with guys. I just wasn’t as friendly like Nova was. Nova was my girl, and I loved her to death, so that’s why I went so hard on her like I did. I knew what it was like to have a reputation and be out there. That shit happened to me in high school and followed me. Coming to Vanderbilt, I was starting fresh and a new life. Everyone has a past, and I just preferred to bury mines.

“Well, just let me know when you’re ready to cash out,” I said as I stood to remove myself from the table.

“I don’t think I was done talking to you, shorty,” he spoke, wiping his mouth and leaning back in his seat. I took in his looks, which was ten times better than me scoping him out across the room. When he smiled, you could see the glimmer of the grill that occupied his mouth. He had one dimple that stood out, and it went perfectly with his dark skin.

"My name is Jon Jon, what's yours?" he asked.

"Kelly. Is that your real name Jon Jon, or is that your nickname?" I inquired.

"For now, that's all you need to know. Here this will cover my ticket, get your things and come with me unless you're scared?" he said, lifting his brow to watch my reaction.

True enough I didn't know this man period, but the way he took charge made me want to see just what he had up his sleeve. I stood up from the table, grabbed his money for the ticket, and went to the back to gather my things.

After paying for his things, I grabbed my purse and walked back out to leave with Jon Jon. I was able to look at him and peep the way he dressed. I could tell he probably was your average dope boy but then again who knew. He held the door opened as we walked outside, and the night breeze caught me off guard.

"Where's your car?" he turned around and asked.

"I actually took a Lyft to work." I held my head down in shame.

"That's cool, ain't no need to hold your head down. You got to do what you got to do," he said.

"Come on." he grabbed my hand and led the way. We stopped in front of a matte black Ford F-150. I watched as he opened the door and helped me in.

"Thank you," I said. He walked around the truck and got in. I said a small prayer to myself.

Lord, please don't let me regret this decision. I don't know this man, but all I ask is that you get me home safely and let me live to tell somebody about this tomorrow.

After my prayer, I opened my eyes, and he was staring at me with a grin on his face.

"You good, shorty. I didn't want to interrupt your prayer." He laughed I couldn't help but chuckle myself.

"Yes, I'm fine. I'm so sorry. I don't normally just up and leave with strangers," I admitted.

“That’s understandable. What’s your address so that I can take you home?” he asked. I called off my address, which wasn’t far from my job.

“Do you always pick up girls that stare at you?” I asked, being funny but trying to start a conversation.

“Nah, but I had been watching you for a minute. So, I decided to shoot my shot,” he responded.

“Oh, you can pull in right here in front behind that Rover,” I told him as we pulled up at my crib. He pulled in behind Nova’s Range and turned the car off. He got out and walked around to the passenger side and opened the door.

“Thank you. You can come up if you want,” I whispered. I didn’t want him to get the wrong impression, but I was also trying to be nice.

He nodded his head and followed me upstairs. Unlocking the door, I moved to the side and let him as I locked the door behind us. Throwing my keys on the island and hanging up my purse, I took notice of him checking out the place. Thanks to Nova our shit was decked out.

“Your place is nice, but um you must pull a lot of hours waitressing to live like this?” he asked. He walked over to the picture that was on the mantle and picked it up.

“Your sister?” he asked. I walked over and placed the picture back on the mantle.

“No, that’s my roommate Nova, and Nova has a good paying job so a lot of this she paid for,” I groaned. “My main focus is school right now,” I told him. He nodded and took a seat on the couch, patting for me to sit beside him.

“Well, then tell me all about Kelly, I got all night,” he said as he placed his phone on silent. I peeped that. I don’t know why but he made me comfortable and this feeling I missed so much.

Nova

My ass was stuffed from that dinner mama cooked. It had been awhile since I had a home cooked meal. My mind was only on one thing, and that was the conversation I had with Muzaini. Everyone was still in the main house, and I had come back to the guest house to retrieve my laptop. I had found me a quiet little spot, the Hamsteads gazebo they had in the backyard. Turning the computer on, I lit my blunt and started to lose myself in the words that I typed out.

"If you don't want to be found, then you shouldn't spark up gas. That shit is strong. I didn't take you as the smoking the type." I heard Muzaini's voice walking towards me.

"I really wasn't hiding. I just didn't want to smoke so close to the house. Plus, it helps me focus when I'm writing," I said, looking back down at the computer.

"What are you writing?" he asked, walking behind me. I closed the top on the laptop.

"A book I plan on submitting to Mz. Lady P. She like the dopest author in the game and she have her own publishing team, and I would love to be a part of it. I'm taking my time on this because I don't want to submit just anything. I'm sorta writing as I go," I told him. Muza hovering over me was starting to make me feel uncomfortable. I guess he could feel in the way that I was shifting my body.

"I really came out here because tonight you're on the clock. I have to make an appearance at this charity event, and I have to have my lady on my arm," he said, smiling like a Cheshire cat. For this nigga to act like he ain't feeling me, he needs to work on his poker face.

"This is so last minute Muza, and I don't have anything to wear. Well I know I didn't pack nothing fancy," I said, standing up and grabbing my things.

"You don't have to worry about anything, Nova. I had my stylist pick out a couple of pieces for you. I asked my auntie to guess your size. She had them placed in the guest room in the house because she didn't want your ma to freak out," he said. I looked at him from head to toe. This man knew he was fine.

"Well, I guess I go get ready," I said, walking towards the house and Muza grabbed me by the arm. I knew I had to be tripping by the volt of electricity that ran through my body when he touched me.

"I need you to be yourself tonight. You don't have to adjust to the people you are around. I think our connection will be better if we just be ourselves around each other," Muza said in a stern voice.

"You thought I was going to be something I'm not just to appease you and your colleagues. Sorry, I don't get down like that anyway," I said then turned to head into the house. This man was making me feel like a queen already, and I could see myself getting used to the benefits of pretending to be his woman.

Muzaini

Watching the glow that radiated off Nova's face when she walked into the room and saw everything my stylist had brought her made a nigga feel special. I couldn't wait to take her out on the town tonight. It was hard for me to act like I didn't like her and to remind myself to keep my guard up. I was dressed and sitting in the living room waiting for Nova to make her appearance. Scrolling through IG, I ran across Cru, and she had her nerve to be on the red carpet of the charity event I was attending tonight. I ran my hand over my waves and let out a sigh. I pray that tonight don't be a mess.

I stood up and walked over to the bar and poured me a drink because I needed it to take the edge off. I wish I had whatever Nova was smoking on earlier.

"Aw hell nah, I'm about to go change," I heard Nova say.

I turned around and smiled. I peeped her taste it was very similar to mine. I was wearing a Gucci Chevron acetate bomber jacket with the matching joggers, and Nova was wearing a Gucci bomber jacket with the tracks pants and a pair of red Gucci pumps to set it off. She had her locs pulled up in some sort of style, which showed the prettiness of her face and bright red lipstick on her plump lips.

"What you need to change for? I think your outfit is perfect," I said, licking my lips.

"Muza, we look like the fucking Doublemint twins," she said sliding her shades on.

"Girl, bring your ass. You already had me waiting long enough," I told her. After a slight eye roll and a smack of her lips, we were headed out the door to the car.

After entering the car, I waited until Nova placed her seatbelt on before pulling off. We were riding to the sounds of Deroz De'Shon "P.I.L."

I know dem niggas gone hate on me
I pray my niggas don't trade on me
I know if I get a case today these hoes ain't gone wait on me
Keep that sucka shit away from me
Keep it G that's the only way to be so

If I tell you I love you don't play with me

I noticed Nova rapping along to the lyrics of the song. She looked like she was meant to be for a nigga. She was made for my arms only. I reached and turned the radio down so that I could talk to her. I wanted to inform her that Cru would be at the party.

“Cru is supposed to be here tonight. You gone be straight? We can always turn around and not go,” I mentioned. Nova turned to me.

“Nah, nigga I done got dressed to turn heads, and that’s what I intend to do. That’s our purpose of coming to this event right to make ole girl jealous and start letting people talk about the new woman on your arm, right? Keep on driving. This will be fun,” she said, putting me in check.

We finally arrived at Pinewood Social, the Tennessee Titans were hosting a charity bowling event for ALS, and the crowd was thick. Walking around, I opened the door for Nova, and as soon as her foot hit the pavement, the cameras started going off, and the reporters were swarming a nigga with a million questions.

"Muza, is this the new lady in your life? What happened to Cru?" they were asking.

I placed my hand on the lower part of Nova's back and made our way to the red carpet. Nova was a natural posing for the camera like she was made for the media. She held my hand and pulled me close, placing a kiss on my lips, which caught me by surprise. My dick jumped, and I pulled her in front of me leaning into her ear.

"You can't be getting my dick hard in these pants with all these photographers out here, girl," I whispered.

"I'm sorry. I saw your little Cruella standing over there looking right at us stank, so I had to do something," she said. We both laughed because, of course, the cameras were still snapping away.

Once we made our way into the bowling alley, I started making my rounds and introducing Nova to a few friends.

"I'm going to run to the bathroom, I'll be right back," Nova whispered in my ear, and I gave her a quick peck on the cheek before she walked off.

"So, I see you were serious about leaving Cru. Who is ole gal?" my homie Bishop asked.

"Hell yeah, but she is a friend of the family that happened to be in the right place at the right time when Cru popped up at my uncle crib. We kind of owe each other in a way, so she's helping a nigga out," I told him, I trusted Bishop, so I felt I could tell him the truth about Nova.

"Nigga, if I don't know nothing else I know you, and I know you like her, fuck all that fake shit you yapping about. You about to fall straight for her ass," he said. One thing I knew was that he was telling the truth.

"Just pray she is who you want and hope she is nothing like Cru's ass," he said, sipping from his glass.

Nova

When I made it to the bathroom, I pulled out my phone because somebody was blowing me up. After looking at the many emails, it was one of my clients needing me for a last-minute emergency show up to none other than this fucking charity event that I was at. I sighed, ignoring the email. Most likely, this nigga had already seen me here. I hated to ignore this email because he was a double payer. I pray to God that I didn't run into him while being with Muza. The bathroom door opened, and I looked up into the face of the bitch that was supposed to be my competition. Placing my phone back in my Gucci clutch, I pushed myself off the sink I was leaning on and crossed my arms because I knew this bitch was about to fly off at the mouth. One thing about me was there was no hoe in my blood, but I also had to keep it classy for my man. *Wait, did I just call Muza my man?* I let out a slight giggle.

"Oh, so I amuse you?" Cru fumed. I knew she was pissed.

"You have no idea how much you amuse me," I answered still smiling. She was so mad that I could see the steam radiating off this bitch sew in.

"Why are you so mad, I can tell that I'm bothering you so much but, yet I haven't even done anything yet my girl," I said.

Cru sucked her teeth and walked a little closer to me. "You really think that you're doing something with Muza? You have no clue this is the norm for him. Muza has commitment issues, he gets bored, but he always comes back home to me when he's done playing like the dog he is," she had the nerve to say. I was laughing so hard I started to choke and had to pat my chest.

"Baby, I hate to tell you this, but the issue isn't with him it's you. You're why he gets bored and why he roams like a dog, because one you allow that shit, but it's also something you're not doing at home that's making him not want to stay. Muza is with me now, and the shit you allowed him to do, he won't be doing that shit with me. He's not a fucking dog; he is my T'Challa, you know king. You disrespected him as a man. If you want to be treated like a queen, then you treat your man as a king. Now, I'm not going to keep having run-ins with you because this conversation was a fair warning. I'm going to have to get real ghetto with your ass the next time you get in mine and my man's space and I even think you're being disrespectful. Now, I have to get back out here with my man before he thinks I'm in here taking a shit.

You have a nice evening," I said, leaving her standing there with her mouth wide opened.

"Close your mouth," I said, glancing back over my shoulder and exiting the bathroom.

I couldn't believe the shit I let roll off my tongue. I was playing this part a little too well. Who the hell was I kidding, I was feeling this nigga. Shit, that little speech made me believe what I said. When I walked back over to Muza a large lump formed in my throat, he was chopping it up with Delaunn Fleming. Delaunn was my double payer who was just blowing my fucking phone up. He is a linebacker for the Tennessee Titans. Muza looked up and saw me

"Damn girl, what took you so long?" he asked, placing his arms around me.

"I had a little issue in the bathroom with your lady friend, I had to put her in her place," I said.

"Novanna, I didn't know you would be here," I heard Delaunn say. I said a silent prayer to the Lord above that he wouldn't blow my cover, because if he did, this shit wouldn't turn out nice.

"Oh, hey. Delaunn, right?" I asked, trying to act like I ain't know him but giving him pleading eyes.

"You know my girl?" Muza asked. *Oh shit.* I thought.

"I do his girl's hair," I lied. Jesus, I was starting to lie like a damn pro.

"Yeah, that's all homie," Delaunn spoke, and he pulled his phone out. I looked at Muza who wore a strange look on his face. This shit was already starting to go south. I smiled trying to ease the tension.

"Oh baby, this my song," I said as I started rapping "BBO" by Migos

Bad Bitches and I know some savage bitches
Get it on they own they don't have to ask you bitches
Postin pictures on the Gram and at you bitches
Secure the bag, lifestyle real expensive

I was so into the song that I made sure I had my eyes locked on Cru on the posting pictures on the gram part. My phone buzzed, and I reached into my clutch and retrieved it. There was an email from Delaunn.

D. Fleming: So, you out the business now or you on a job? I got the hint you didn't want your cover blown.

Me: I really don't owe you an explanation because my personal life aside from what I do should remain personal. My job is not the type of job you broadcast on a bulletin board. Sorry I couldn't assist you tonight.

I sent the email off, and at that very moment, I was ready to leave.

Mona Lise

It had been a long and drawn out day. After cleaning up the main house and coming to shower, I was finally able to relax in my bed. I had no clue where Nova had gone, but my guess was somewhere with that damn boy that I told her to stay away from. Sitting on the edge of my bed, I ran the brush through my long tresses. I had this habit ever since I was a small girl. I loved my natural hair; it was so beautiful to me. It was long and beautiful, but it felt like the more that I brushed it now, the more it would fall out. I heard a light tap at the door.

“Nova must be back,” I said to myself and placed the brush on the nightstand and made my way to the door. Opening the door, Malcolm barged in right fast. Placing my hand on my chest, I spoke

“Malcolm, what in the hell are you doing down here?” I asked. He stood in front of me with one hand in his pocket and the other scratching his beard.

“Mona Lise, you can’t drop a ton of steel on a man and not expect him to holler out in pain. I have a daughter that I knew nothing about, the more I think about it, it pisses me off. Yeah, I may have said I never wanted kids, but hell, I made one, and I don't know shit about her. I feel like I owe her my life. Why did you bring her here knowing that I would see her and not question you?" Malcolm said with worry and concern all in his voice.

I closed my robe over my nightgown. The guilt I know it showed on my face. I had lied all my life to this man, and now that I may need him, I didn't know how to tell him the truth, so I had to take drastic measures.

"Malcolm, I'm sick," I blurted out.

"What you got the flu or something? You need a couple of days off?" he asked. I rolled my eyes.

"I only brought Nova around because I'm sick and if something happens to me, she needs to know who her father is. I've been battling cervical cancer for some time now. Nobody knows, not even Nova," I spoke out in shame.

"Mona Lise, damn is there any more secrets? I know I'm a married man, but you also know that you have a place in my heart and in this family. Why would you keep that a secret? We could have been getting you the best medical treatment!" he yelled. The tears started to fall.

"I don't want y'all sympathy or help. All I ask is that you don't hurt my daughter. If things don't go right with your wife, don't you dare let her hurt my daughter. I'm not saying I'm dying tomorrow, but I have to figure out a way to tell Nova all this. I need this job to finish paying for Nova's college, so I know once Elizabeth finds out I will lose that," I cried.

Malcolm paced the floor and was shaking his head. I assume stressed out like I was.

"You got to give me some time, Mona. I can't just spring this shit on my wife like this," he said. I nodded my head in agreeance.

He walked over to me and placed his hand on my shoulders. I looked into his eyes, and he looked into mines. Without a word being spoken with our mouths, everything was said with our eyes. He leaned in and placed a kiss on my lips and then my forehead. I placed my hand on his chest and rested my head enjoying his scent.

"I have to get back to the house before Elizabeth finds out I'm missing," he whispered.

"Ok," I said, nodding my head.

I watched as Malcolm opened the front door and my eyes bulged out my head when I saw Nova and Muza standing there.

"Unc," Muza said.

"Nova," I gasped.

"Mama," Nova said.

"Muzaini," Malcolm said.

"What you doing down here?" Muza asked Malcolm.

"Boy, bring you ass. Asking me questions like this ain't my damn house," Malcolm said and walked off with Muza.

Nova walked in, and I stood there with my arms crossed ready to tear into her about where she been with Muza.

“Mama, are you sleeping with that man?” she asked me first.

“Nova, that is my boss, if you must know we were actually talking about you and Muza. Didn’t I tell you to stay away from him.” I quickly asked changing the subject.

“Look, mama no disrespect but I’m grown. Muza just wanted me to accompany him to a charity event tonight. That’s it. What’s the reason why you want me to stay away from him so bad?” she asked.

“Nova, he is a man of high caliber, and I need you to focus on graduating,” I told her. Nova looked at me trying to digest the first part of what I said.

“A man of high caliber, do you not think I know that, or are you saying I’m not good enough to be with a man like him? He’s just another nigga with money. I can’t do this anymore,” Nova said reaching into her purse. She handed me a check for $25,000.

“What is this, Nova?” I questioned.

"That's half of the money I owe you. Mama, I haven't been enrolled in college since sophomore year. I only went to college to satisfy you, but that's not what I wanted to do. To see you struggling to pay that high ass tuition pissed me off even more. I want to write," she said.

"Novanna Collier, you been lying to me this whole time about your schooling? What the hell have you been doing all this time?" I asked. I was so mad my head started to hurt.

"I've been writing and working. I take care of everything. I'm not hurting for any money. Maybe one day I'll go back to college, but right now it isn't for me. You can take that money and go find you somewhere to stay rather than live here," she said.

"Nova, it is my job as a parent to work and send you to school. You just want to throw your life away. You can always write and still go to school. Hell, by now, if all you've been doing is writing, you could've been done dropped a book or two you been out of school long enough!" I yelled.

"See, this is why I don't like telling you things because you don't ever listen to me. You know what, I don't even want to stay here the rest of the weekend." She sighed and headed to the bedroom to grab her things.

I wanted to follow her and tell her about my illness, but tonight wasn't the night. I watched as she grabbed her bags and walked back in the living room. I sat on the couch in silence. I felt Nova's eyes burning me.

"I love you, mama. Hopefully one day I can make you proud and show you just how great of a writer I will be," she said, placing a kiss on my cheek.

I listen to her heels walk away and out of the house. Closing my eyes, the tears started to fall. It was so much I wanted to tell her, and I pray that God gives me enough time to do just that.

Malcolm

"Unc, you sure you ain't messing with Mona Lise? I was just playing earlier, but to see you in the house, I ain't gone say shit." Muza said still pressing me about the issue. We had stopped in the kitchen to have a drink.

"I know you ain't gone say shit because it ain't shit to say. What are you doing with Nova? Don't play with that girl's heart," I told him. Muza was my nephew by marriage, but I also knew him, and now that I knew Nova was my daughter, I was not gone tolerate him playing games with my child.

"Nova's cool. She fit right in tonight. I may take her out on another date. She put Cru in her place too," he said. Finishing off the drink, I placed the glass in the sink.

"Clean that shit up. I'll talk to you some more tomorrow," I mumbled. I had to go lay it down.

A nigga head was on ten. I slowly walked the steps to the bedroom that I shared with my wife. Entering the room, I started to unbuckle my shirt. Elizabeth was sitting at her vanity with a smug look on her face.

"I saw you," she said. Removing my pants, I looked up at her.

"You saw me what, Elizabeth?" I asked. Elizabeth looked at me in the mirror.

"Why were you at the guest house? You were in there for quite some time, Malcolm," she asked as she turned around in her chair.

"Yeah, I went down there because I needed to talk to Mona Lise. Were you aware that she is sick?" I threw out there. There was no way I was going to tell my wife my real reason for going there.

"Sick how? I'm aware that her daughter looks like your grandmother and have some of your features. Malcolm, have you ever cheated on me? Don't you dare lie to me. I have this weird feeling about all of this. Nova is a beautiful child, and I have no ill will towards her, but Malcolm Dewayne Hamstead, I'm no fool so if you don't tell me the truth all hell will break loose in this house, and neither you nor Mona Lise will like it," she said. I could see the South Nashville coming out of Elizabeth. I know I promised that I would wait and tell her, but I had to keep the wife happy.

"From what I was told today, she is my daughter that I never knew about," I whispered.

"Oh my god nooo!" Elizabeth burst out in tears. I ran over to her and tried to comfort her.

"Get off of me, Malcolm. How could you do this to me and have her working here all these years?" she asked.

"Elizabeth, it isn't like that, it was a one-time thing," I lied.

I knew I should've told her the truth, but I couldn't have her knowing the truth about me and Mona Lise past and present. The truth was I loved both of them, and this whole time, I literally was having my cake and eating it too.

"Elizabeth, listen to me. I know I am wrong on so many levels but imagine my surprise when seeing her for the first time. You know I never wanted any kids, so that's why she never told me. She has worked here and raised Nova on her own for twenty-three years. Mona Lise is dying, and she felt the need to tell me now because I will be all

Nova has. Nova doesn't even know yet," I said, holding on to Elizabeth's hands.

"This is a lot to take in, Malcolm. How can I walk around knowing this woman slept with my husband and gave him something that I couldn't give him? How do you expect me to just overlook all this?" she asked. Closing my eyes, I let out a huge sigh.

"I'm not asking you to pretend or overlook anything. I really just need patience with all of this, especially with approaching Nova. Please, Elizabeth, I'm sorry, but please don't say anything to Mona Lise." I pleaded.

I knew this was asking her a lot because I knew I had just caused her so much pain. Elizabeth was always a forgiving person, so maybe she could forgive this situation.

"I can't promise you that, but out of respect for Nova and Nova only, I will not say anything to her or her mother at least until I find out she knows that she is your daughter," Elizabeth spoke, removing her hands from mine and walking towards the bed. That would have to do for now.

Nova

Leaving my mother was the hardest thing I had to do, but I'm glad that I was able to finally tell her the truth. I knew she would be mad for a while, but that was one less thing I had to deal with. She was stubborn at times, and now I knew who I got that shit from. I walked to the front of the Hamsteads house and ranged the doorbell, I knew it was late, but I had no other way to get Muza's attention.

"I got it!" I heard Muza yell as he came to the door. When he opened the door, he was dressed in the Gucci joggers he wore earlier and a wife beater and some Gucci slides. His chest was sitting on swole, and he had arms of steel. Them motherfuckers were big when he crossed his arms.

"Girl, what are you doing out here?" he asked.

"Um. I actually was about to catch an Uber home, but we needed to exchange numbers you know for business purposes," I said.

"What the hell are you going home for? Bump that hold on," he said and turned to run upstairs.

"Who was at the door?" Mrs. Hamstead asked as she peeked out over the banister from upstairs.

"Sorry, it was me. Muza is taking me home. Thanks for the hospitality," I said.

"Is everything ok, why are you going home? It's late dear," she asked.

"Long story and my mother needs some space, we sort of had a small disagreement," I told her.

"Oh, I'm sorry for that, maybe she will come around," she said. Muza was making his way back downstairs.

"I'm going to drop her off, and I'll be back, Auntie," he said. I could've sworn I seen her wipe her eyes as if she was shedding a tear. I didn't know what that was all about.

"Come on," he said and grabbed my bags.

This man was everything. I had to keep telling myself this was only for the money, but a bitch was feeling a type of way. I watched as he hit the lock and opened the door for me as I got in. He placed my bags in the back seat and made his way up front. When he got in, he looked over at me.

"What?" I blushed.

"What happened with you and your moms?" he asked. I was scared to tell him the truth because then he would have a reason to back out our little arrangement.

"I just went ahead and told her about school because she keeps preaching and tryna dictate my life. I wasn't being disrespectful, but I told her I was grown. I have no clue why she's so adamant for me to leave you alone, like I'm not on your level," I was rambling on.

"Damn, Mona Lise feels a certain way about me, huh? That's fucked up," he said as he started the car.

"You do know that you still gotta keep up our little deal at least for a few weeks. I don't want folks to think of you as a little industry freak.

I peeped that shit with Delaunn, so what was that all about because I know you don't do his chick hair," he said coolly but shocking the hell out of me.

I busted out laughing to try to keep from embarrassing myself.

"How you just gone call me an industry freak. In Nashville running into a Titan is nothing. They asses be everywhere. We have been out on a couple of dates, but that's it. Nothing major. It wasn't like I knew I would meet yo ass. Wait, what does it matter it ain't like this shit we doing for real anyways. You could've been stepping on his toes, I could've been his first, and then what would that make you?" I asked, looking at him as he kept his eyes on the road.

"Well, if you were his first, you're mine now until I say otherwise," he spoke glancing over at me. I couldn't do nothing but laugh.

We pulled up in front of my apartment, and I saw a truck parked behind my Range, which was my guest parking spot.

"Who the fuck is in my guest spot? Kelly's ass don't ever have no company," I said aloud.

“Well, I’m going up with you anyways, so if it’s an uninvited guest, he can get served real quick,” Muza said, stepping out of the car.

I followed and got out and met Muza as he walked around the car. Walking upstairs to my apartment, Muza trailed behind me carrying my bags. Using my key to unlock the door, we entered the apartment, and I flicked the lights on.

“You can just sit those bags right there,” I told Muza.

I watched as he placed the bags on the floor beside the couch and took a seat on the sofa. I gave him the side eye like why was he making himself comfortable. It was going on three in the morning. I heard moans coming from Kelly’s bedroom, which piqued my interest. Muza and I both looked at each other, and he started laughing.

“Damn, somebody is getting they back blown out.” He laughed, placing my hand over my mouth.

“Oh my god, my roommate never gets off, so I’m dying to know who this is. Shit, I leave for a weekend, and she goes wild,” I said, taking a seat beside Muza. My thoughts drifted to my mother, and I wonder how she felt.

“You good?” Muza asked. His voice alone made me feel comfort. It made me feel a little too comfortable. Don’t get me wrong I know how to be with a man for paid companionship, but it was something about Muza was making me want more. I let out a deep sigh.

“Yeah, I’m straight. A little tired, but I did have a good time tonight with you,” I admitted.

“It was nothing; you were a natural. When you blow up, you already got that star attitude. What really went down in the bathroom between you and crew?” he asked, looking at me with his deep brown eyes.

“How you know I’m gone blow up, you saying you believe in me? I will never have a book that gets me recognized like that. Them people that were at that charity event was all over you,” I said, and Muza grabbed my face.

“Why do you not feel you will be like that? You can do anything you put your mind to if you put in the hard work and speak that shit into existence. You can't put yourself down just because the next person does it," he spoke in a serious tone.

How could this man that I barely knew see the potential in me and I couldn't?

"That meant a lot. But nall, she came in the bathroom just staring at me and shit and I laughed at her ass, so she was like "Do I amuse you?" in her little bougie ass voice. I told her actually you do, then she went on to say how you were a dog and you always come back home because you get bored. I told her she was the boring one and you weren't a dog you were T'Challa, a king, and should be treated as such."

"Damn, so I'm yo *Black Panther*?" he asked, leaning towards me. His cologne started playing tricks with my nose.

"Come on to Wakanda then," he said, getting closer and placing his lips on mine.

I don't know what the hell came over me, but I tried to suck his lips off his face. Muza's big muscular ass had me pinned down on the couch and climbed on top of me as our kiss was becoming more and more intense. Part of me was wanting all of this, and the other half of me knew I needed to remain focus.

"No, no, stop. We are not supposed to be doing this. Remember this is business," I panted.

"Business for who, we got to act the part right? It has to be believable to everyone including us so that we don't get caught slipping," he said with his eyes locked on me. My panties were already soaking wet, and I could feel his third leg busting through his jogger pants.

"Not here," I whispered.

I pushed Muza off of me and stood up from the couch looking at him. I held my hand out for him to grab and lead him down the hall to my bedroom. Entering my room, I thought I was going to be able to take control, but Muza had other shit on his mind. As soon as I closed the bedroom door, I was tossed on the bed like a rag doll. The hungry look he had was how a lion looks at his prey right before he attacks. This nigga removed my panties and pants in one pull.

"Damn," I mumbled.

Muza licked his lips and pulled his beater over his head. Placing his big frame on top of me, he placed small kisses on my stomach and made his way further down. Using his thumb, he gently played with my clit before placing his thick tongue in my center. The warmth of his tongue caused my body to get hotter. Lil baby was hungry, and he was getting all his nourishment.

"Damn, you taste good," he moaned.

Placing my hands on top of his head, Muza inserted his tongue in my pussy, and I felt my juices oozing out. Grinding into his face, this nigga's tongue was long, and he was snaking that bitch and sticking it in and out playing with me. He slowly inserted two fingers and kept his mouth on my pearl as he sucked for dear life. This nigga had my eyes rolling back to the back of my head. I grabbed ahold of my knees because I knew I was about to cum. Snapping my legs closed, I placed a grip around Muzaini's head.

“Shitttttt!” I yelled. Muza lifted up and removed his pants while I worked on my breathing cause a bitch was woe.

“You got a taste of the mouth, you sure you want this dick?” he asked.

Opening my eyes, I glanced down at his shit and kept a poker face, but inside I was screaming and wondering where in the hell he was about to put that big ass thang.

“We here now, ain’t no turning back,” I said.

Muza slapped his dick against my lips teasing me, and I was really like please hurry up and stick this shit in. Pressing against the gates, he eased himself inside. I placed my hand on his chiseled stomach while he pushed himself further inside of me, and he stopped and looked at me.

“Move your hand,” he demanded, smacking my hand away.

Muza had made his way inside and was pounding the shit out of my pussy. This nigga’s size was unbearable, and I was trying my best to take that shit like a pro, but every time I eased my hand back up, he would smack it away.

“Oh my god, Muza,” I whimpered in pain and pleasure because now the pain was subsiding.

“Shut up and take this dick,” he said as he used his thumb to massage my clit with each stroke.

“Look how she’s reacting to this dick. Girl, you creaming all over this dick,” he said, looking down. Pulling out he laid on his back

“Come ride this shit,” he demanded.

I did what I was told, eased over, and glided down his pole. Muza placed his hands underneath my ass and assisted with me bouncing up and down on his dick. Closing my eyes, I bit down on my bottom lip as I could feel this nigga all the way in my stomach, but that didn’t stop me from putting on a show. His moans were turning me on, and I had this thug ass nigga singing like a bitch. He grabbed ahold of me, and I felt his dick twitch inside. I sped up, and about three minutes later, he released all in me.

“Damn girl, where you learn how to ride dick like that? I thought you were going to have a hard time since at first, you couldn’t take the dick. You almost got your hands broke," he said as I was walking back out of the bathroom. I shook my head at him.

"I never back down from a challenge," I told him as I sat down on the bed beside him giving him a hot soapy rag. Muza grabbed the rag and cleaned himself up.

"So, I guess this just makes our job even better. Don't be spazzing out over the dick," he had the nerve to say.

"You wish," I said, but honestly, I knew down inside that the energy between us had already intertwined, and the sexual experience was going to make things tough. Here we were supposed to be pretending, but this shit was just getting deeper and deeper.

Kelly

I don't know what happened between Jon Jon and me, but one minute we were talking, and the next he had me screaming his name. I glanced over at him, and he was snoring lightly. I heard noises coming from Nova's room, and last I checked she was staying at her mom's for the weekend. Slipping my feet in my slippers, I put my glasses on, eased out the bed, and walked out of the room. Walking towards Nova door, I placed my ear on the door, and I heard talking. *I just know she didn't bring work back to the house.* I tapped lightly on the door. I could hear movement, and finally, the door opened, and Nova stood there in her bra and panties.

"I thought you were at your mom's for the weekend?" I asked.

"I was, but now I'm home. We will talk about this after my man leaves," she whispered.

"Your man? Nova, who you got up in here?" I asked, trying to peek over her shoulder. Nova closed the door some and leaned towards me.

"Girl, I think I should be asking who the hell Jon Jon is, the way you were hollering his name in there. Yep, I heard you. We will talk tomorrow," she said, laughing and closed the door.

I stood standing at the door for a few minutes before I walked back to my room. Entering my room, I slowly sat back on the bed so that I didn't wake Jon Jon.

"Where'd you go?" he mumbled. I looked over my shoulder, and he was scratching his beard.

"I was trying to see where that noise was coming from because my roommate was supposed to be gone for the weekend," I told him. Jon Jon sat up in the bed, and he grabbed his phone off the nightstand. I wonder if he had a woman that he needed to get back to.

"What you over there thinking about?" he asked.

"Nothing, what makes you think I'm thinking about something?" I asked.

"Because I know, but look, check this out. I need you to call yo boss and tell him you won't be back," he demanded.

"Wait a minute. I won't be back? I can't just up and quit my job. I have bills and school that I have to take care of," I told him. I don't know what this nigga was thinking, but the shit wasn't logical.

"Look, I'm feeling you, and I can't have my girl bussing no damn tables for $2.13 an hour. I just want you to focus on school. I got everything else covered. You help me, and I help you. We'll both be good. Trust me," he said.

I gave him a complex look because I didn't know who the hell this man was, and yeah, the sex was good, but how he gone call me his girl after one night? I sat there and kept pondering and finally I gave in.

"Ok, if you say so," I said. Right then and there I had a bad feeling about this, and I should've gone with my gut, but you only live once, right.

With a smile on his face, Jon Jon pulled me into his arms and laid back down. I got comfortable and laid there contemplating until I dozed back off.

Malcolm

Making my way downstairs, I wanted to talk to Mona Lise a little more about Nova. Entering the kitchen, the smell of freshly brewed coffee hit my nose. Mona Lise knew exactly what I wanted every morning. She leaned against the counter sipping from her cup staring into space as if the weight of the world was on her shoulders.

“Good morning,” I said, startling her. Mona Lise looked up.

“What’s so good about it?” she asked. I looked around

“Where are the Cheerios?” I asked. With her face screwed up

“Malcolm you don’t eat Cheerios. What are you talking about?” she asked me.

“I’m just trying to find the bowl of Cheerios that you were eating out of that someone pissed in,” I told her. Grabbing my cup of coffee, I took a sip of the hot liquid.

“Where’s Nova?” I asked.

“Nova left last night. We had a little dispute, and she decided to leave,” she said.

“You didn’t tell her, yet did you?” I asked hoping that wasn’t the reason she left.

“No, I haven’t told her any of the things that I needed to tell her. You know this whole time I been sending her checks for school, she hasn’t been attending school since her sophomore year. Nova has been lying to me this whole time. I just can’t see how she wants to throw her life away then turn around and gives me a check for twenty-five grand!” she yelled.

“Maybe she has a different plan for her life. As a young adult, I’m sure she didn’t want to hurt you. You have to let her find her own way through life,” I told her, taking another sip of my coffee. Mona Lise shook her head.

“No, that’s what you not gone do is try and play daddy now. I’ve done just fine for twenty-three years. You can’t tell me how to raise my daughter!” Mona Lise spat.

“What you will not do is talk to my husband like that. It isn’t his fault that you raised Nova on your own. He is only trying to offer some helpful advice," Elizabeth said, startling us as she walked into the kitchen.

"You told her?" Mona Lise asked me with a look of shock on her face.

"He had every right to tell his wife, I'm being the bigger woman and trying to accept this, but the disrespect will not be tolerated if you would like to keep your job," Elizabeth scolded Mona Lise like a child. *Lord, please don't let Mona snap off.*

"You know what, my health is way more important anyway. I'm going to leave before I continue to work under these circumstances. I might as well leave with what little dignity I have left. Ms. Elizabeth, I do apologize for dropping this on y'all the way that I did, but I'm dying, and I wanted Nova to know that she does have a father. I will remove my things from the guest house and get out of your hair," Mona Lise said.

To hear those words, leave Mona Lise mouth made my heart shatter. This was all bad the way I loved this woman, and here my wife stood beside me loving me more than I could ever love her.

“You don’t have to leave Mona Lise. Where would you go?” I asked, not even catching the side eye Elizabeth was giving me.

“Excuse me. It isn’t your concern where she goes, Malcolm. Now Mona Lise, I wasn’t firing you, but I understand your need to leave,” Elizabeth said.

“Elizabeth, whether she is here or there, I have to communicate with her about Nova. I have a daughter now that I can’t neglect. I have to make sure she gets decent medical treatment,” I told Elizabeth, digging a bigger hole for myself. The way Elizabeth looked at me before she turned and walked away was enough to know that my marriage may be on the line.

“Mona Lise, I’ve always had your back, and I will continue to have it,” I told her as I walked over to her. “Nobody should battle cancer alone, especially the mother of my child. I will have my guys come pack up your things and take them to a property that I have that Elizabeth knows nothing about. I will continue to pay you as you still work here.

You know I love you, right?" I whispered. Mona Lise lifted her head and looked up at me.

"Yes, Malcolm, and I love you too.

Muzaini

My phone was beeping like crazy, and that shit was pissing me off because a nigga was tired from fucking Nova all night. I laid on my back and looked up at the ceiling and noticed the painting of the Nova that she had on her ceiling. I looked over at Nova who was out like a light. Checking my phone, I had texts, missed calls, and photo tags on Facebook and IG. One tagged caught my attention, and it was something that Delaunn had posted on his IG.

It was an older photo of Nova and him looking real comfy on somebody's beach. *Why in the hell was this nigga tagging me in pictures?* See this is the type of shit a nigga didn't like to deal with. I wasn't the type of industry nigga that beefed over pussy. I never have and wasn't about to start no time soon. I slid my arm from underneath Nova and sat up on the side of the bed. I had some things that I needed to take care of today. I wiped the crust from my eyes and stood to walk in the bathroom.

"Where are you going?" Nova mumbled.

“Freshen up, I need to head home,” I told her. I felt bad because I was feeling salty about this shit with Delaunn, but at the same time, I believed Nova and what she said about them.

“It’s an extra toothbrush under the sink, and the towels are in the basket on the shelf!” Nova yelled. I nodded my head and made my way to the bathroom.

After taking care of my hygiene, I walked back in the room, and Nova was holding her phone shaking her head. I wonder what that was about. I grabbed the shit I had on last night and put it on in silence.

“I’ll hit you up later. I got some things that I need to take care of,” I told her. She stood up and made her way over to me.

“You good? You seem a little standoffish this morning?” she asked.

“I’m forever straight,” I told her and turned to walk out the room.

I felt Nova walking behind me as we made our way down the hall. Entering the kitchen, I spotted a light skin chick and some dude, which I figured was her roommate and the guy sticking it to her last night.

"Oh my god, Muzaini Muhammad is in my crib. The world must be about to end," she boasted, causing me to chuckle.

Whoever the dude was hit me with a head nod, and he looked back at his plate to finish eating.

"Nice to meet you," I said.

"Muza, this is my roommate, Kelly. Kelly Muza," Nova spoke, introducing us. I caught the eye that Kelly gave Nova.

"Well, I've got to head out, nice meeting you," I said and continued on the door. Nova was behind me.

"I enjoyed your company last night," she whispered.

"Likewise, you just make sure to tell Delaunn that," I said leaving her to ponder what the hell I meant. I shook my head as I walked off and headed to my car.

Muzaini Muhammad acting like this wasn't me. I was that nigga and could have any bitch I wanted, but why, I ask myself again was this shit with Nova bothering me.

After leaving Nova's I headed back to my aunt and uncle house, a nigga's head was gone. When I pulled up, I saw a moving truck and movers moving shit.

"The hell going on?" I mumbled. I parked my whip and made my way to the house.

Upon entering, I saw my uncle and Mona Lise talking, and the conversation looked to be serious.

"What's going on?" I asked. My uncle held his hand up dismissing me, which I didn't like.

"Rude ass," I said, walking into the house. I headed straight in the house and went looking for my aunt. Walking upstairs, the door to her bedroom was closed, so I tapped lightly and entered.

"Why do you always knock and still walk in. You are to wait until the person invites you in," she said, standing at the window I assume watching was taking place downstairs.

"My bad TT, I was just trying to see what the hell was going on, but your rude ass husband was too busy to talk," I said.

"That's because he is too busy making sure his baby mama gets moved out," she said finally looking over at me, and her face was stained from crying.

"Huh baby mama, what's really going on?" I asked.

"Seems like Malcolm and Mona Lise had a rendezvous some years ago, and it resulted in a child that we are just now finding out about," she said. I was kind of confused.

"Talking about a little kid, I ain't ever known for Ms. Mona to be pregnant," I told her.

"That's because the child ain't little, Muza, she is twenty-three years old," she cried.

"Nova?" I asked.

My aunt just nodded her head, and the tears just fell. Now all the times I asked him about Mona Lise I see why he was so secretive. He'd been bussing her ass down.

"Does Nova know?" I asked.

"No, and I know you guys have been kicking it. So, it isn't your place to tell her. Let her mother and father deal with that," she said. Rubbing my hands over my head, I couldn't believe this shit.

Cru

I didn't know who this Nova chick was, but she was fucking up everything I had worked for. I was currently on IG scanning hashtags of last night's event and trying to find pictures of little Ms. Thing so I could know for a fact what I was working with. There was a picture under Muza name of Nova and another guy who I also remember seeing at the party last night, but this picture was most definitely not from last night. I click on the guy's page whose name was Delaunn Fleming, and he appeared to be a linebacker for the Tennessee Titans. Not only did he have one picture, but he also had several pictures of him and Nova, and Muza was tagged in all of them. I instantly knew this was a man scorned.

Rubbing my hands together, a small grin spread across my face, because he just didn't know how he was going to help me get my man back. I typed up a nice little DM, hoping he would return my message.

A loud knock at the door caused me to close my laptop. Walking over to the doors, I looked through the peephole shocked at who was on the other side. Unlocking the door, I pulled it opened and placed my hands on my hips.

"Well, what do I owe the pleasure of this visit?" I asked Muzaini. Muzaini looked me up and down, and I knew he was taking in all that he was missing. He brushed past me and walked towards the living room.

"This isn't a pleasure call Cru. I need to know what the hell was your point of approaching my girl last night?' he asked.

"I know you didn't come here to talk about someone so irrelevant, like Muza what is wrong with you dating the help's daughter?" I said.

Yeah, I had done my research I knew exactly who this peasant bitch was, now I was just trying to get enough dirt on her so that Muza will come back to me. Muza walked up to where his mouth was damn near touching my nose.

"I need for you to get this in that thick ass skull of yours, I don't know if your sew-in is too tight, and it's fucking up your common sense, but Cru me and you are done, sweetie. It is nothing you can do for me anymore. I have been knowing this for a long time, but I admit I fucked up and kept you around longer than you should've been. And if you ever disrespect Nova again, I will see that your career or whatever it is you're doing these days will go down the fucking drain. Do I make myself clear?" he said through gritted teeth.

"Crystal," I told him just to shut him the hell up.

He could think whatever he wanted, but I was too far in to back out now. Muza smirked and turned to walk back out the door, leaving me standing there.

Nova

When Muza left, I went to take the sheets and shit off the bed so that I could wash them. Kelly was saying goodbye to her little piece from last night, and I couldn't wait to tear into her ass about him. I walked to the washroom and placed the sheets in the washer. As soon as I got in there, my phone dinged. Running back to the bedroom hoping it was Muza hitting me up, I grabbed the phone my smile faded when I saw it was an email from Delaunn.

I need you tonight 4,000 you know where to come. Delaunn

I threw the phone back on the bed. One thing I couldn't do was let my cash cow go because escorting was my only means of income. Even if Muza was slowly coming off change, I needed to have a rainy-day fund. I sent him a reply letting him know that I would be there. When I sat the phone down, Kelly was standing in the doorway with her arms crossed with a grin longer than Lischey on her face.

"Bitch, spill it. I've been waiting all night for this shit," I said, patting my bed so that she could sit down. Kelly twisted over to the bed, and I busted out laughing.

"You're telling me to spill it, but I think your tea is way hotter than mine," she said.

“Ok yeah, it sort of is,” I admitted. So, I started to tell Kelly everything that transpired.

“Oh my god, well it seems like your story is way more interesting than mine. So how is this going to work? Are you doing this just for the money, or do you really like him?” Kelly asked.

I thought about how I wanted to answer that. Because I knew it was all about the bag, but I can’t front and act like he ain’t winning me over slowly.

“You know I’m always about securing the bag, but I would like to keep my occupation a secret. Not that with you I have anything to worry about, so tell me about this Jon Jon cat. How the hell did that happen? He looked way out of your league,” I asked Kelly.

“That nigga just popped up at my job. He had been coming in there for a little minute and shit. He told my ass to sit down, and he ends up bringing me home. I ain’t gone lie he caught me off guard at first, but I couldn’t deny the way that nigga had me feeling. You know he asked me to quit my job?” she said, looking over at me and my ears perked.

“Wait, so he must gone cover you half of the bills?” I asked not meaning to come off offensive, but I could tell that Kelly took it that way. Kelly stood up and walked off shaking her head.

“That’s fucked up that that’s the first thing that popped up in your head!” she yelled as she went in her room and slammed the door.

Delaunn

Now of course y'all may think a nigga is coming off as crazy but see Nova thinks she can play with niggas feelings then move on to the next. See Nova ain't tell y'all all that. Don't get me wrong I had gotten Nova's number from one of my teammates when I moved to Nashville for the new season. I never went in treating Nova like she was an escort because when I first laid eyes on her, I thought she was the most beautiful woman I had ever seen.

She was different from the rest, and she made a nigga want to wife her. So of course, we started off as strictly business, and I was paying her more than usual because I enjoyed her company. She had even mentioned quitting and giving this relationship thing a try. So how you expect a nigga to act when she showed up to an event with the next nigga. That shit wasn't cool, and then she wanted me to keep her secret as if my feelings wasn't shit.

Sitting in the room, waiting on Nova to come through, I was going back and forth in my head with what I wanted to say to her. The whiskey I was drinking was taking the edge off, and I was getting more comfortable. I had the lights dimmed low so the mood would be set and I had her favorite wine chilling. There was a knock at the door, I stood from the couch and fixed my shirt as I made my way over to the door. When I opened the door, there stood Nova looking sexy as ever. Her locs had been curled, and she wore them down.

"Wassup," I said as I moved over letting her in.

"Hey, I'm surprised you wanted to meet," she said, placing her purse on the counter as she went straight for the wine.

"Oh, you thought I was gone trip about that little shit that happened at the party?" I asked. Nova took a sip from the glass.

"Delaunn, you were about to show your ass then to top it off, that shit you pulled on social media was messy as hell. What was your point?" she asked. This wasn't the route I wanted to take this conversation, but I knew that she would bring it up.

"Novanna, let's be real like we always have with each other. What happened to us that quickly? We were just discussing being with each other, and now you want to be with Muza?" I asked.

"Dammit Delaunn, I know what it looks like, but it isn't what you think. I'm only helping him, and he is helping me. Our families are sort of intertwined," Nova said.

"So, he doesn't know about your little escort business, this just an appearance thing for the both of you?" I asked. I knew Nova was taking in circles and not telling me everything.

"Look, I'm here with you now, and once this is over you and I can talk about what's going to happen with us," she said. I grabbed Nova's hand, pulled her towards me, and placed her in my lap. Caressing the side of her face, I leaned in and kissed her.

"Wait, you know we are not about to go there," she said. I felt the heat rise behind my ears; she had never turned me down.

"What you mean? Ain't this what I pay you for since I'm a paying double. I'm back to being a customer now right, so what's the problem?" I asked. Nova snatched her arm away from me. I had no clue that I had tighten my grip on her arm.

"I'm sorry, Nova. I ain't mean nothing by it," I told her. The frightened look softened on her face, and she leaned in and kissed me.

Nova

Delaunn had every right to be mad, and he made sure he called me out on my shit. Ok yeah, I had an issue with falling with guys with a little bit more money than your average person. The way that I feel about Muza was how I felt about Delaunn at one point, but Muza was different. Don't get me wrong it was nothing wrong with Delaunn. I was just bored with him. I needed to protect my secret because Delaunn's ways reminded me of a bitter scorn ass woman. So, I leaned in and kissed him like my life depended on it.

Delaunn's hands roamed over my ass, and I could feel him hardened through the sweatpants that he had on. He lifted me and removed his dick from his pants all in one swift motion. Delaunn was packing in that area, but Muza was much bigger. Why in this moment I felt bad or felt that my morals were being tested like I owed Muzaini. I wanted to be faithful to a man that I wasn't even committed to.

"That feel good?" Delaunn asked, bringing me out of my thoughts.

"Huh?" was all I could say.

"I asked if that felt good?" he said as he lifted me and eased me back down on his dick.

"Aw yeah, baby. You know you the only one that can satisfy me," I said, putting it on thick.

I was ready for this moment to be over, so it was time to bust out the prize so that I could get my money and cash the fuck out on this nigga. I hopped off Delaunn and got on my knees in between his legs and started sucking his dick like my life depended on it. I knew Delaunn was feeling it because he had damn near slipped off the couch. I had him exactly where I wanted him. In three minutes tops, he was spilling like a broken faucet, and I swallowed every drop.

"Damn Nova, shit!" he yelled out in ecstasy as he tried to get control of his breathing. I wiped my mouth and gave him a tantalizing smile. I stood up, made my way over to the bathroom, and freshen up so that I could take my ass home and ask God to forgive me for being a hoe. Well, make that a paid hoe.

Delaunn

As soon as Nova walked off to the bathroom, I got up, walked over to the entertainment center, and cut the camera I had recording off. Call me a dog ass nigga and say I was wrong, I don't give a fuck. I know one day this tape will come in handy if she decides not to act right. I walked towards the bathroom and joined Nova in freshening up.

"I'm going away for a few weeks to meet with this new trainer, so I might fly you out on the weekend if that's ok with you?" I asked her. Nova looked at me as if she was thinking hard about her answer.

"Ok baby, that sounds like fun, even though I don't want to come off as a distraction. You need to focus on training. This is your year, baby," she said as she leaned in and kissed me on the lips.

This was how I fell for Nova. She was always concerning and motivated a nigga. I swear a nigga was going to make her wifey.

Muzaini

I had been blowing up Nova's phone. I just needed to be around her for some reason. After seeing that shit that went down at my family's house and then the five minutes, I had to deal with Cru's ass my head was on ten. One of my groups had a gig tonight, and I wanted to bring Nova. Then on top of that, I had to fly out to the distillery in the morning to check on the new batch of Muzanac I was pushing out for summer. A nigga had a lot on his plate, but that didn't stop me from wanting to spend time with her.

"Stop right here," I told my driver as we pulled up in front of Nova's house.

Her car wasn't there, so I pulled out my phone and dialed her number again. While the phone was ringing, Nova pulled in like a bat out of hell rushing out of the car. She fumbled with her phone, and she finally answered.

"Hey, Muza," she answered all out of breath. I wanted to go in on her ass immediately, but I had to remember this wasn't my damn girl.

“Damn girl, you’re hard to contact, what are you doing?” I asked, watching her from the car she didn’t even know I was sitting in.

“Nothing just got out the shower, my ass been knocked out,” she said. I shook my head as the lie rolled so freely off her tongue. That shit was a huge turn-off. Why the hell was she standing right here lying? She finally walked up the steps and headed inside her apartment.

“Aw, I didn’t mean to disturb your beauty sleep. What you about to do?” I asked.

“Oh, Me and Kelly finna hang out,” she mentioned.

“You think y’all would want to go to see my artist perform tonight? That’s why I was calling. I ain’t want to spring something on you last minute,” I said, getting out the car making my way to Nova’s door. I tapped lightly on the door.

“Um, I’ll have to ask Kelly and get back with you,” she said, opening the door. Nova gave me the side eye, and I shrugged it off and made my way inside hanging up the phone.

"So, you just popping up now?" she asked. I looked at her fully dressed purse still on her shoulder. Details were everything, and I paid attention to everything.

"Where you headed?" I asked.

"I'm not headed anywhere." She walked off and threw her purse on the couch and headed to her room to undress. All this shit was funny to me. I could tell me being here had thrown her off, and she was confused as shit.

"I thought you just got out the shower? Nova, you're a horrible liar. I have been watching you since you got out the car, talking bout your ass was sleep. It's not my place to question what you do because you ain't my girl, but obviously it's something you don't want me to find out since you felt the need to lie anyways. With that being said from here on out, I advise you to keep it funky with me like I have been with you and how I'm bout to be with you," I told her. She was stoned face and embarrassed.

"So, you're stalking me now?" she questioned. I busted out laughing.

“Girl, don’t insult me. Sit down so that I can tell you what I need to tell you then you can go on about your night,” I told her.

“Why I got to sit down?” she asked, shaking my head because Nova was hardheaded as fuck. I learned that much about her already.

“After I tell you what I tell you, trust me you gone need to take a seat,” I reassured her. Nova sat down and placed her arms on her knees waiting for me to open my big mouth.

“What I’m about to tell you, technically I’m not supposed to be telling you. Today, when I went back to my uncle’s, your moms was moving out. I tried asking him what was going on, but he dismissed my ass. So, I went inside the house and talked to my aunt. She was crying and upset and shit. Has your mom ever told you anything about your father?” I asked Nova. Nova's face was all twisted up

“No, why?” she asked. I let out a huge sigh and took a seat beside her on the couch.

“Nova, the reason why your mother was moving out today was because my uncle was moving her out to her own place. It seems like some time ago he and your mother had an affair, and it resulted in a baby," I slowly told her. Nova busted out laughing.

"My ma ain't had no other kids, what she look like?" Nova laughed. The look on my face was a concerning one, and Nova took notice right away.

"Nova, my Uncle Malcolm is your father," I said. Nova was quiet. I didn't know what type of reaction to expect.

"My mother would've told me this shit, hell nah so the whole time I was at them people's house they knew this shit?" she yelled.

"Look, I don't know all the details, I wasn't even supposed to tell you this much, but I knew you needed to know this. Now what you do with the information is all on you," I told her. I stood up from the couch and turned to look at Nova before I left.

"Call me if you need me. I'll leave and come back," I said, making sure to make her feel comfortable. I just prayed that she handled this the right way and not go all off and shit.

Nova

Staring into space minutes after Muza left, I was fighting inside with the information I had just received. *Why on earth would my mother keep this from me? Why on earth would my mother work for this man and sleep with him too?* Lord, I had so many questions. I quickly dialed my mother's number on the phone. After a few rings, she answered.

"Nova!" she said in the phone like she was happy to hear from me.

"Mom, where are you?" I asked, getting straight to the point. This wasn't a telephone kind of conversation. This needed to happen face to face.

"I have a new place. I'll text you the address, sweetie. Is everything alright?" she asked.

"That we will see," I said, hanging up and grabbing my keys. I was scared yet mad as hell.

I skipped to the truck and unlocked the door. I didn't care what my mother thought now, I was driving my damn Range Rover over there, and I dare her to ask me where I got my shit from. Malcolm Hamstead was the richest motherfucker I knew besides Muzaini's ass, and my mother had us penny pinching all my damn life. It was something more to them, and I knew it. This was why she stayed around all this time talking about they were family. Oh my god, I wonder how Mrs. Elizabeth is taking it?

The sounds of horns blowing brought me out of my trance. I pulled through the light and kept driving. Wherever Mr. Malcolm put mama up at it sholl wasn't on the bad side of town. Mama was loving this shit. She has been a damn side chick all her life. I pulled up in front of Terrazzo condos and looked up at the fancy ass building. Shit, she was doing it big. Stepping out of the truck, I hit the locks and walked inside.

Entering the building, I looked around the lobby and took everything in. I spotted the elevators and made my way to them. While on the ride up, my stomach started hurting and I started to get hot.

Not right now, Nova, get your shit together. Go in here and get straight to it, I told myself. The elevator stopped, and I walked off the elevator and headed to my mother's door. I raise my hand to knock, and I froze. I started to pace in front of the door.

"Nova," I heard a male voice.

Turning around there stood Malcolm, the man that was supposed to be my father. All I could do was look at him. I was trying to find where did I look like him, or if I even looked like him at all. He walked closer to me, and I backed away shaking my head.

"Where is my mother?" I asked walking passed him.

Entering the apartment, my mother stood in the kitchen with her arms crossed and devastation on her face. Malcolm came in behind me closing the door. Here we all were standing in the kitchen looking at each other stupidly.

"Well shit, since the gang's all here, does anyone want to tell me about this shit I'm hearing about this man being my daddy?" I asked, looking at mama. Mama shifted on her hip and placed her hands on them before she spoke, I knew she was about to chew into my ass.

“Novanna Collier, now I know you’re mad, but you’re not about to step up in here with all this damn cussing and being disrespectful. I let that slick shit you were talking yesterday slide, but today I’m gone slide my hand right across yo damn face if you keep playing with me. Now play with your life if you want to!” she yelled. Rolling my eyes, I crossed my arms and waited for someone to talk.

“Nova, I don’t want you to be mad at me because I found out the day you stepped foot in my house, even though even then I had to drag it out of your mother,” Malcolm spoke. I looked at my mother in disbelief.

“Malcolm, don’t even try to be the good guy in all of this. If you hadn't been so adamant about not wanting kids, this wouldn’t have been an issue,” she said.

“I just want to know why? Why in the world would you allow me to grow up thinking you had no clue who my father was, but for your own selfish reasons you made sure you stayed around him and his wife all your damn life,” I said as calm as I could.

"Don't you ever talk to me like that. You don't know shit about what I had going on," mama said.

"I know that's exactly what I'm trying to figure out. This looks really bad on your end, mother. It looks like you settled with being a side chick all your life. No wonder you never had a man because you had somebody else's the whole time."

SMACK! The stinging from the slap my mother just gave me had me wanting to pounce on this woman.

"I told you to watch how you talk to me. This was my man first. Your father didn't want to marry her, but since he did to satisfy his family, he made it to where he could be with me also. I love this man!" mama yelled then grabbed her head before she passed out on the floor.

"Mama!" I yelled, running to her side. Malcolm bent down.

"Mona Lise, Mona Lise!" he called out to her, reaching into his pocket he dialed 911.

Mama slowly opened her eyes, and she tried to speak, but her words weren't coming out. She reached and grabbed Malcolm's hands and nodded her head. Malcolm looked at me.

"Nova, your mother is dying of cancer. Now, I don't know what's going on now that caused her to pass out, but she just told me this the same day that I found out I was your father. She wanted me to know and make sure that if anything happened to her that I look after you. I know that this isn't the best time, but I apologize for everything, I'm sorry I wasn't there. Had I known, I would've been there. I would have never denied you. You look just like my great-grandmother, and when I saw you, I knew some shit was in the game. But, do not hold this grudge because your mother may not have much longer here with us," Malcolm said, looking back at my mother.

I looked down at my mother, and my heart broke into a million pieces. Why was she keeping all these secrets from me? I couldn't understand, and I just prayed that I had enough time left with her to figure this all out.

Jon Jon

Sitting in the driver seat, I had my hand on the back of Kelly's head as she was bobbing for apples on a nigga's dick. I was going to have her ass gone, and that was the plan. Most motherfuckers look at me as a dark ass nigga. Not dark as in complexion wise, even though I was, but a nigga was grimy. I didn't give no fucks about nobody, and everyone I encountered was for a reason. I made a living being a grimy nigga. I was discreet in everything I did. I was a storm that nobody knew was coming. Old girl Kelly was gullible. She gave off that look that all she needed was some good dick and a nigga to pretend he cared, and she would do anything for a nigga.

"Damn," I moaned as I shot all in her mouth and she did like a good girl was supposed to and swallowed my kids. Kelly leaned back in her seat, and I put my dick back in my pants, starting the car and pulling off.

"I need a favor from you. Are you gone help your man out?" I asked, looking over at her.

“Sure, what’s up?” she asked. I’ll see if she be that down when a nigga tell her what it is.

“How deep are your roommate and that Muza nigga?” I asked. Kelly fixed her glasses on her face.

“He and Nova aren’t that serious yet, but soon as she gets her hooks in him, I feel sorry for his pockets. Why?” she asked.

“You beefing with your girl or something, why you speak on her like that?” I fished around with the question. I could sense a hint of something in the way she said her answer, but I wasn’t sure.

“Nova is my girl, but we butt heads every day. Nova is all about her money. So long as whoever she’s with got a lot she gone hang around. What’s up with all these questions?” she asked, facing me.

“I want you to set something up. Help me get some money,” I flat out said. Kelly looked lost

“Set something up like what?” she asked.

“I’m gone rob that nigga, and I’m gone rob your girl too,” I said, giving her an evil look.

“Wait a minute. You want me to help you rob my best friend and Muza of all people?” Kelly asked me.

I nodded my head.

“Muza ain’t nothing but another nigga like me. He can be touched like any other nigga. There ain’t gone be no harm done except for in the pockets. All I need for you to do is fish around with your girl talk her into some double date shit, poker night. They come through we hehe haha, and get fucked up. I’ll have one of my colleagues come through, rob the spot, and we all get robbed, making it not look suspect. They will never know you were behind it,” I told Kelly. That was just what a nigga was thinking at the moment; I had to work out the details.

“They will never know I was behind it because I’m not doing no shit like that, and for you to even think that I would cross my friend like that, you’re a bigger fool than I thought!” Kelly yelled.

One thing I hated was for a motherfucker to raise their voice at me, and this bitch just tried it. Not even thinking twice, I grabbed the back of Kelly's head and slammed it on the dashboard of the car. Kelly cried out in pain. With my hand still wrapped around her hair, I spoke slow enough for her to catch all the syllables I was about to throw at her ass

"You must want to die right along with Nova and whoever else I got to kill. I don't even know why I asked you because whatever plan I come up with you gone do that shit anyways. One thing you need to know about being with me is that I get whatever I want. I wanted you, and you gone be my shorty because I might wife you one day," I lied. A nigga wasn't thinking about no damn wife and not even thinking about her ass, but I had to get in her head.

"So, you gone set that shit up for me or not?" I asked Kelly, letting her hair go.

Kelly raised her head and took her hand to rub the front of her face. Kelly was a red light skin chick, so her forehead was red as fuck, and I knew that shit was gone leave a mark.

“Yeah, just please don’t hit me again.” She trembled.

“Don’t try no funny shit either. If I even think you are thinking about doing some sneaky shit or run your mouth to them, it’s gone be ugly for you,” I told her. Kelly nodded her head. Starting up the car, I pulled off and headed to take her ass home.

Kelly

On the inside, I was crying and dying. Who the hell was this nigga? How the hell did he change so quickly? I was scared out of my damn mind, and I couldn’t believe the shit he asked me to do. There was no way I was going to be able to do my girl like that. The ride was eerily quiet. I was scared to breathe wrong around him. He might bash my damn head again. I slowly touched my head, which was aching in pain from being slammed on the dashboard. I looked over at him, and he looked as if he didn’t have a care in the world.

When we got back to my place, thank God Nova’s truck wasn’t there. I had to think of a way to get out of this shit. I reached for the handle of Jon Jon’s truck, and he grabbed my arm.

“Hold up, my love. I was going to get that for you. I’m coming up with you,” he said. I sighed because I thought he would be dropping me off, but I could tell he wasn’t going to make this shit easy for me.

“I’m sorry bae, I got to pee,” I told him.

He cut the truck off and exited the vehicle and made his way to the passenger side where he opened the door for me acting like the perfect gentleman. This nigga was motherfucking loco I can’t even front. We made our way upstairs to the apartment, and once inside, I darted to the bathroom. Closing the door and locking it behind me, I stood in front of the mirror, and a single tear rolled down my cheek as I look at the bruise that was forming on my light skin.

“Motherfucker,” I whispered to myself. I closed my eyes and silently cried.

I let my pussy get me in some shit, fuck I would’ve rather for this nigga to give my ass an STD or something. Here I am getting stuck with something that I might not get rid of. Flushing the toilet to make it seem like I used the bathroom, I quickly came out the bathroom. Jon

Jon was parked on the couch looking at his phone. I sat in the chair across from him and crossed my arms. He looked up at me and caught me rubbing my forehead.

“Why you all over there, you can’t sit by a nigga now? I’m sorry for that shit, man.” He sighed, pointing at my face. He stood up and came stood behind me bending over the chair he placed his arms around me and placed a kiss on my neck.

“For real Kelly, a nigga is sorry. I won’t put my hands on you again,” he said, sounding sincere. The sound of the front door opening and slamming caught me off guard. Nova walked in looking a mess, and I could tell she had been crying.

“You ok, Nova?” I asked. She looked up, and I had completely forgotten about the damn knot on my head.

“The fuck happened to your head?” she asked instantly sizing Jon Jon up and down. Fuck. I touched my head and looked at Jon Jon, and he gave me a cold look.

"Girl, we were in a little fender bender, and my head hit the dashboard. I'm ok. What's going on with you?" I asked. Nova wasn't buying it, and I knew it.

"We need to talk privately, I don't need everyone in my business," she said, looking at Jon Jon. He chuckled, which made me nervous, and he took a seat on the couch.

"Baby, can I call you later I really need to talk to Nova?" I asked. Jon Jon rubbed his beard and placed his hands together.

"Can't y'all go in the bedroom, I just got here?" he asked.

"You have had enough for today, don't you think? You need to leave!" Nova yelled.

"Wait, Nova, you can't put him out. He is my company, and we just got here," I said.

"I don't care nothing about that. We need to have a family meeting, and it doesn't concern him, so his ass needs to go!" she yelled.

I don't know what came over Nova, but she was pissed, and clearly, Jon Jon was fuel to the fire. Jon Jon stood up, and I placed my hands on his chest. For some reason, I thought he was about to hit Nova.

"Don't," I said.

"Don't what, that nigga ain't finna hit my ass. He probably knocked the little sense you had left right on out when he did whatever he did to you. Fender bender my ass," she said.

"Nova, really. I can't believe you being such a bitch right now," I said. Nova had me fucked up.

"You mad at me, but he's the one knocked you upside your head!" she yelled.

"Look, my girl. I ain't put my hands on Kelly. What she's telling you is the truth. I don't know what's going on with you and why all of sudden the sudden distaste in me, but I apologize. Kelly, I'm gone leave and let y'all talk. Hit me up as soon as y'all are done, and I'll come back and get you," Jon Jon spoke, squeezing my hand when he said soon. I nodded my head and watched him walk out of the door.

“What the fuck is your problem, Novanna?” I asked, throwing my hands in the air.

“What really happened to your head and don’t lie to me, Kelly? My spirit is giving me bad energy from the both of you. I’m finna have to cleanse the whole damn apartment,” she said.

“I was telling the truth, we were at the light in one of his other cars, a car rammed us from behind, and I didn’t have my seatbelt on because I had just finished sucking his dick, so my head hit the dashboard hard as fuck.” I shrugged.

“I still get a bad vibe about him,” she mumbled.

“Well, what happened to you? You walked in like you lost everything,” I asked.

“You wouldn’t believe the day I had. Muza comes over saying we needed to talk. Why he tells me that his Uncle Malcolm is my father.” Nova said.

“I know you lying.” I gasped.

"Hell no. Girl, my mama was moving out, his aunt was crying and shit, and she told Muza what was going on. Girl, Malcolm done set mama ass up in this bad ass condo downtown. The whole time I'm thinking she was working for them because she was close, but really it was because she was being Malcolm's side chick. I go to talk to mama and Malcolm over there. I was so mad at her girl that I was talking out the side of my neck. Malcolm didn't find out about me until the day I showed up at his house. Mama's been keeping this shit secret all my damn life. Then she passes the hell out, and Malcolm told me my mother was dying of cancer," Nova cried.

"Shit girl, you have had a long day. Is your mother ok?" I asked. I care about Ms. Mona Lise a lot. She was a sweet woman, and she played no games.

"They were running tests on her when I left the hospital. I had to leave. I couldn't see her like that," she sobbed in my arms.

“I’ll go back up there with you. You don’t need to be here. You need to be by her side at a time like this. Where’s your phone so that I can get Muza number out and call him.” I asked,

“No, don’t call him!” she shouted.

“Why not, I’m sure he wouldn’t mind being around you. You like him, don’t you?” I asked.

“No, but I’m not his girl, he isn’t required to be here during this time,” she said.

Rolling my eyes, I held my hand out so that Nova could give me her phone. Dialing Muza, I prayed he answered for Nova’s sake and mines.

Muzaini

The night had been hectic trying to make sure my group was ready for this showcase. A nigga had finally sat down in the booth and was enjoying a bottle. I was overlooking the club, so I kept my eyes on everyone behind the Gucci shades I was rocking. I was dressed in Gucci from head to toe from the Gucci button down I wore to the Gucci sneakers I rocked on my feet.

"Mr. Muhammad, do you need anything?" one of the many workers asked.

"Nah, I'm good." I dismissed the worker.

My phone started to buzz I looked down at the number and didn't notice it, so I sent it to voicemail. Bopping my head to the sounds of NBA YoungBoy "Solar Eclipse", I was feeling good. My phone buzzed again, and I looked down at the number, this time it was Nova's number. I answered the phone quick as hell.

"Wassup?" I yelled in the phone. I stood up and made my way to the back of the club so that I could hear.

"Muza, this is Kelly," the girl said. I instantly perked up praying that nothing had happened to Nova.

"Is Nova ok?" I quickly asked.

"Well kind of, as you know, some things took place today, and her mother got sick and ended up in the hospital. Nova is sitting here when she should be up there with her mother. Now I have talked her to going back, and I will sit there with her for a little while, but I called because I think she much rather you be there than me," she said.

"Say no mo. What hospital are y'all heading to?" I asked Kelly.

"Centennial," Kelly said.

"I'm on my way," I told her and ended the call. I walked back to the booth. I had and sent a text to my head assistant to come upstairs so that I could speak with him.

I was already heading down when we met halfway.

"Wassup boss?" he asked.

"I've got a family emergency, and I can't stay. Make sure everything runs smoothly, and after the set, they are to have a meet and great with the five winners from the radio contest. If there are any issues, call me," I told him. I trusted him. Hell, he could run the damn company alone if I allowed him. My driver was waiting outside when I exited the club. I got in told that nigga where to go and get me there asap.

* * *

When I got to the hospital, you would've thought something happened to Nova the way I came up in there. I had to calm myself down before I made it to her. In order for me to be her peace, I had to bring it to her. When I got on the sixth floor, I saw my Uncle Malcolm standing outside of the room on his phone, and he looked like he was stressed. I bet that nigga was. Shit, being in the doghouse with your wife and then your side chick sick, he needed a nice drink and a blunt. He looked up, and we locked eyes. He hung up the phone.

"Did Elizabeth send you up here?" he asked. I laughed.

"Hell nah, I'm here to comfort Nova," I said, sizing him up. I loved fucking with my uncle. His temper was just like mine. I wanted to fuck with him, but I knew he wasn't in no playing mood.

"Speaking of which, you know that's my daughter. I wanted her to stay away from your ass, but one thing I know is when you try to keep someone away from someone, all it does is bring them closer. That's what happened with me and Mona Lise.

Now, I love your aunt, but when we married it was somewhat organized. Our parents made us do that shit. My heart was with Mona Lise first. Over the years, I began to love your aunt, and I wouldn't change anything except wishing that I knew about Nova so that I could've been the father she needed. Please don't end up like me loving two women and being selfish not to let one go. Plus, nephew or not, you hurt Nova and I will kick your ass," he said. All I could do was shake my head. A lot of things he said made sense.

"Well Nova and I are friends, but I do like her, I don't know how much longer I'm going to be able to pretend to be in a relationship with her for the media. Hell, it's only been a couple of days, but I can tell I'm digging her," I admitted.

"Aw, so that's what the hell y'all doing. This is for the media and let me guess Cru, right?" he asked. The door opened, and Kelly walked out the room.

"Oh, I was just about to call you. I have to leave. This nigga keeps blowing my line up. She's in there staring off into space," Kelly told me.

"Thanks for calling me," I told her.

"No problem. Maybe once all this blows over, we can do a double date game night. I'm sure Nova will like that because she's been talking about it," Kelly said.

"Sounds like a plan," I told her.

I walked into the room, and Nova was sitting in the chair staring at her mother. I walked over and placed my hands on her shoulders, causing her to jump a little. She looked up at me, and a smile eased on her face.

“So glad you’re here,” she whispered.

“I can’t leave you hanging when you a need a shoulder,” I told her. We both smiled. My uncle came in and pulled another chair up on the opposite side of the bed, we all sat there in silence.

Cru

After exchanging details with this Delaunn dude, I couldn’t wait to meet up with him today. I needed some ammunition, and he was it. I could’ve sucked that shit up, took it like a champ, and went on my way, but hell no, Muza was made for me and me only. I truly loved him, and I wished he could see that. I was sitting in the parking lot of Walmart waiting on him to pull up.

When Delaunn pulled up beside me, I unlocked the door so that he could get in the car. This man was some eye candy. Hell, if things didn’t work out between me and Muza, maybe I’ll take the other man in Nova’s life. The door opened, and Delaunn slid his big frame in the passenger side of the car. I removed my shades and smiled.

“It’s a pleasure meeting you,” I spoke first.

"I'm just trying to see what the deal is. Me meeting you don't mean nothing," he said.

"Oh, someone doesn't seem to be too friendly. Nevertheless, we both want something that if we work together, we could have. You want your hoe Nova, and I want my man Muzaini back," I told him.

"Why she got to be all that?" he asked. I laughed. This guy was really in love with this girl.

"That is her profession, right? I mean if it isn't I take that back. I figure if we come up with a nice plan, something that will anger Muza to the fact that he doesn't want to be with her anymore," I told him. Delaunn remained silent. I didn't know if he was going to take the bait or not.

"I got a video of me and her, matter of fact it was today. She came over, she told me how we were going to get back together and shit, and then we had sex. I needed my own ammunition just in case she tries to back out what she is supposed to do," Delaunn said, pulling out his phone and showing me the video. And sho nuff it was Nova.

“Can you send me that video, I’ll pay you top dollar for it?” I asked. Delaunn rubbed his beard and chuckled.

“Girl, I don’t want your money. A nigga ain’t hurting for shit. Do you know who I am?” he said. Shaking his head, he airdropped me the video from his phone.

A slick smile crept across my face. I was so excited at the thought of ruining her precious little life.

“Thank you, oh and I will be in touch. If the video doesn’t work, he needs to find out about Nova’s occupation,” I told him. This nigga just shook his head at me and got out of the car.

I mean I don’t know why he was being rude about the whole thing. If he loved Nova and wanted her to himself then he should’ve been jumping at the chance of this. I wonder why he was sitting on that tape.

Novanna

It had been a whole month, and my mother was still in the hospital holding on. The cancer wasn't letting up. She went from looking full of life to a whole different person. I hated seeing her like that. The relationship between Malcolm and I had grown because we spent a lot of time at the hospital. He and Elizabeth were still married. After she got over the initial shock, and I'm sure he docked it up a little about him and my mother endeavors, she lightened up. Muza was extremely busy, but he made sure I at least got an hour out of his day if he was in town.

Delaunn had worked my damn nerves constantly blowing my phone up. He knew my mother was sick and that most of my time was spent at the hospital, which to him was great news as long as I wasn't with Muza. Kelly hasn't been back up since the day she made me come up here. She is so in love with that Jon Jon nigga that she is always up under his ball sack. I'm happy for her I guess. I still think it's some shit in the game with them two.

Coming out the bathroom, I made my way over to my chair. Mama was in and out, but her eyes were opened glued to the TV. Once I sat down in the chair, I got hot all over, and it felt the room was spinning. I shook my head and reached on the table for the water I had been drinking on. Taking a sip and using an old newspaper to fan me. I was burning the fuck up. Then there it was. I felt it coming up my throat, so I darted to the bathroom and spit of my breakfast from this morning. I flushed the toilet and stood there on the wall. After catching my breath, I came out of the bathroom and went to the sink to wash my hands and rinse my mouth out. I used some of mama's mouthwash to rinse my mouth out.

"I hope I can hang on long enough to see my grandchild," Mama whispered, causing me to turn around. Tilting my head to the side, I walked over to the bed.

"Mama, go back to sleep. Them pain meds got you delusional," I told her.

"I been dreaming it Nova, and I may not hold on that long, but watch what I tell you. You need to go ahead and take a test so that we can know for sure. Even though I know I'm right, I want to know," she said.

My mama was on some other shit. There was no way in hell I was pregnant. I thought about my last two encounters. I had sex with Muza unprotected, and I had sex with Delaunn, but he didn't cum in me, I swallowed his damn kids. *Ching, Ching* went off in my head. Oh my god if I was pregnant by Muza, this shit was a huge plus, I would definitely be securing the motherfucking bag by giving him his first child.

I stood up so damn fast. I was finna take my ass to the drugstore and get a pregnancy test. I got dizzy and tried grabbing the side of mama bed, and my ass hit the floor.

* * *

Waking up, I noticed I was in a hospital room of my own in the emergency department. I started to panic because I ain't know what the hell was going on. The last I remembered was talking to my mama about being pregnant. There was a knock at the door.

"Come in," I mustered up. The door opened, and my father peeked his head in.

"Girl, don't you go giving my old ass a heart attack. Between you and your mama, I can't take no more damn hospitals," he said.

"My bad, I don't even know what happened," I said honestly. There was another knock on the door, and the nurse peeked her head inside. The little white chick was too damn excited for my liking.

"Hello Ms. Collier, I just love coming to bring good news. We ran some tests on you while you were out and had them sent off to the lab and congratulations are in store," she said. My father looked at the nurse.

"Congratulations on what exactly?" he asked. The nurse looked at me.

"Ms. Collier is with child, five weeks to be exact. All of your tests were good, so you passing out sometimes happens during the first trimester, but here are your papers, and you are free to go whenever you feel up to walking," she said, handing me my papers. I looked at the papers and there it was I was indeed pregnant.

"Lord, is it by Muza? Elizabeth is gone have a field day with this. So y'all gone make it official instead of this damn game y'all playing?" Malcolm asked.

I was starting to feel overwhelmed. Hell, I haven't even talked to Muza yet so I couldn't be answering questions and making decisions yet.

"Yes, it's Muza. I don't know what's going to happen. I guess I have to wait and see," I told my father. My mind then flashed to Delaunn. Oh Lord, he was gone lose his shit. I placed my hands over my face and took a deep breath. I had to find a way to get rid of him and quick.

Muza

My night had been long as hell. I had to catch a redeye flight this morning back to Nashville. All I wanted to do was lay down. My energy was at an all-time low, and normally my ass be on the go. A nigga never gets tired. Before I went home and crashed, I stopped at the hospital to check on Nova. Her mother wasn't doing good at all, and she wouldn't leave her mother side for long periods of time if she did my Uncle Malcolm was there. My aunt had finally come around which was shocking. That nigga had the juice. Sometimes Malcolm confided in me about a lot of things. I guess since he was my uncle only by marriage he considered me one of the homies. I walked into Mona Lise's room, and she was sitting up watching TV. The room was empty, and neither Nova nor Malcolm was in sight.

"Hey, Muza," Mona Lise spoke barely audible.

"Hey, Ms. Mona Lise. Are you here by yourself today?" I asked, walking closer to her bed so that I could hear her.

"No, Nova passed out and had to be taken downstairs to the emergency room, and Malcolm went down there to be with her. I'm just trying to stay awake so that she can tell me about my grandbaby she carrying," Mona Lise said, cracking a slight smile.

"Grandbaby, Ms. Mona Lise, what are you talking about?" I asked.

"I've been dreaming about babies, and I know Nova is pregnant. I feel it," she whispered. Now, I don't know if Mona Lise was tripping or not, but I needed to find out what the hell was going on and asap. I pulled out my phone and called my Uncle Malcolm.

"Aye, y'all still in the emergency room?" I asked him soon as he picked up.

"Yeah, come on down here so I can check on Mona Lise," he said.

"Say no mo," I said, hanging up the phone. I looked over at Mona Lise

"I'm about to go downstairs to the ER and Malcolm is on his way up here," I told her. She nodded her head and turned back to look at the TV.

I walked out of the room speed walking to the elevator. I had to mentally prepare my mind for the things that were about to transpire while on the way to the ER. Nova is pregnant, first off is it mines? Does she want a baby because this is all I ever wanted was a family? Will she be willing to give this relationship thing an actual try? I was feeling Nova, and from the vibes she gives off, she might be feeling a nigga too. When I reached the ER lobby, my uncle was waiting for me.

"Nova has actually been discharged. She was getting her things together. She doesn't know that you are here, so just meet her when she comes out. Congratulations," he said, patting me on the shoulders and walking off.

"For real?" I asked. He shrugged his shoulders and got on the elevator.

I placed my hands over my head and smiled. I couldn't wait to see Nova. When I turned around, Nova was walking through the double doors. She looked so pretty. Ok, a nigga sounding corny as fuck, she really looked miserable like she was fighting a million thoughts herself, but I just wanted to make her feel better. I walked over to her and met her.

"Sup, you ok?" I asked. She moved her locs out of her face looked at me with sad eyes.

"I'm pregnant, Muza," she said. I chuckled.

“So, I heard. Let’s go to the cafeteria and talk before we head back to your mom's room,” I suggested. Nova nodded her head, and we headed to the cafeteria. Entering the cafeteria, we found a table and took a seat.

“You want something to eat?” I asked Nova. Nova shook her head so fast.

“Hell no, I don’t want to throw up again,” she said.

“Well, you can’t go the whole pregnancy not eating. The baby still got to eat, how far along are you anyway?’ I asked.

“Five weeks and yes it’s yours,” she said. Well damn, I ain’t even ask her ass all that.

“Why you say it like that? I just wanted to know how far along you were, I never asked you was I the father or not. What type of nigga do you think I am?” I asked.

“I’m just saying, before the thought even crossed your mind, Hell, we had sex one time and look at me.” She pouted. Now she had me worried.

"So, you're not happy about being pregnant?" I asked.

"It's cool. I wonder what they gone say now?" She laughed.

"Honestly I don't give a fuck what they got to say, but I do want to make this thing official with you. The one thing I always wanted was a family. I want to be in my kid life fully in the same house. I know we barely know each other, but it doesn't change the way I feel about you. If I had any doubts about you, I wouldn't even pursue this, but this is what I want?" I told her.

Nova

I was shocked as hell that Muza came in and stood up like a real man. I didn't mean to come off all crazy when he asked me how far along I was. I was slick scared he was gone try and say he wasn't the father. I swear if he knew that I had messed around with Delaunn, he wouldn't be saying all this shit. Now, he wants to be in a real relationship with me. How did this go from me just wanting this man for his pockets and the development of feelings amongst us both, to becoming parents and actually being in a relationship? Well, guess what, the bag is secured bitches, and I got his heart right along with it.

"Well, Muza, I never knew that I would actually turn out liking your ass either, but I am willing to give this thing a try since we are about to be someone's parents," I told him. Muza smiled and got up from the table. He lifted me up and hugged me spinning me around.

"I have to go tell mama. She swears she knew what was going on already. I'm just scared. The reality of me losing my mother is starting to sink in. You know she said she wouldn't be here when the baby was born, but she wanted me to find out for sure if I was pregnant and to tell her. It was scary, and no matter how I prepare myself for the day that she leaves, I don't think I will ever be ready," I admitted to him. Muza held my hands.

"You gone be straight, God is going to prepare you for your biggest battle, plus I'm not going to let you go through that alone, but come on, we done kept your mama waiting long enough," he said. The smile on my face no one could take it away. We walked back upstairs to share with my mother the great news.

Walking into the room, Malcolm was standing by the bed holding a cup for my mother as she drank from a straw.

"Mama, I guess your dream was right. You are going to be a granny," I told her. The smile that graced her face melted my heart.

"Told you, that's all I wanted to hear, you guys will make great parents," she struggled to say. I instantly walked over to the bed and grabbed her hand.

"You ok, mama? Don't try to strain yourself and talk," I told her. She brought her fingers to her mouth in a peace sign and kissed them placing them on my flat stomach. I felt a knot form in my throat, and my eyes started to burn.

"I'm tired, baby. I'm going to get some rest. I love y'all," she whispered. Mama closed her eyes.

Muza rubbed my shoulders, and I took a seat in the chair beside her bed. Malcolm did the same. We were going to let mama get her rest, and when she woke up, I would still be here so that we could talk more about the baby.

The sounds of the machines beeping caused all of us to jump up. I touched my mother, and I knew she was gone. The nurses entered the room.

“Excuse us,” one nurse said as she picked mama arm up and checked her pulse while the other nurse was fiddling with the machine.

“What is going on?” I asked trying to hold back the tears, regretting what I already knew to be confirmed. The nurse looked at me with sad eyes.

“I’m so sorry. Ms. Mona Lise has passed,” she said. I slowly sat down in the chair and let out a gut-wrenching cry that I know came from deep down in my soul.

Malcolm

Watching Mona Lise die took something from me. You know they say God prepares you for things like this, but I think I missed that. I just know that the pain she was in was no longer there. She held on long enough to hear my daughter tell her about being a grandmother. Mona Lise would've been an awesome grandmother. Poor Nova, I don't think she could've prepared herself for that either. Leaving the hospital was hard on all of us. I was going to make sure that Mona Lise had a beautiful home going celebration.

When I arrived home, I walked straight to the bar and poured me a drink.

"Long day?" I heard Elizabeth asked. She took a seat on the sofa, and I grabbed my glass and went and sat down beside her. Letting out a huge sigh, I opened up.

"Let's just say crazy, good, and sad. When I got to the hospital today, Nova had been taken to the ER for passing out in her mother's room," I said.

“Oh my god, poor child, is she ok?” Elizabeth asked.

“She’s fine. Well, she was fine, just pregnant. It looks like Muza finally got you a baby to spoil,” I told her. Elizabeth clapped her hands she was extremely happy.

“Yesss, Lord. See, I knew I liked Nova and him together when I first met her. So why do you look so down and out? Please don’t tell me you’re tripping about Muza getting your precious daughter pregnant?” she asked.

“Nah, not at all. The news is great news, but after Nova told Mona Lise she was happy that she was going to be a granny, it was like she was just holding on for the news because shortly after she passed. Nova is taking it extremely hard,” I told Elizabeth. Elizabeth was silent for a minute, and I wondered what was going through her head.

“You know I don’t like whatever went on between the two of you. I still felt like I was played, but I don’t wish death or sickness on anyone. I hate that Nova has to go through this, especially with her being pregnant, but I will reach out to her and give her some comfort.

You make sure you put Mona Lise away nicely. She did dedicate her life to our family for all these years," she said, getting up and walking away. I watched as the other woman I loved swayed her hips out of the room. Taking another sip of my drink, I knew now that since Mona Lise was gone, I had a lot of making up to do with my wife because she will forever hold that over my head, no matter how ok she seems to be.

Nova

I was staring off into space as I sat in the car with Muza, and I felt numb. I couldn't believe my mother just died. This shit was unreal. How could a person get good news and devastating news all in the same day?

"You want me to come up with you while you get what you need?" Muza asked.

He had brought me home to get my laptop and stuff. I was going to his house with him because I didn't want to stay here. I hadn't seen or spoken to Kelly, and I rather not be around the bitch honestly. She had me feeling a type of way since she went missing with her little nigga. And from the looks of it, both they asses was here.

"I'm cool, I'm just gone run in and run back out," I told him.

Opening the door, I got out the car and made my way upstairs. Unlocking the door, I walked in, and Kelly was sweeping up some glass and had the nerve to be wearing some shades at nighttime.

"Sup, Nova," she said, trying not to look at me.

"Oh damn, you still remember my name?" I asked being sarcastic. Kelly shook her head. I walked passed her, and Jon Jon was sitting on the couch.

"Wassup, Nova? Kelly and I are tryna set up a game night with you and Muzaini. Think you can get that popping?" he asked. I rolled my eyes.

"I don't know, Jon Jon. I haven't talked to Kelly in almost a month. I have other things on my plate right now like being pregnant and making arrangements for my mother's funeral," I said, walking towards my bedroom.

I walked into the room and slammed the door behind me. I sat on the bed and let a few tears fall. I was beyond frustrated. The door opened and in walked Kelly. Wiping my face, I stood from the bed and started to gather the things I came for.

"Nova, I'm so sorry I haven't been around like the friend I should have. You have to understand that I want to be, but Jon Jon is very jealous. Congrats on your baby, is it Muza's?" she asked. Shaking my head, I didn't even bother answering.

"I never thought I would see the day that Kelly would let a man dictate her life. You're way smarter than that," I said. I reached up and grabbed Kelly's glasses from her face. She quickly moved back, and I noticed her black eye.

"Really Kelly, I knew that nigga was beating on you. Why in the hell are you taking this shit from him? You need to leave this nigga asap. Matter of fact, I will put his ass out of my shit right now," I said, marching towards the door. Kelly grabbed my arms.

"No, Nova! It's fine. I am going to leave just don't say anything to him right now. Sorry about your mother," she said, trying to change the conversation. I knew what she was doing.

"You said you were running in and out," I heard Muza's voice enter the room.

"My bad, baby. I was coming," I told him, grabbing my things.

"Damn, what happened to your eye?" he asked Kelly.

"That's none of our concern. Let's go!" I told Muza, grabbing him.

"What type of nigga would I be to notice some shit like this when the nigga is in the next room, and he apparently needs to be addressed?" Muza asked.

"You will be a nigga who walked away from someone that doesn't want any help, ain't that right Kelly?" I told Muza but shooting Kelly an evil look. This bitch was bonkers, and I couldn't believe this shit.

"Come on, Muza," I said, walking out of the room. He followed. Making our way towards the living room, I turned to Jon Jon

“Look a here lil nigga. You got to get out of my house before I call the police and have you escorted out. You’re no longer allowed here. If you want to visit Kelly, you take her to your own house and beat her ass,” I told him. I meant every motherfucker word.

Muza motioned me to head towards the door before he added his two cents.

“She meant every word, don’t come back here, bruh,” he said. We left out of the apartment and headed back downstairs to the car.

Kelly

Oh my god, what the hell just happened? I was scared to leave out of Nova’s room because I knew it was about to be some shit with Jon Jon. Jon Jon came flying around the corner.

“What the fuck did you tell them? You done messed up the plan!” he yelled, grabbing me by the hair.

"I didn't tell them nothing I was congratulating Nova on her pregnancy and she took my shades off and seen my eye. I told her to leave it alone," I cried. I had to think fast.

"I have a plan that's way better than the first, but you have to hear me out, under one condition though," I mentioned to Jon Jon, hoping he like the idea.

"It better be good, or I'm gone get in your ass," he said, letting my hair go.

"Look, Nova and Muza both want me to leave you, so all I got to do is wait a couple of days call her asking for help because I left you. I'll get her to give me Muza's address so I can come over, then I can send you the address, and you and your men can run in. The only thing I ask is that you don't hurt them. Nova is pregnant," I told him. He started stroking his beard like he always did when he was in deep thought.

"You better hope this works. If this shit goes right, I'll let yo ass go for real," he said. My ears perked up at what he just said. Lord, I would give anything to get away from his ass. I guess that even means setting up my friend.

Novanna

My mother's funeral was so beautiful. Malcolm had truly shown out with the arrangements. Her colors were white and lavender. The white and gold trim casket was fit for a queen. Even Mrs. Elizabeth showed her respects. Today was extremely hard for me because it really hit me that my mother was gone. The last few weeks of our life together was terrible. Even though we hashed things out, I just wish I would've had time to deal with everything. I would've told her sooner about my schooling, and just a lot of things would've been done differently. Tomorrow is never promised and now I know to cherish the ones I have and who have helped me on this journey.

I was ready for this day to be over with. I was tired of being around all the fake nosey people hitting me with a million questions, especially concerning Malcolm and Muza. Everyone knew who the hell Malcolm and Elizabeth Hamstead were. Muza ass was getting slipped mixtapes and sales pitches from cousins that I didn't even fuck with. I was over the circus.

Immediately after the repast, I was gone. Instead of going all the way back home, we decided to stay in Muza's condo in town. I didn't care, I just wanted a shower and to lay up under my man. That sounds so crazy now. I had to end up blocking Delaunn from all my social media and get my number changed. Hopefully, he got the picture because I didn't need any drama in my life, but if I knew him, I knew he was pissed though, especially how I just up and vanished. Lord knows what he might do.

Upon entering the condo, I started peeling my clothes off one by one. I undid the bun that I had my locs in and let them fall freely. Standing in the bathroom mirror, I just stood there and looked at my body. I ran my hand over my belly, it was flat, but I can only imagine when it gets big. I really have a human being growing inside of me. Novanna Collier is about to be somebody mother. *Lord, give me the strength.*

Opening the glass shower door, I got in and turned the shower on, letting the water cascade down my body. After washing my body with some Dove Anti-stress body wash, I felt somewhat better. Opening the shower, I stepped out and grabbed the towel from the back of the door, wrapping it around my frame.

When I came out, I walked into the room that Muza and I shared, and he wasn't in there, so I took my time applying body cream and throwing on one of Muza big t-shirts. Climbing up to the top of the bed, I pulled the covers back and slid underneath. The slumber that took over me was oh so peaceful.

* * *

The ringing of a phone made me stir in my sleep, and then I heard Muza's deep voice. I didn't know who he was talking to, but I kept my eyes closed and played sleep.

"Why the fuck you still calling my phone? You need to find you somebody else to harass," he whispered, but I could tell he was mad, and he ended the call. I heard him let out a sigh and wrap his big arm back around my body.

"I know your ass ain't sleep," he said, rubbing my stomach. I giggled.

"Well, as long as you got your hoes in check ain't no reason for me to question you," I told him.

"You silly, girl," he said and planted his chin in the nape of my neck. We nestled back in and tried going back to sleep that was until my damn phone started to ring. My stomach instantly formed in knots because I'm praying this ain't Delaunn.

"Now here go your hoes calling," Muza said. I reached over and grabbed my cell off the nightstand. I frowned up at the sight of Kelly's name. I placed the phone back on the table.

"Why you not answering, who is it?" Muza asked.

"It's Kelly, and first off it's two in the morning. She can't do nothing with me at that time," I said, brushing it off. The phone rang again.

"You may need to answer. It may be something serious since she called back," Muza said. I sat up and reached for the phone, answering it.

"Hello!" I yelled in the phone. Kelly's crying caught my attention.

“Nova, I left, but I’m scared to go back to the apartment because he might come back there,” she cried.

Hearing that she left Jon Jon was great, so I take it she was done being stupid. I placed the phone down and looked at Muza.

“She left him but scared to go back to the apartment because he might show. Is it ok if she stays here?” I asked him.

“Yeah, that’s fine,” he said. I placed the phone back to my ear.

“I’m going to text you Muza address. You can stay with us for the night until we figure out something,” I told her.

“Thank you so much. I’m on the way,” Kelly said, and we hung up the phone. I looked at the phone then at Muza.

“What, you didn’t want to help your girl?” he asked me.

That was something that I was playing around with in my head. It wasn’t that I didn’t want to help her, I just felt that our friendship had been compromised since Jon Jon came in the picture. This girl who I considered my friend played me to the left for a nigga that she barely knew.

"It isn't that. It's just I know our friendship will never be the same. I just feel weird about some shit," I admitted. I stood up from the bed and headed to the guest room, to make things suitable for when she got here.

I placed her some towels on the bed, and Muza walked in and leaned against the doorframe. This man was fine, and he knew that shit.

"What you over there thinking about?" I asked him, walking over to where he stood.

"A nigga is far from corny so don't think that shit, but I'm just thinking about you. It's just crazy how this shit all played out. I ain't gone lie though a nigga went in knowing I was going to be with you. Yeah, we were faking this shit for the media and Cru, but I knew what I was doing. I want you to know that as long as I got breath in my body, you gone be straight. You're giving me something that I always wanted, and that was a family. Yeah, my aunt and your dad raised me, but it's nothing like a mama and daddy. He or she is gone have nothing but the best," he told me.

I immediately felt bad because I was harboring a lie I know he wouldn't ever forgive about my past. I would never tell him he was a walking lick to me at first.

"Well, I admit when I first saw you to I knew I was going to catch feelings," I told him, bending the truth a little. I did have feelings for this man— I actually loved this man. You would've thought we had been together for years, but you could never deny chemistry this strong.

Kelly

My plan was working like I knew it would. I was so anxious to get the fuck away from Jon Jon that I wasn't thinking straight. Jon Jon agreeing to this was perfect. I just prayed he didn't get carried away whenever they came up in there. When I arrived downtown, I drove to the address that Nova had given me. I had to get in character mode and make sure I had my story all put together. Making my way inside, I took the elevator up to the top floor, stepping off the elevator I was greeted by a big burly ass security guard.

"I'm Kelly, Nova and Muza are expecting me," I told the man.

He simply spoke into some kind of damn device, and I watched as he nodded his head. Shortly after, he moved out of the way and allowed me to head to the door. *Damn, I must tell Jon Jon about that security.*

Nova stood there at the door in an oversized shirt and didn't look to thrill to see me. One thing about Nova it was hard to get shit past her because she was into all that energy shit and that shit always turned out to be right. I still was going to keep my cool.

"Thank y'all so much for allowing me to stay here. I couldn't go back to the apartment. He threatened to kill me," I cried.

"You should've left when we tried to get you to leave. Come on," Nova said.

I followed Nova through this bad motherfucker he had the nerve to call a condo. This was the whole damn top floor made into one damn apartment. I knew this nigga was pissing out money. Nova stood in the door and pointed into the room.

"This is where you will be sleeping for tonight," she said. She wouldn't even look at me.

"Nova, I'm sorry for everything," I apologized. Nova squinted her eyes, and I swear it felt like this girl was looking in my soul.

"Either I never really knew who you were as a person, or you just got weak for a man to the point that you let him alter your mental. It's something going on with you that you're really not telling me. You left me at my weakest point, something I would've never done to you if it had been your mother. I'm letting you stay here for maybe a couple of days then you have to leave. I'm paying out of the lease on the apartment, so you need to find you somewhere to go or you can have the whole thing transferred into your name. It's up to you. I'm glad you chose your life over that nigga though," she said before turning on her heels and heading back down the hall.

"Bitch," I mumbled.

Ok yeah, I know I ain't been the best of a friend, but damn how can she be so cold. At least I asked Jon Jon to spare her fucking life, what the hell am I saying. I laid back on the bed and text Jon Jon, letting him the know the eagle had fucking landed.

Jon Jon

"Look I got everything covered on my end. I have my own personal issues. This ain't got nothing to do with all that you talking. When the time comes for us to link, we will. There's no need to rush the shit," I said calmly in the phone as I walked into the crib, throwing my keys on the table. I scratched the top of my head while the person on the other end of the phone was going on and on. I swear this was why I hated answering certain phone calls from certain people.

"Well aite, sorry to cut you short, but I got some shit to take care of, so I'll hit you later," I said, hanging up the phone while they were still running off at the mouth.

Checking my messages, the message I had been waiting on had finally come through. The address to the hit. I already had my crew on it. Kelly also sent me a message saying that a guard stood outside the elevator stopping everyone going to Muza's crib. I knew doing this I would have to face some sort of security off top just because of Muza status, but it wasn't nothing me and my team couldn't prepare for.

I kicked my shoes off and propped my feet up on the couch. Looking around at my crib, a nigga had done pretty good for myself. A nigga was so lowkey motherfuckers that once knew me probably thought a nigga was dead. That's just how I chose to operate considering the type of work I did. I pressed play on the flick that I kept in the DVD player and started to beat my meat until I dozed off.

Cru

I flung the iPad across the room listening to it shatter into pieces. Seeing the shit I just saw had me in an outrage and sick to my stomach.

"Bitch, you gone replace my shit. I know you mad and shit, but you can't just be busting up shit that don't belong to you. Everybody ain't rich like you!" my cousin Kesha yelled.

I was so mad I wanted to cry, but I wasn't about to let my cousin see me like that for her to go back and tell all her broke ass friends what I had going on.

“This shit can’t be real, I see now that’s why he’s sticking with her ass because she done fucked around and got pregnant. Damn!” I yelled, placing my fist in my hand.

“If your ass weren’t so selfish Cru, you would’ve had your man. If you would have given Muza a baby, but nope, all you care about is Cru and only Cru. You can’t get mad at him,” Kesha said.

“Why the fuck is you even here if you gone be taking his side. All that shit may seem all good now, but I got something that’s gone shake that fucking household and have his ass back eating out of the palm of my hand,” I told my cousin thinking about the video that Delaunn had given me.

Oh my god, I wonder did Delaunn know about this little pregnancy. Opening my phone, I went to the post I saw of Muza and Nova’s pregnancy and screenshotted that shit and sent it to Delaunn. If he didn’t know, well now he knows.

Shortly after sending that text, my phone rang. Looking down at the phone, I laughed because it was Delaunn calling me.

"Well, hello there?" I cooed into the phone.

"Bra, that shit a joke, right?" he asked. Shaking my head, I wanted to laugh, but I had no room hell he was feeling just like I was, I just wasn't about to show it.

"Yes, it's true meaning we need to move forward with our plan asap," I told him.

"Man, that could be my baby. Fuck all that other shit!" he yelled.

"Look, calm down. I swear I understand your pain. Muza has a huge function coming up, and media will be everywhere. That would be the perfect time to expose our lil Nova and crush everything," I told him while plotting that shit in my head. I was actually getting turned on just thinking about that shit.

"I'll let you know the details because I'm sure you won't get an invite." I laughed. Delaunn was steaming, and he hung up in my face. My cousin stood there sucking her teeth.

"All the measures you taking to be with a man who don't want you. I wouldn't even want to be with a man if I had to do half the stuff you were doing?" she had the nerve to say.

"Bitch, your own baby daddy don't even claim you or your kid!" I yelled at her.

"But do you see my ass plotting or ruining lives just so that he would. Me and my son are great. All these niggas out here, how you think what's his face gone react. Ain't y'all together? I swear y'all made for each other grimy and grimier," She spoke as she grabbed her purse and keys.

"I'm getting my ass far away from you because I don't want to be around no bad juju. That shit might come back on me," she said, walking out the door.

"Bye, then!" I yelled. I didn't care, and sholl didn't need her ass.

Muza

It was early as hell, and I was sitting in the bed working from my laptop. Nova was sound asleep, and her little snores were kind of cute. She was sleeping like she didn't have a care in the world. We spoke last night about her friendship with Kelly, and she was adamant that she wanted out. Females are way different than men, but who was I to tell her about her friendship with Kelly when I haven't been around that long. The only thing I could tell her was to do whatever made her happy. She was carrying my child, and I didn't want her stressing over nothing. I knew Nova always kept her own cash, but I took the initiative to set her up her own account so that she could spend freely. She hasn't been doing hair in a while, so I knew the money she was making was probably dwindling down. Money was never a biggie for me. I had a great accountant, and I always kept my ducks in a row so that I can continue making money and never went into debt.

My 3rd annual Muza Entertainment ball was in about a week, and I couldn't wait for the surprise that I had planned for Nova. Nova stirred in her sleep, turning towards me. She opened her eyes, and I hit her with a head nod.

“What in the world are you doing up?” she asked. I turned my nose up.

“Damn girl, you cute and all, but your breath is not matching your face right now,” I said.

“Fuck you, Muza,” she said, shoving me.

“Speaking of which, a nigga ain’t hit that since I got you pregnant. I’m a needy nigga and you gone have to come up out them draws sooner or later, my girl,” I told her, I was dead ass serious. Shit had been so hectic that sex hadn’t even crossed my mind.

“I know you got needs baby, and I got you. As soon as I go throw up,” she said, hopping off the bed and flying to the bathroom. That shit was funny to me. I placed the laptop on the bed and went in the bathroom to check on Nova.

“You good, baby?” I asked. She grabbed the toothpaste off the sink and applied some to the toothbrush.

“I will be, I’m already over this shit, and it haven’t even really started yet,” she moaned. I wrapped my arms around her and looked at her in the mirror.

"You got this, baby," I told her, wanting to reassure her.

"Look I got to head to the office today and wrap up some things, and I also need to stop by the venue to handle some things for my annual ball. But look, I got something for you," I told her, leading her back to the bedroom. I grabbed the black card and handed it to her.

"Muza, what the hell is this?" she asked me with her eyes wide.

"I know that you haven't been working lately with everything going on, so since we together now, and you're the mother of my child, you need some spending money and shit. This card you can use for whatever and the other card is your bank card. I got you an account set up and ready to go. I don't want to hear no independent rah rah shit either. I'm gone take care of you," I told her. Nova just stood there looking at both of the cards.

"Thank you, this means so much," she said and leaned in to kiss me.

I welcomed her kiss. I miss the touch of her soft lips. I slid my hand underneath her shirt and started palming her ass. A small giggle came from her mouth. I pushed her back towards the bed and laid her down.

"I thought you had to go to the office?" she asked.

"I do, and I will, but I'm going to work in that office first," I told her pointing to her pretty pussy.

Making my way in between her legs, I used my thumb to massage her clit just a little bit. Using the tip of my tongue, I toyed with it some more. I was done teasing her and used my tongue to whiplash the cat. Nova was wet as fuck already.

"Damn, girl," I whispered.

BOOM!

Kelly

Once I sent Jon Jon the address, I could've sworn this nigga said he was gone wait a couple of days. This nigga just texted me and told me he was walking in the building. My stomach was doing flips. I paced the floor back and forth and used my hands to fan my face because all of sudden it had got hot in the room. Nova and Muza were in the room, and I wondered how he was going to bypass security. Whatever the fuck he had planned, that shit worked because when I looked up, and Jon Jon crazy ass was standing there looking at me like I was the enemy.

"Shit, you scared me," I said. Even at this moment, this man was turning me on, and I knew I hated his guts. He stood there dressed in all black and had his ski mask rolled up sitting on top of his head.

"Where the fuck they at?" he asked.

"In the bedroom, how did you get past security?" I asked.

Jon Jon grabbed me by the hand and pulled me to the living room where there were three other mask men. All of them had their masks pulled down, so I couldn't make out anyone. The big ass security guy was tied up laying on the floor with his mouth gagged and taped up.

"Show me to the room," Jon Jon demanded.

It was time. I tried to turn and walk off, but my feet wouldn't move. It felt like someone had poured some cement on my shit. Jon Jon grabbed me by my hair and shoved me.

"Let's go I ain't got all day. Come on two of y'all," he said to the guys that were standing there. I lead them down the hallway to the room, and once at the door, I stood there.

Jon Jon

Standing outside the door, it was go time. I held my hand up and counted to three.

"One, two, three," I counted and on three, we busted into the door.

"What the fuck!" Muza yelled. Pointing my gun at him, I signaled for my homie to go take care of Nova. These niggas had the nerve to be in here tryna fuck. I couldn't help but take a nice look at Nova's body.

"Damn homie, I ain't mean to bust up yo groove. But, I'll be out of your hair in no time if you cooperate," I told him.

Man nigga, how the fuck you get in here?" Muza asked. I laughed.

"You really need better security. But enough chit-chat, I know you got a safe around this bitch, so I need cash and jewelry, or your precious fine ass Nova will be touched in a way you might not like," I told him.

"I don't keep no money here," he said.

I felt this nigga was trying to play me. Using the gun, I came down across his face, causing him to drop in pain. I walked over to Nova and used the gun running it down her chest and across her belly.

"Muza, get up!" she yelled. It was time to play with his head now.

“Nova, you really love this nigga, don’t you. I thought once you gave us the address you were coming back to daddy,” I taunted. The look on her face was of anger and confusion.

“You tripping. I don’t even know who the hell you are,” she said.

“You don’t have to play dumb, it’s ok,” I told her. Looking at Muza, getting up off the floor, that nigga was steaming the muscles in his face was tight as fuck.

“So, you gone give me what I came for, or am I gone fuck yo bitch again,” I said, making sure to piss this nigga off some more. Kelly stood in the doorway quiet as a mouse.

Muza walked over to the closet and entered something into the safe. I threw him the bag that I had, and he stuffed it with money. I placed the gun to the back of his head in case he tried something stupid because I saw the gun he had in the safe.

“Don’t even think about that shit,” I told him.

“Who the fuck sent you?” he asked.

Grabbing the bag out of his hand, I said, “You don’t listen much, do you? Didn’t you hear me say your girl gave me your address?” I laughed, backing out of the closet with my gun still pointing at him.

Making my way out of the room, I threw the bag at my homie, and he walked out of the room. The looks on Nova, Muza and Kelly’s faces was priceless. When I got to the door, I stopped and looked at Kelly. Drawing my hand back, I punched her dead in her shit and ran out the room. With my homies following behind me, we hit the elevator and got ghost.

“Pull over right here,” I said as we got some distance away from downtown. My lil nigga whipped into Exxon parking lot, and I opened the bag and pulled out a stack thumbing through it.

“This is about 30-40 thou,” I said. I lived for this shit.

This was the first robbery I done and actually let motherfuckers live. That’s why I knocked the fuck out of Kelly. I left too many damn witnesses, and all it would take is for her ass to feel bad and speak on that shit. Even though I did enough damage by telling all them lies about Nova, maybe that shit won't come back on me. I told Kelly I was gone let her go free, but I realize now that's something that I can't do. I got to get her ass back and make her my bitch just to keep her ass quiet.

Muza

Standing there in the middle of the floor, I was pissed. The confusion that hit me had me thinking hard. It was so many unanswered questions. Who the fuck was this nigga that came up in my house? This nigga had an address that he claimed my girl and mother of my child gave him. Some shit wasn't right. Nova ran over to me and tried touching my face.

"Muza, are you ok?" she had the nerve to ask. I was really looking at her sideways right now.

"Don't touch me. Who the fuck was that nigga? You really had somebody come in here to rob me?" I yelled. Nova was shaking her head.

“I don’t know who the hell that was. Why the hell would I send somebody to rob you, Muza? That doesn’t even make sense. I wouldn’t dare bring nobody to do no shit like that!” she yelled back.

I looked at Nova in her eyes to see if I could tell if she was telling the truth or not. She looked sincere, but at this point, nobody was to be trusted. I just lost 40 thousand dollars even though that was just chump change. Kelly, who had regained consciousness, turned to walk out of the room, and Nova was on her heels.

“Hold up, bitch!” she yelled she grabbed Kelly. Kelly looked frightened.

“You know something. I find it mighty funny how this nigga knew so much about me and then turned around and blacked your eye in the same damn place that was blacked earlier. That was a familiar hit. I have been having these bad vibes about you and your little boyfriend. I find it so weird how when I tried to get you to leave that night you wouldn’t leave, and you were scared, then all of sudden you get the courage to leave with no other bruises. I have never given Muza address to nobody but you. I have been staying with him for a while and nothing has ever happened, then the one time I give out his address, and you show up, he gets rob. It was Jon Jon, wasn't it?" Nova asked, Kelly.

I was dying to know the answer. My shit was leaking from being hit with the gun, but I was going to find out what the fuck was going on. Kelly smacked her lips.

"Nova, I'm so sick of your shit. For the longest, you have tricked everyone, and I do mean EVERYONE that you just a perfect goody two shoes. But in reality, you just a money hungry dick jumping hoe. That's all you know and all you will ever be. Who the fuck gives up school to..."

SMACK! Nova hauled off and smacked Kelly so hard that she flew back against the door. Kelly grabbed her face and laughed.

"Well Muza, there's that guilt anger right there. Nova knew who that was that ran up in here we were in it together," Kelly said. All I saw was red.

“GET THE FUCK OUT!” I yelled. Kelly walked out the room, and Nova stood there.

“WHY ARE YOU STILL STANDING HERE, BYE!” I yelled so loud Nova jumped.

“You’re really going to believe that lying bitch. She is mad, and I don’t know why she is doing all this lying, but nothing she said is true, Muzaini. I would never do nothing like this,” she pleaded.

Her pleads fell on deaf ears. All I heard in my head was sirens, deep down inside I didn’t want Nova to leave, but I didn’t know what to believe I had to take some time and get my head together.

“Just leave Nova please, take whatever I gave you and just leave.” I sighed. This woman was still the mother of my child.

“I don’t want shit you have to give, if I leave Muza don’t try and contact me because I have told you nothing but the truth, and you taking her word over mines is foul as fuck,” she said as she turned and walked off.

“The fuck you mean don’t try and contact you? You are carrying my damn child, so I contact you whenever the fuck I get ready. You’re dismissed,” I said, walking out the room leaving her ass there. She had me so fucked up.

Novanna

Muza was on some other shit right now. I knew he was mad but to really put me out. Kelly had better be glad she got ghost before I left out because I was going to beat that bitch senseless whenever I saw her again. As soon as my life started to be going well and everything was in place, shit just had to go sour. I will be lying if I ain't say I deserved it though. Even though I had absolutely nothing to do with the robbery, I had been lying to Muza about my past and how he was just another come up at first. I couldn't help the feelings that eventually came along. I should've let that shit been known when Kelly called herself throwing me under the bus.

When I stepped back in my apartment, the shit was trashed. Shaking my head, I closed and locked the door behind me. My space was tainted. It was so much evil and negativity up in here that it was screaming at me. I immediately started to clean and pick up things. It took me a total of three hours to get my place back right. I had completely stripped Kelly's room and placed everything in trash bags.

The rest of the house had been bleached, saged, and recharged. I was tired as shit. Sitting down on the couch, I did something that I hadn't done in a long time, something that I loved dearly that I had tucked away since my mother's illness. I pulled out my laptop, and I started to write. I wrote from my soul because baby I had a story to tell.

* * *

BOOM! BOOM! BOOM!

Jumping up out my sleep, I looked around and realized I dozed off on the couch writing. I looked at the time it was 9:37 a.m. The loud knocks came again. Who the fuck was this beating on my damn door? I got up and walked over to the door pulling it open, wishing I would've looked out the damn peephole first. It was Delaunn's crazy ass.

"What the hell you want?" I asked, not letting him in my apartment.

"So, you run off and get pregnant by that nigga and leave me to find out from the internet? You played me I thought we was better than that," Delaunn asked. I rubbed my temples because I didn't have the strength to do this with him.

"Delaunn, ok all bullshit aside, why can't you just move on? I'm not with anyone right now, not even Muza. Yeah, I lied to you to spare your feelings and to keep my secret safe, but you know what? I don't even care anymore. You can tell Muza whatever it is you want about me escorting whatever. That was just a part of me that I wasn't ready to share yet, but he will eventually find out anyways. I'm focused on my pregnancy and trying to remain drama free, so if you'll excuse me, I'm going to go throw up now," I told him, slamming the door in his face and making sure to lock it. I was sick of these niggas.

I bolted straight to the bathroom and was bent over the toilet in seconds. While hovering over the toilet, I kept hearing more beating at the door.

"I swear for God this nigga better leave me the hell alone," I mumbled.

Stomping back towards the living room, I looked out the peephole this time before opening the door because if it was Delaunn, his ass would've been out there knocking. I think I'm gone have to take a restraining order out on him if he doesn't come to his senses. Unlocking the door, I pulled it opened.

"Wassup, dad?" I asked from the look on his face he didn't seem to be too happy. He walked his milk dud head ass clean pass me and stood there waiting on me to close the door. Closing the door, I turned to him.

"What you looking all crazy for?" I asked.

"What's this shit about you sending somebody to Muza's house to rob him? I know this shit a joke." He chuckled sarcastically.

"I don't know what Muzaini told you, but like I told him, I didn't have anything to do with that. He so angry he can't even think straight. What reason do I have to rob him, I'm carrying his child. I'm set for life, so why do I need to rob him? Just being real he stood there and watched me confront Kelly, and Kelly stood up there and lied like I was in on the shit. How long have I been staying with Muza even at his other crib where he keeps a lot of his money like a dumbass, why nobody never robbed him there? I only gave the address to Kelly because she lied and said that she was leaving her abusive boyfriend and she couldn't come back here and stay because she was scared he would hurt her. So, Muza said it was ok for her to come to the condo. I only gave her that address then all of sudden we get robbed. The robber was talking like I had been involved with him. He was saying shit to make it play out like I really was in on it. Muza fell for that shit. If he doesn't want to believe me that's on him because I would never do no foul shit like that," I told my father.

"Who the hell is this guy that she was involved with?" Malcolm asked. I could tell he was tryna stay calm, but I could see the hood coming up out him. It felt weird that I had a father that had my back, or did he have my back?

"Some nigga name Jon Jon she just met that was beating her ass and brainwashed her silly ass. Wait, what were you coming over here to do? Did you think I would do something like this?" I asked, crossing my arms over my chest.

"No, I know good and well your mama ain't raise you like that, but I wanted to hear both sides of the story before I passed judgment on anyone. I actually had to talk some sense in Muza's head because I think he more so hurt than anything. It's like a battle with him. He loves you and wants to make sure you and the baby are ok, but he also realized he might have said some fucked up shit, and he is embarrassed to face you right now," Malcolm said.

"I understand all that daddy, but he put me out like I was nobody. Good thing I still had my own shit. I even told him if I leave don't bother trying to find me, and of course, he went off about the baby and shit. Can I tell you something?" I asked my father who was now sitting beside me on the couch.

"Sure, sweetheart you can tell me anything, I'm just glad I get this opportunity to have a meaningful conversation with my daughter," he said. He was saying that shit now, but let's see how he handles the real Nova.

"What I have to say though you have to promise it stays between me and you. I understand your loyalty with Muzaini, but as your daughter and your flesh and blood, you now have a loyalty with me," I told him, and I was dead ass.

"Damn girl, is it that bad?" he asked. It was all or nothing, and maybe then, he could help me in the future, if this problem comes about.

"I have sort of being lying to Muza about who I am and the way I was getting money. This is also a secret that I was keeping from mama and thank God she never found out. She probably would've gone to her grave sooner. The main reason I dropped out of college was because school just wasn't for me. I had found a fast and easy way to make some money, and I got addicted to that life. I got addicted to not having to worry about struggling with bills, and I got addicted to buying nice things whenever I wanted to. I was escorting," I mumbled, but I knew he heard me. Malcolm leaned in.

"You were what?" he asked.

"You heard me. I was escorting. I wasn't half-assing though. I was really just accompanying rich ass men to events, dates, and some even just like having conversation where I boosted their egos or made them feel superior or better about themselves. These men were paying top dollar. I would get paid from two to ten thousand a night. There was one guy that plays for the Titans that we kind of grew to like each other and there was sex. He is fucking crazy, and he literally just left here before you arrived. It made me money hungry, so the first time I saw Muza in the mall, I was instantly attracted to him because he screamed money. I never knew who he was. I came home and researched him not knowing that I would run into him at your house. So, when the chance came about for me to pretend to be his girl, I was like hell yeah all I saw was dollar signs. I never knew that I would actually like him, well love him, nor be carrying his child. Kelly kind of let it slip today at the house, but he was to mad to catch on. I just know that when he finds out the truth about my past, he is not going to want to have anything to do with me," I admitted. Malcolm let out a huge sigh and rubbed his head.

"As a man one thing we hate is for our women to have a whorish past, not saying you a whore, but that is what he might label you as. Now, this is complicated for me, but as your father, I'm going to keep it real with you because I raised Muza. He is not going to accept this too well," he said.

"I don't see why not. I haven't done a job since I started dating Muza," I told him.

"That's not the point, Nova. You were with many different men. Muza is a very high profiled person who lives in the spotlight, so this will be displayed everywhere. You will have people paying to destroy the both of you guys' lives. So there going to dig into your past. Now since there is a child at hand, things may be different because Muza is big on family. I just don't want you to get your hopes up, and things go a different route. You have to tell him though sooner than later and before someone else tells him. That Kelly girl her life is ruined, so if she knows anything about your past, that's a quick cash come up from anybody wanting a story. You have to watch people," Malcolm said. I nodded my head in agreeance.

"That's so true, thank you for listening to me. You don't know how hard that was for me to tell you that. I know I have to talk to Muzaini, so hopefully, I can tell him really soon," I said.

My father and I continued to talk. I was blessed to finally have a dad.

Muzaini

A week later, Muza Entertainment's 3rd annual ball

It was the day of my annual ball, and before I started running around like a chicken with my head cut off and doing interviews and photo ops, I had to make a very important stop. I stood there thinking about what I was about to do, and it took a lot of long nights and fighting with myself to bring me to this point. Lifting my hand, I knocked on the door and waited patiently. To calm my nerves, I couldn't find shit to do with my hands, so I placed them in my pocket of the pants I had on. The door opened, and there she stood looking like a goddess.

"What's up?" Nova asked. Just hearing her voice did something to me. I know it's been a week, but it felt like years. She stood there wearing a pair of shorts and a sports bra and had her locs in a high bun on her head.

"Look before you flip out on me, I'm sorry for popping up at your spot, but I was heading to the venue, and I wanted to do this face to face. I know we have a lot to talk about which we will get to all that, but I sort of don't have the time right now. I wanted to apologize for spazzing out on you and asking you to leave. I understand I was wrong and I should've believed you wouldn't do anything like that. As you know, tonight is my annual ball, and before all this shit happened, I was going to take you as my date. If you say yes, my stylist is downstairs and ready to take you to handle everything you need to do in preparation for tonight. Nova, will you please do me the honor of escorting me to the ball tonight?" I asked. I could tell she was stunned.

"Muza, we really do have a lot to talk about, but yes, I will go with you tonight," she said. Hearing her say yes was music to my ears. I leaned in and placed a kiss on her cheek.

"Thank you. I have to run but get dressed, and a car is waiting for you downstairs," I told her. This shit was going to be great. I went back to the car and headed to my first stop.

I knew the step I was taking tonight was a huge one but being away from Nova the way that we were I knew that I loved her and wanted to spend the rest of my life showing her. I just pray that she felt the same way about me and can forgive me for the way that I handled that little shit.

Nova

To open my door and see Muza standing there looking fine as ever, I was shocked but happy at the same time. So, hearing that he wanted me to go to the ball with him was all I needed to get my foot back in the door and get things back on track with my baby daddy. I knew he had someone waiting on me and I didn't want to keep them waiting long, so I threw on a pair of Victoria Secret PINK yoga pants with a matching top and grabbed my bag and headed downstairs to the car.

"Sorry for taking so long," I said once I got inside the car. The stylist seemed pretty cool.

"It's ok. I'm on your time. Well, we do have to have you ready before a certain time, but Mr. Muhammad has everything set for you. While you're getting your hair done, I will show you a few pieces that we had flown in, and you can narrow the choices down from there. Also, you will be getting your nails and feet done during your hair process.

My name is Tammara by the way," she spoke rarely making eye contact. She had her face glued to her phone and tablet.

"Cool, sounds like a plan, I know getting this head of mine done can take some time," I told her. She finally looked up.

"I'm sorry, I had to make sure Mr. Muhammad suit is just right. As you know I'm his stylist, and I also handle the designs for his clothing line, so you may find me working on three things at once," Tammara said, taking a sip from the energy drink she had. I laughed. She was wired.

The first stop we made was to the salon. Once inside, I was treated like royalty. Baby the way my head was washed, I'm sure I came on myself. While the retwisting process began, everything that Tammara told me about started to happen. In she rolled a big ass rack full of dresses. There was so many to choose from. I swear I could use to this type of treatment.

"I'll show you a dress, and you say yay or nay then we can go from there," Tammara said, holding up the first dress.

I know I shook my head to the first five dresses she held up then the next one she held up I knew it was the one. It was giving me Rihanna and Cardi B vibes.

"That's it. I don't need to see anymore. I want that one," I told Tammara, and she nodded her head.

"Ok, I see you got taste; this is an Alexander McQueen," she said.

This dress was everything it was a petal pink midi knitted dress with a vintage corset like bustier top. The dress had grosgrain details on the shoulder straps with metal adjuster and metal zipper fastening on the center front. This shit was bad.

After Tammara left to go get my shoes, the lady finished up my hair. Then I was off to makeup. I couldn't believe I had been here almost five damn hours. A bitch was sleepy and hungry, but I was scared to eat anything because this child of mine wouldn't let it digest. I was literally snacking on crackers and ginger ale, which was pissing me off even more.

“Are you ready to see yourself?” Tammara asked while standing behind me.

“Yes, I’m nervous though,” I admitted.

“Don’t be because girl you are finnne, and you are rocking the hell out of that dress,” she said. I slowly turned around, and my mouth flew open. I knew I was the shit but damn.

“Lord, I swear all our problems gone go away when he sees me in this dress,” I admitted. Tammara laughed.

“I don’t know much about you, but I can tell Muza genuinely cares for you. I can vibe with you. That Cru wench he used to date This is so unprofessional, but I couldn’t stand that bitch and the broom she flew in on,” Tammara admitted. I busted out laughing.

“Yeah, she’s a mess. Thank you for helping me today,” I told her, leaning in and hugging her.

“Let’s get you to your man because I know he is waiting on you boo,” she said, and we both walked back to the car.

Muza

Looking down at my watch, I was watching the time like a hawk. Nova should've been here by now. A nigga was nervous, hoping she ain't back out on a nigga. The majority of all the interviews I had done so far today were asking about Nova and the baby. I swear living the life I live, a nigga didn't have no privacy thanks to the paparazzi. It was almost time for me to walk the red carpet. I spotted my Maybach pulling up, and I noticed it was my driver. Walking down the steps, I headed to the carpet and waited for the car to come to a complete stop. My driver got out and made his way to the back of the car, opening the door there she was.

"Damn," I mouthed.

Nova looked like she was made to be beside me. I mean I honestly didn't have any words to speak. She was breathtaking. I swallowed the lump in my throat and placed my hand out for her to grab.

"Girl, you are so damn fine," I told her. She was blushing so damn hard.

“Thank you for all of this, and thanks for the compliment,” she said.

“Well, I know you a natural and shit, but are you ready to hit this red carpet because every damn interview I did today I was asked where is Nova and questions about the baby, so you’re gone get bombarded,” I told her.

“I’m fine. It’s nothing I can’t handle,” she answered. I placed my hand in the small of her back, and we made our way to the red carpet.

The cameras were flashing, and Nova was working that shit like she always did. Each mic we stopped at asked us the infamous questions about the baby and our relationship. Nova shocked me when she told them that we were expecting, but that part of her life she wanted to remain private until she was ready to share certain aspects with the world. She did better than I would have. She was early in her pregnancy, so she didn’t want to do too much too soon, and something happened, so I understood that fully because I didn’t want anything to happen to my baby. Some shit most pregnant woman lived by, so I could dig it.

We finally made our way inside after a good thirty minutes of interviews and photos. Nova didn't leave my side, I told her she could mingle, but she wanted to be right by me. Malcolm and my aunt had made their way over to us, and we started laughing and talking, Nova and Elizabeth were talking about the pregnancy, and Unc and I was chopping it up about the announcement I was going to make tonight.

"Ahem!" we heard, and we all turned around staring at Cru and Delaunn. I knew my ass should've put a ban on the party.

Nova walked over to me and stood beside me to make her presence known.

"What do you want Cru, and if you try any shit I will throw your ass out of this party so fast," I said through gritted teeth but making sure to keep calm because I knew cameras were on me at all times.

"You don't have to be so rude. I was only coming by to congratulate you both on your child. I can honestly say I'm happy for you," she had the nerve to say, causing me to raise my eyebrow. I couldn't help to notice the look that Delaunn was giving Nova, and she was looking dead at Cru.

“Thank you, stick around it’s more to congratulate on,” I told her walking past her and Delaunn, taking Nova with me. Malcolm and my aunt followed.

“Come on stage with me, I have to introduce the performers,” I told Nova.

“Ok!” she said excitedly. Walking up on the stage, I grabbed the mic as the crowd cheered us on.

“Thank you, guys, for coming out tonight and thank those that have supported this event each and every year. As you guys know, all donations from this event goes to the women’s foundation for those who suffer from drug abuse, physical abuse, or just need help period. I have dedicated my life to this because of my mother. A lot of y’all been asking about this lady right here and yes, she holds a special part of me. A piece of me that I’ve always wanted. That’s why I can only do what's right and pray that she will accept what I'm about to do," I spoke to the crowd as they cheered on.

I reached into my pocket and got down on one knee. Nova was shaking her head, and everyone was screaming. I spoke into the mic

"Novanna Collier, will you marry me?" I asked.

Loud moans came over the loudspeaker catching me off guard. I turned around, and there was a video on the screen of Nova and Delaunn fucking.

"Oh my god!" Nova cried.

"Turn that shit off right now!" I yelled. Everyone had their phones out recording.

"Don't tape that shit!" I yelled. Nova ran off stage, and I followed behind her. She ran dead smack into Cru and Delaunn who were both wearing mischievous grins.

"Oh, what was that other congrats you were talking about?" Delaunn asked. I reached behind Nova and rocked his ass to sleep while Nova had pounced on Cru.

"Worldstar!" I heard someone yell.

Nova

"Get the fuck off me!" I yelled as my father was pulling me off Cru. This bitch had just ruined my life in the worse way.

"Come on, baby girl. You're pregnant," Malcolm said calmly pulling me away. I looked over at Muza who had a look of pure hatred on his face.

"It's not what you think, Muza," I told him.

"It's not what I think? Y'all just made a fool out of me. Here I am proposing to you because I wanted to spend the rest of my life with you, and you all on video fucking the next nigga. Everyone has seen this shit this shit gone be in every paper and all over social media. Fuck!" he yelled.

My emotions were getting the best of me, and I couldn’t stop crying long enough to even get my words out.

“I swear it’s nothing between me and him,” I cried.

“That’s what you say, hell is that even my baby you carrying or that nigga’s?” Muza asked.

“Really Muza?” I cried.

“You know what, fuck this shit. This right here between us is over. All that shit I said on stage, you can forget that shit,” he said tossing the ring in the trash and walking away. Tammara ran over to the trashcan, reached in, and got the ring.

“This nigga crazy she said.” Looking at the box, I just fell in my daddy's arms and cried.

“This isn’t fair daddy, that video is so old. I told you he was crazy,” I said. Malcolm caressed my back.

“It’s ok. We will get through this like we get through everything else,” he reassured me.

I wasn't so sure about this though. This was damaging to the both of us. I felt so bad for Muza and the worst part I hadn't even had a chance to tell him my secret yet. I knew for a fact he would never want my ass then. Cru and Delaunn were gone see me, and I put that on my unborn.

Muzaini

I had never been so humiliated in my life. Here I was bragging about the woman I love and wanting to make her my wife, but it was apparent that Nova had other things on her mind. Seeing her being fucked by that nigga ignited a fire in me that I wasn't sure I could control. I was hurt, and I'm that nigga, so that was not a good look. It has been two weeks since that shit went down, and I had my people doing damage control, trying to get my ass out of the spotlight. The media was having a field day with it. Somehow, they all wanted to interview Nova, and I hadn't spoken with her, but what she put out for everyone to know did kind of spin the whole thing, and now everyone was attacking Delaunn and Cru.

Nova had told them that Cru and Delaunn were salty about our relationship being the bitter exes, and it was them that tried to leak an old video that she didn't even know was being recorded. Last I heard, she was pressing charges against Delaunn. I didn't let that shit change my life. I just put myself in my work.

"Mr. Muhammad, you have a visitor," my secretary's voice came through the speaker.

"Who is it?" I asked.

"Umm sir, it's Cru. Do you want me to ask her to leave?" she hesitated. Letting out a huge sigh, I wasn't sure if I even wanted to speak with her. Her ass had been blowing me up since the party, and I don't know why.

"Send her back," I told her. I scooted back in my chair and placed my hands on my stomach and waited for her to make her entrance. When the door opened, and she walked in, I couldn't do nothing but shake my head. Maybe it was because a nigga ain't had none in awhile, but damn she was fine. The long jumbo braids she rocked looked nice touching her ass. She showcased her smile that used to have a nigga weak. I kept my poker face on though I didn't want her to know the effect she was having on me.

"I'm surprised that you actually let me come back. I have been reaching out to you," she said, taking a seat.

"I don't know what you are reaching out for. You have caused enough damage in my life," I told her, and it wasn't nothing but the truth.

"Muzaini, all I did was keep you from making a huge mistake. Nova was just about the money. Delaunn told me everything about their relationship, and soon as she seen a bigger payday in you, you know what she did? She dropped him like a bad habit. Are you sure you wanted to marry her? Granted she is possibly carrying your child, and I know that was something you always wanted, but I love you, Muza. I really do, and I couldn't allow that to happen. Now she is spreading these rumors about me like I had something to do with the tape, but that was all Delaunn's doing," Cru spilled.

"If all you were doing was trying to keep me from making a mistake, why didn't you come to me personally, Cru? If you knew this nigga was going to do some bogus shit like he did, why you ain't talk him out of that?" I asked her. I kind of was getting what Cru was saying, but some shit just wasn't adding up.

"Honestly, I didn't. He told me he was going to come and talk to you like a man because he didn't know if the baby was his or not because Nova wasn't speaking to him. I simply was in the wrong place at the wrong time," she said.

"Guilty by association," I told her. Cru stood up and walked behind the desk and stood in front of me.

"Muza, I know that I messed up while we together, but I really love you, and I'm willing to make some changes to prove to you just how much I love you," she said.

I looked at her, and at that moment, my head wasn't thinking straight, but my other head was wanting to do all the talking.

"Show me," I said, unzipping my pants.

Cru dropped to her knees and went to work. I closed my eyes and enjoyed the warmth of her mouth. I knew dealing with Cru's crazy ass that I shouldn't even be doing this because now a nigga wouldn't be able to get rid of her. My heart was still with Nova, and I couldn't shake that shit.

Nova

"Thank you, I will see you Monday morning," I told my lawyer and hung up the phone.

Things for me have been a pain since the night of Muza's ball consisting of many interviews and being bothered or harassed on social media. I was the victim in all of this, and that's why I was going through with pressing charges on Delaunn. What he did was something they call revenge porn, and it was a law that they took seriously in Tennessee.

I missed Muza more than anything, but I knew that it was over for us. The only concern he had was this child I was carrying, even though I wasn't going to be harassing him about that either. He wanted to question if he was the father or not, so I was going to give him a paternity test and gone on about my business. I closed my laptop. I was done with writing for the day. I submitted the first couple chapters of a book to Mz. Lady P and I was waiting on a response. I was moving forward in my life. There was a knock at the door, and I stood up to go get it. Looking through the peephole, I saw that it was Kelly. Sucking my teeth, I opened the door.

"What?" I asked. I wasn't here for her shit, and I most definitely wasn't fucking with her trick ass no more.

"I just came to get my stuff," she said, looking at the floor.

"You got you half of the rent?" I asked, I wasn't hurting for no damn rent money, but this bitch was gone pay.

"What you mean?" she asked.

"I do recall you staying here, and you just left without paying the rent. If you got money, you could get your stuff," I told her, crossing my arms.

"I only have two hundred dollars, Nova," she said, reaching into her bag.

I closed the door, walked to her room, and grabbed two trash bags not even looking inside to see what the contents were. Walking back to the door, I opened the door and sat the two bags at her feet.

"Two hundred dollars for two bags; you'll get the rest when you have the rest of my money," I told her, holding my hand out.

"I swear you're a bitch," she said.

"I'm a paid bitch. You did me so dirty you're lucky I'm even entertaining your fake ass right now. Get the fuck off my doorstep," I told her.

"How did that engagement go? You just wait I got you," she said. My antennas went up to the shit my father told me a minute ago about her ass.

"Bitch, get out!" I said, closing the door in her face. That hoe was going to be a problem.

Jon Jon

A nigga was chilling and enjoying the fruits of my labor. I had moved into a bigger spot since Kelly had come back and told me she was pregnant. A nigga didn't want no damn kids no time soon, but shit, as long as I could keep her ass around so that she wouldn't open her mouth, then the shit was aite I guess. Smoking from the blunt that I just rolled up, I let the smoke feel my lungs. Kelly walked in and dropped two trash bags on the floor. I lifted my head off the couch and looked at her like she was crazy.

"Yo, what is that shit?" I asked clearly pissed off.

"Some of my shit. You know that bitch made me pay her for this shit. She told me I could get the rest of my stuff when I bring the rest of her money," Kelly said, plopping down on the couch.

"You need to get that shit out the middle of my floor. What money you owe her?" I asked.

"Rent," she said.

"Oh. I guess you need to pay that before she takes that ass to court," I told her hitting the blunt again. I blew the smoke in Kelly's face.

"Really Jon Jon, where I'm gone get the money from?" she asked me.

"I don't know, but you need to get them damn bags out the middle of the floor like I asked. I'm not going to repeat myself," I said in a more serious tone.

Kelly jumped up, snatched the bags, and headed out of the room. I laughed because I was just fucking with her ass, I loved getting under her skin. She left my ass alone when she thought I was mad at her.

Muzaini

A nigga had fucked up big time. I end up fucking Cru damn ass in my office. I was gone stop at the head, but shit, I couldn't resist. My judgment was cloudy, and she offered to come over and cook dinner, and my damn dumb ass agreed. I felt bad as fuck. Was that normal considering I'm single, but I felt like I cheated on Nova. I needed to get some things off my chest and I felt now was the time.

I pulled up to Nova's apartment, and I just sat there for a minute. I had gassed myself to come over here and talk. What did I want to know? What could she possibly tell me that was different from what I had already heard? I closed my eyes and let out a deep breath because I was going to have to face her sooner or later. I couldn't ignore this like the shit hadn't happened. I slowly opened the door, getting out of the car. I placed my shades on my face so that she couldn't read me and skipped upstairs to her apartment. It was now or never, so I knocked on the door.

"Who is it?" I heard her yell.

"Muza!" I responded. There was a pause for what I know to be about two minutes, and then I heard the locks on the door. Nova opened the door, and shit, I was speechless.

"Um, hello?" I heard her say, snapping me out of my trance, I looked at her up and down, taking in her beauty.

"My bad, is it ok if I come in? I think it's time we talk," I asked her.

Nova crossed her arms and moved to the side, letting me in. I walked in and went straight to the living room, taking a seat on the couch, which I noticed was new. I looked around the place, and literally everything had been replaced.

“I like what you did with the place,” I said.

She took a seat at one of the bar stools that were in front of the bar area and looked at me as if I was bothering her.

“It comes a time in life when things need to be replaced— *ALL* things,” she said, emphasizing the all. I caught every bit of that shade.

“You’re right about that. I think a conversation deserves to be had about the things that took place that night at the ball. I know things have been overwhelming for the both of us, but it seems like we still have to deal with each other,” I said, pointing to Nova’s stomach.

“Before we talk remove your shades, and you know I was waiting for this day to come because this is the norm for you. You run away from situations until you’re ready to deal with them, but this whole time I have been dealing with this shit. I was the victim in all of this. You were just embarrassed as you say. Like I was trying to tell you from the jump, that video was old, and I didn't even know I was being recorded. Matter of fact, you remember the day you were sitting outside of my apartment stalking me, and I came home? You told me about keeping it real with you because you knew I was hiding something. That was the same day and the last time that I was ever with him. I never cheated on you, and what hurts the most is you had the nerve to question my child as if I lied to you about that. Now don't get me wrong when I found out I was pregnant I questioned myself, but Delaunn never came in me, so I knew then that this baby was yours. The damage has been done, and everyone has seen me in my most private form. Meanwhile, all you're worried about is your name," she said. I could tell she was hurt and had an attitude.

"What do you expect? A lot of things have happened since we tried this relationship thing. First the robbery and then this shit. I'm like damn can I really marry you?" I told her, regretting how I worded that shit the instant it left my mouth.

"And like I told you the first time I didn't have shit to do with that robbery. Like your ass don't know by now that that shit was Kelly and Jon Jon's doing. I mean it's cool you don't trust me and that you may look at me differently because I see some people must have got in your head, and most likely it was a hating ass bitch. Muza, hear me and hear me well when I tell you this. Me and you will never work because this shit will forever be on your mind. Again, it's clear you don't trust me. I just wish that you could see I was always loyal to you and faithful from the day we got together. I love you, but I love me more, and no matter how bad I hate that we have come to this, I will not chase you nor beg you to be with me. If you want a paternity test when the baby is born, you can have that also," she said.

Wait a damn minute she wasn't supposed to be handling this as good as she was.

"So, why aren't you gone tell me the truth about you and Delaunn?" I asked. I wanted to fish around about the shit Cru told me.

“What the hell does he have to do with us? I told you all that happened. He’s just a bitter ass nigga,” she said.

“So, you weren’t with him for his money and then when you met me, a bigger payday, you hopped on me and left that nigga out in the cold like that. That’s why he was tripping, but hell, who wouldn’t? You can’t play with people feelings like that, Nova,” I said.

For some reason I wanted her to hurt like I was hurting. If I couldn’t be happy, why should she be able to be happy?

“You know what how I met Delaunn and what we had going on isn’t your business anymore because we are not together, engaged, or none of that. You’re tripping real hard. I thought this would be a civilized conversation, but I see now this is over,” she said.

“It must be true. I’ll go, but before I do I just need you to know that I will be there for my child, so I need to know about all appointments and shit like that, and you also need to get prepared for Cru to be in the picture once the baby is born,” I said.

"Wait hold on, why do I need to be prepared for that?" she asked, placing her hands on her hip.

"We are back together now," I said, walking towards the door.

"How can you be with someone who played a part in that shit that happened at the ball?" she asked.

"She didn't. She was tryna warn me about the gold digging chick that I was about to marry. Speaking of which, I think Kelly called you the same thing. What was it, a money hungry dick jumping hoe?" I told her. I knew I was wrong and my face felt every bit of the punch that followed.

"Are you fucking crazy?" I yelled.

"No, but you are. Get the fuck out of my house before I black your other eye!" Nova yelled.

I knew I fucked up, and I asked for that shit.

Novanna

I was so turned up that I was pacing the floor like Yvette on *Baby Boy* right before Jody knocked her ass out. This nigga had me messed up. I wanted to cry because this wasn't Muza. I just knew Cru had gotten in his head. It wasn't nobody else but her. I laughed at the fact that I had punched Muza in his eye, I'm glad his ass ain't have no reflex.

My ass was hungry, so I headed to the kitchen and grabbed me some pickles and Chester's Hot Fries to satisfy my craving. My phone rang, and I grabbed it. It was my dad Malcolm FaceTiming me.

"What's up, Pops?" I said, looking into the phone taking a bite of my pickle.

"Nova, why you over there putting your hands on folks?" he asked. I shook my head. This nigga had the nerve to tell on me.

"Man, he was disrespectful as hell. I ain't never took no shit from nobody, and I'm not about to start letting him think he can disrespect me. Did you know that he and Cru are back together?" I asked him.

"No, I didn't. Who told you that?" he asked.

"He did that was before he called me a money hungry dick hopping hoe," I said. My father's face changed like he was instantly pissed.

"He let that girl fill his head up with bullshit. I don't care what she says. I know she played a part with Delaunn and that shit he pulled. Then he got the nerve to be laying up with her talking about get used to her being around my baby. He got me fucked up, daddy. I will put my Louboutin on that hoe's neck if she thinks she gone play with me," I told him.

"Nova, calm down and don't get all stressed out with my grandchild. I'm gone have a talk with him because he ain't think to tell me all that shit. Did you tell him about you know what?" he asked, referring to my escorting.

"No, I didn't, and what's the point now. It's done between us," I mumbled.

"Communication is key. Yeah, he's mad right now, but he's gone be even madder when he hears it from somebody else rather than from you all this time. I'm just trying to tell you," Malcolm said.

"I understand. Well, I'm about to finish my snack. Tell Elizabeth I said hi, and I will talk to you guys later.

"Aite then, love you, baby girl," he said. I laid the phone down and continued to eat my snack.

Cru

I was walking around on cloud nine. I had stopped by my house to pick up a few items before heading over to Muza's. Things were finally going to get back to how they use to be. I knew once I broke him off some and planted that seed in his head about Nova that he would come running back. *Manifest in your life sis and watch it become what you want* was what I lived by. Grabbing my overnight bag, I flew out the door and headed to my man.

I hopped in my Telsa and turned on my boo Ella Mai banging "Boo'd Up" the whole drive to Muza's

Ooh, now I'll never get over you until I find something new

That get me high like you do, yeah yeah

Ooh, now I'll never get over you until I find something new

That get me high like you do

Listen to my heart go ba-dum, boo'd up

Biddy-da-dum, boo'd up

Pulling into the driveway Muza's cars were lined up, and I pulled right behind one. I checked my makeup and adjusted my breasts as I got out the car, making my way up the steps. I ranged the doorbell while checking my clothes, making sure I looked nice. The door opened, and my mouth dropped.

"What happened to your eye?" I gasped.

"Nova is what happened," he said, letting me in.

"What the fuck, Muza? You should have her ass locked up. She shouldn't be putting her hands on you," I told him. We walked in the kitchen, and I looked at his eye.

“Ain’t nobody about to press charges on her. Shit just got emotional, and I said some fucked up shit,” he said.

“That doesn’t justify her putting her hands on you. Let that had been you blacking her eye, and you wouldn’t be sitting her talking to me right now because you would be in jail,” I told him. He stood up from the table.

“Look, just cook whatever it is you were about to cook. This conversation is over,” he said, walking upstairs.

This nigga had to be in his feelings about Nova. I wasn’t no dummy, and I knew he still cared for her very much, but I was just going to have to take his mind off her. It was nothing if I gave him everything he wanted.

I walked over to the refrigerator and pulled out the things that I requested his shopper to get for dinner. Usually, Muza had his meals cooked by his staff, but I wanted him to have a home cooked meal from the heart. One thing about me even though I rarely cooked because you wouldn’t dare catch me in the kitchen, I could get down. I pulled out the pork chops and rinsed them off seasoning and battering them ready to drop in the fryer. While the chops fried, I peeled the potatoes and made some homemade mashed potatoes along with some green beans and gravy for the mashed potatoes and pork chops. After everything was done, I fixed Muza a plate, grabbed him a beer, and carried his plate upstairs.

When I walked in the room, Muza was sitting up in the bed going through his phone.

“I brought you your plate,” I said, causing him to hurry up and put his phone down. *I wonder what the hell he was up to.*

“Thank you, Cru, and you cooked my favorite. I’m about to fuck this shit up,” he said, reaching for the tray. After saying a quick prayer, he dug in. I climbed into bed beside him and clicked on the tv.

“Girl, you keep cooking like this and a nigga might just keep you around,” he said with a mouth full of food.

"Damn, I thought I was good enough to keep around without the food. Muza, I really hope you give me another chance. I promise you won't be disappointed," I told him.

He looked at me like he was thinking about what to say next. He placed his fork down on his plate and looked at me. His brown eyes carried a sadness as he licked his perfect lips.

"You are aware that I do have a kid on the way. I know I'm the father of Nova's baby, and I'm not about to be no deadbeat. I let your ass feed me some bullshit earlier, and I said some things to her that wasn't cool, and it might mess up our parenting relationship. That can't happen because she will be around, and hopefully if I decide to be with you for the long run, you have to respect the mother of my child," he said. What the hell did he mean *if* he decides to be with me for the long run?

"What exactly do you mean by if you decide to be with me for the long run?" I asked.

"Cru, my girl, we can't just pick up where we left off because we left off on bad terms. You're on like a trial run," he said. This nigga had me ready to flip his whole plate over on his ass, but I kept my cool.

"It's cool. You will see this is the right decision in the long run," I told him, feeling confident.

Novanna

Eight Months Later

My pregnancy was at the end of the road, and I was miserable as shit. This child had turned me into the biggest bitch ever. I was always irritable and snapping off on motherfuckers. I couldn't wait to push this child out. I kept my end of the deal by allowing Muza to come to all doctor appointments to keep him in the loop and that was it. I still loved him of course, but I had lost some respect for him after that blow up we had in my apartment. We literally met at the doctor office, and after the appointments, we would go our separate ways. Sometimes he did try to reach out, but I shut that shit down. I knew that he and Cru was an official item again because they asses were all over the entertainment headlines. When it first made headlines, I use to see shit like SHE WON. No bitch, I let you borrow him I use to scream.

Delaunn and I ended up settling out of court, and I was awarded 1.2 million dollars simply because he admitted to setting up the camera and recording me without permission with the intent to use for revenge purposes. The video went viral and was shared amongst many social media sites, so that helped also. I bet he thinks twice about doing some shit like that again. Delaunn was suspended from the team and probably wasn't going to be signed for another season with the Titans. I ended up moving out of that damn apartment and buying me a house. It's nothing huge but big enough for my baby and me. My dad had his friends set everything up, and Muza hired somebody to do the nursery.

I had also heard something back from my book submission, and your girl was signed to Mz. Lady P Presents. It was a feeling that I couldn't explain because I stepped out on faith and turned a dream into reality. I had a lot of time on my hands, so I spent the majority of my time writing anyways. I eased up from my desk and walked out of my office to head to the kitchen and get me some ice. I heard the front door open, and I rolled my eyes, I should've thought twice about giving my father and Elizabeth a key. Elizabeth turned the corner carrying a bag.

"Well look at you looking like you're ready to pop. I was just in the area, and I thought of you," she said, placing the bag on the counter.

“What did you bring me this time, Elizabeth?” I asked, filling my cup up with ice.

“Oh, don’t act like you don’t like my surprises or me popping up over here,” she said, reaching into the bag and pulling out two frames. I damn near choked on my ice.

“Elizabeth what is this and what will possess you to get something like this done?” I asked, grabbing both frames.

This lady was crazy. She had gotten two pics that Muza and I had taken together the first night we went out and the night of his ball blown up in black and white and placed in a golden frame.

“This is for the baby. It has to have something to look at. Maybe it will send a blessing over this house because this is what is supposed to be. I can’t believe you are sitting around here and letting him date that Cru wench and parade her around like that. What happened to fighting for your man?” she asked.

I knew it was coming. It never failed. Elizabeth always made it her point to try and talk me into some bullshit.

"Ms. Elizabeth I've told you time and time again that I'm cool on him. If that's what he wants, then he can have that. I will always love him just from a distance," I told her.

"Bullshit, I like to see the two of you try and co-parent with both of y'all still having feelings for each other. It's just a big ass mess if you ask me," she said.

"How you know he still has feelings for me?" I asked.

"He is my nephew. Do you think I just be over here harassing just you? He gets it too," Ms. Elizabeth said.

She grabbed the frames and went upstairs to the nursery, and I followed. Walking up the steps, I felt a trickle of water run down my legs then a big gush.

"Ooooh My God!" I slowly yelled.

"What. girl?" Ms. Elizabeth turned around. I looked at the ground then up at her.

"Oh, hell. Ok, let's get you back downstairs and let me call your father and Muza. Do you have a bag packed?" she asked. I nodded my head yes.

"It's a small suitcase in the nursery beside the dresser," I told her. I was keeping calm and trying not to panic because I was controlling the level of my pain. Elizabeth came back downstairs with the suitcase.

"Muza and your father will meet us at the hospital," she said, helping me off the couch. I had started doing my breathing that I had learned in Lamaze the whole walk to the car. It was time, and I was about to become someone's mother.

When we got to the hospital, Muza was waiting at the entrance with a wheelchair.

"Come on, Nova. How are you doing? You in any pain?" he asked. I could tell he was nervous.

"I'm fine. The contractions are coming more and more though," I blew. I was pushed upstairs to a private suite, where I got comfortable and waited on the arrival of my bundle of joy.

I was given an epidural and decided that I would try and get some rest because I haven't dilated fully yet. Muza was sitting by my side, and my father and Ms. Elizabeth were sitting in the corner knocked out. I felt like I was being stared at, so I opened my eyes, and Muza had his eyes locked on me.

"Why are you staring at me?" I asked, rolling my eyes.

"I'm just thinking. I wish we could've enjoyed this pregnancy together. I feel like I missed a lot. You know like being able to rub your stomach and run out and get your cravings. That's how it was supposed to be," he had the audacity to say.

"Well, it wasn't my fault. You could've had all that had you not let all the bullshit interfere or let your girlfriend Cru get in your head. I told you the truth from the start about the Delaunn situation right then, and there we could've fixed the issue and moved forward, but nah we didn't, so now we here," I told him.

"I know you still got feelings for me, Nova, no matter how you try to play it," he said.

I chuckled.

“And I know you still got feelings for me while you over there playing with Cru’s head. Do you really want to be with her Muza? Or is this a get back thing?” I asked because I had to know.

“I don’t know what it is, but I do have feelings for you and always will,” he said. That wasn’t good enough for me. I rolled over and turned my back to him.

“Don’t do that me, Nova. Don’t shut me out like you been doing? We can’t keep doing this,” he said. He was right we couldn’t.

“If you don’t want to be shut out, back out of that shit you got going on with Cru and come back to your family. If you can’t do that, then it really isn’t nothing left to discuss,” I told him, and I meant every word. I felt like I started feeling pressure in my bottom.

“I think it’s time,” I told him. A nurse walked in as soon as I said that,.

“I noticed a spike on your monitor, I’m going to check you,” she said, lifting the covers.

"Whatever you do, I know you may feel some pressure in your bottom, but do not push. I'm paging the doctor," she spoke and ran out of the room. My father stood up.

"I'm gone step outside. I don't want to see all that," he said.

"Oh, Malcolm, you are such a wuss. It's natural," Elizabeth said.

"I'm good. As soon as I hear cries, I will step back in. Good luck baby girl, you got this," he said, kissing my forehead.

Ms. Elizabeth was on one side of the bed, and Muza was on the other. The doctor came in and put his gloves on, and as soon as he lifted the sheet, his eyes widened. The nurse nodded her head.

"I told you," she said. I started to panic not knowing what the hell was going on.

"What's wrong?" I asked. The doctor looked up.

"Ok, I'm going to need you to give me one big push. You guys hold her legs if you want to. Your baby is right here, that's why you feel the urge to push. On the count of three, you're going to push. One, two, three, push!!" he said, and I did just that. I pushed with all my might.

"Give me another one," the doctor said. I pushed down until I damn near passed out, and I heard the cries of my baby.

"It's a girl!" he said.

They handed me my baby, placing her on my chest, and I was in love. Muza leaned over with tears in his eyes.

"Oh my god Nova, she is beautiful. You did a great job. Thank you for her," Muza said. My father entered the room and walked over to stand beside Ms. Elizabeth who was already taking a thousand pictures.

"This princess needs a name," she said excitedly. I looked at Muza, and we looked at our daughter.

"Star Mona Lise Muhammad," I said. It was official. She was my shining star.

Muzaini

Man seeing Nova boss up and give birth to my daughter like a champ made me fall in love with her even more. The conversation we were having before she made her grand entrance was her giving me a chance to make my decision. The way my daughter was trying to come out was a sign. I was going to end things with Cru and get back with Nova. It was only right.

My Uncle Malcolm had given me a cigar with a pink ribbon, and we snapped it up while I held my baby girl.

"I think I made my decision, Unc. I'm gone get back with Nova," I told him.

"I'm proud of you making the right decision. Have you guys had a chance to really talk about everything?" he asked.

"I mean yeah we discussed some stuff. I just got to talk to Cru, and she ain't gone take this too well. I need to run downstairs and get Nova's push gift. I think she ready for it before she passes out," I told him, handing him his granddaughter.

"You gone spoil that girl to death. Leave me some shit to do," he said, laughing.

I walked out of the room and headed towards the elevator. I pulled out my phone and sent Cru a text that we needed to talk. Getting off the elevator, I made my way through the lobby. I was busy responding to Cru. She must have known it was some shit because she texted back instantly going off.

"Darn, watch where you going?" I heard a female voice say. I looked up from my phone.

"My bad," I said, noticing it was Kelly. The sight of this hoe I wanted to strangle her ass then I looked down at her huge belly. She looked like she was about to pop.

"Well, if it isn't Muza. Nova must've had the baby. You guys still going strong?" she asked.

"Don't sit up here asking me questions like I don't know you and your lil boyfriend robbed me. I swear you lucky you pregnant," I told her.

"So, I assume Nova must've put that in your head. I wonder what else has she told you," she said, shifting all her weight to one side.

"What's that supposed to mean?" I asked. I knew I should've walked off instead of entertaining this chick.

"How well do you really know Nova? You guys were getting engaged until that little shit with Delaunn happened, right. Do you know how she and Delaunn met? Your Nova ain't so sweet. She's an escort," she said. I grabbed her by the arm and pulled her over to a couch that was in the lobby and sat down.

"Come again?" I asked.

"Nova dropped out of college to be an escort. She has had quite a few clients, and they were all rich ranging from politicians, business owners, football players you name it. That's why we always butted heads because I would try to get her to stop but she was addicted to the money. You were her next victim. She bragged about you buying them bags in Burberry that day and instantly came home and researched who you were," Kelly said.

I felt the heat radiating off my back and rising up my neck. This shit all made sense. I done had a baby with a hoe.

"Why should I believe you after the bullshit you done?" I asked her.

"You don't have to believe me, but it's the truth, I'm surprised she hadn't told you yet, but why would she? She got you already, and she had your kid." She laughed.

"Was she still doing that shit when I started coming around and when we got together?" I asked I had to know.

"I don't know," she said standing up.

"It was nice talking to you." She smiled and walked away.

I continued to sit there and digest all that I was told. What in the hell did I get myself involved with? I guess it was true that I really didn't know Nova. I placed my head in my hands and said a prayer because I knew I was about to go upstairs and raise hell. I couldn't go in there without knowing if it was the truth or not, but I was going to ask her first. I didn't even bother going to my car and getting the keys to Nova's push gift. I had upgraded her Range and got her a Bentley Bentayga truck. Nah, she can have the truck. I'm not going to deprive my child because she did just give me the most precious gift.

See, this was the shit that irritated me. I loved Nova's ass to death, but at the same time, I was hating her ass if this shit proved to be true. I walked to my car, retrieved the keys, made my way back inside the hospital, and headed to Nova's room.

Entering the room, Nova was breastfeeding Star. She looked up and smiled.

"I was wondering where you went," she said. I gave her a half smile and scratched my head.

"I had gone downstairs to get your push gift," I said, giving her the box. She took the box and opened it with one hand. Lifting the key, her eyes grew big.

"No, you didn't. A Bentley?" she asked. I nodded my head.

"I ran into somebody downstairs in the lobby," I told her, walking closer to the bed.

"You know Nova while you were giving birth to Star I had made the decision to try and work things out with you. You know you sort of gave me an ultimatum beforehand. I was going to go home call it off with Cru and gives us that chance, but you know relationships should always be built on trust and being honest with your partner, right?" I asked. Nova nodded her head and removed a sleeping Star from her breasts, placing her on her shoulder.

"What are you getting at? I feel you fishing around with this big speech. Who did you run into downstairs?" she asked. I knew she wasn't getting aggravated with me. I was the one that had the right to be pissed and aggravated.

"Kelly," I said, crossing my arms. Nova looked at Uncle Malcolm in fear.

"Baby, I think we need to step out and let Nova and Muza talk," he told my aunt.

"No, y'all stay put. Nova, do you have something you need to tell me or should've been told me before I got your ass pregnant," I fumed.

"Nova, just go ahead and tell him," Malcolm said. I turned to him.

"Oh, so you knew she was turning tricks?" I asked.

"Boy, you better watch your mouth before your ass be down the hall in another room," he said.

"Ms. Elizabeth, can you get her please?" she asked, and my aunt walked over to grab Star.

"So, I take it Kelly told you about my past? And that's exactly what it is. Once again Muza, once you entered my life, I left everything alone, including that part of my life," she said.

"Yeah because you seen me as a come up, researching a nigga and shit!" I yelled.

"First of all, ok yeah when I spotted you in the mall I saw you and was like he's fine and looks like he got money. However, I didn't even know who the hell you were at the time. Even after you asked me in the store that day and paid for my shit after I told your ass no, I could buy my own stuff. I did my research after them damn girls in the store was like "*oh my god! You don't know who that is?*" Who was to say that I ever saw you again? I had no clue when I came to see my mother that I was going to see your ass again. Don't get it twisted. When you needed me to pretend to be your girlfriend and offered to pay me, it wasn't a problem because I needed you to keep my secret also. I couldn't help that I started to catch feelings for you. But for you to stand up there and call me a hoe and regret getting me pregnant is fucked up," she cried.

"I don't want to hear none of that crying because you should've told me. I told you about keeping it real with me when I caught your ass lying to me the first time. How I look being with somebody and you done been on different niggas arms and ain't no telling who you done slept with," I told her.

"Just like you have a past with different women I can't judge you for that, so why should I be judged by something that I use to do? I didn't sleep with every client that I had. This isn't fair Muza. That's all you care about is what the next motherfucker gone say. Everybody in the industry got a damn past, hell it's life," she said. I shook my head.

"Nova, this shit ain't cool. You were a damn prostitute, and you expect me to be like oh ok?" I asked.

"First of all, I wasn't no motherfucking prostitute. I was a damn escort! You slick paid me for services, did you not? You needed me on your arm to portray to the media you had moved on from Cru. You took me to events as your eye candy. It's the same damn thing except you did get some pussy out the deal, which I turned down, but you were like *"we need to get in character it will only help us"* Did you not say that shit? Please tell me how the fuck is it different?" she yelled while clapping her hands. She was pissed now, and that ratchet side was coming out.

"She does have a point," my aunt said. I looked at her like she was crazy.

"Man, y'all tripping. Let this had been Cru's ass and y'all wouldn't be so damn lenient," I said.

"This ain't Cru. This is the mother of your child. The shit is in the past Muzaini. You have a beautiful, healthy daughter here, and she needs both of her parents. How can you say you always wanted a family but run every time some shit displeases you? God forbid you ever get married and do that shit. Everyone has a past, even me. You wouldn't think my ass came out of University Court projects. Grow the hell up Muza," Elizabeth said. Everyone was really acting like I ain't have a right to be mad. I was done with this shit.

"So, you don't have anything to say?" Nova asked.

"Nah, I'm good. I'll be back later," I said, turning to walk out of the room.

"In no way will I ever keep you from your child, but if you leave, I take it as you are giving up on us as in me and you," she said.

"How can you not give me a chance to digest this?" I asked.

"What are you digesting? You either want to be a family or not?" she asked.

I let out a huge sigh and placed my hand on the door opening it. I looked back over my shoulder at all of them staring at me and walked out. I had to leave. The man in me couldn't see the woman I love just parading around with different men. I loved her more than I loved myself, but I wouldn't do nothing but hurt her if I stayed simply because every time I look at her that shit would be in the back of my head. I couldn't give myself fully to Nova just yet.

Novanna

I couldn't believe Muza, then again, I could this was the typical shit that he did. He was all for self, and he cared what everyone thought regardless of the way it made others feel. Here we had a whole kid together, and he left me. I couldn't control the crying after he left. My father and Elizabeth tried they best to console me.

"Nova, don't even worry about him. You focus on yourself and your child. He will come around. I know him. He just being a man and he's hurt. Give him some time," she said.

"I mean I understand all that, but I told him if he left I was done. He could've stayed and still had the chance to digest whatever it was that he needed to digest. He can go live his happy life with Cru," I cried.

"Ain't shit gone change, and don't you start acting differently because he around. You're my child and you are welcomed in my home. You don't have to want for anything, so that little past life you lived ain't no going back to that. You have made a nice home for you and Star, and your writing is about to take off. I see it. So, stay focus," Malcolm told me. I heard everything he was saying, but was there a prescription for heartbreak because I needed one.

The first night was long for me. I didn't even want to have the baby in the room with me, so I sent her to the nursery. I thought I was going to be able to get some much-needed rest, but that didn't happen. My mind was in overdrive.

* * *

When I woke up the next day, I had paged for the nurse to bring me Star. The door opened and in walked the nurse without my baby.

"Ms. Collier, you were sleeping, and her father is in another room visiting with her," she said. That shit caught me off guard.

"It's time for her feeding so can you tell him he needs to bring her in here please," I told her.

"I sure will," she said as she walked out of the room. Well, at least he came and seen Star. A few minutes later, the door opened, and Muza came in pushing the cot that had Star inside.

“Heyy, mama’s baby. You ready to eat?” I said in baby talk as if I didn’t see Muza standing there.

I wanted to look at him so bad, but I wasn’t about to do it. I reached in and grabbed Star, placed her on my breast, and watched as she ate. She was so beautiful she looked like a mixture of the both of us. He took a seat in the chair while I fed Star.

“I don’t want things to be uncomfortable between us whenever I come and visit Star,” he said. I didn’t even look up.

“Things wouldn’t be uncomfortable if you hadn’t left how you did. I’m not the one uncomfortable. Like I told you I would never keep you from seeing Star,” I told him.

“Nova, you are making this hard being cold and acting as if I’m not sitting here,” he said. This nigga was seriously delusional.

“How do you expect me to act? I have to digest all of this. I just had my heart ripped out my damn chest, and you seriously want me to welcome you with open arms. You’re crazier and more selfish than I thought," I said. I started to burp Star, and he just continued to sit there looking stupid.

"Things will happen on its own time," I told him.

"I will give you money weekly for her, neither of y'all don't have to worry about anything," he said.

"You are not obligated to take care of me, Star is your responsibility, plus I have more than enough money put up for a rainy day. I'm sure your girlfriend will not like you taking care of the woman you love," I said I hope he caught that because I threw that shit.

"I know I'm not obligated, but what kind of man would I be if I didn't make sure you were straight?" he asked. I was growing tired of this shit.

"Muza, take care of Star, and that's it. Call before you come to my house, and she will not be leaving my presence for the first six months, so if you have any plans where you think she's coming to your house. I suggest you reconsider," I told him, and I was serious.

"Wait why is she not allowed at my house?" he asked.

"You really have to ask? Cru and I do not like each other, ain't no faking the funk at all. You just wait until I get evidence, but I know for a fact that she played a part with Delaunn. I know it, and I feel that shit down in my soul. I do not want that evil wench around my child because one thing you gone find out about me is, I'm not going to play about my child, and I don't mind going to jail," I told him with a serious look on my face.

"I'll respect it for now, but eventually the both of y'all are going to have to get along," he said, which angered me more.

"You say that like you plan on being with her for a long time," I said. Muza shrugged his shoulders.

"I don't know shit to be honest," he said. I didn't even have a comeback. We both sat there in silence. What had we become?

* * *

It had been two weeks since I been home from the hospital. This motherhood thing was whooping my ass. I had started a schedule so that Star and I could get have some teamwork things going on, but she wasn't going, Before the baby, I was a night owl, I did my best work in the wee hours of the morning. But, it seems like Star was taking after me because she would sleep all day and stay up all night. Elizabeth and my father stayed over a few nights so that I could try and get some rest. I couldn't even sleep during the daytime while Star was asleep because I was either taking care of stuff around the house or working on my book.

My child knew exactly what she was doing because she was a damn daddy's girl. One night I was so tired that I couldn't think straight, so I had no choice but to call Muza. I wasn't trying to be disrespectful to his relationship, but a bitch needed help. Nah ok, I really didn't give a damn if I was being disrespectful or not. Fuck Cru. But, don't you know that as soon as her daddy got there, that lil girl went to sleep and slept the whole night. I didn't know what she thought she was doing, but that was not about to become a habit. I ended up hiring a nanny, especially for the daytime, so that I could at least get some rest so that I would be energized for the night in case Star wanted to show out.

Tonight was Ms. Elizabeth birthday dinner, and I asked the nanny to stay over so that I could attend. Star was still too young to be out and about just yet. Looking in the mirror, the baby weight was filling me out just right. My stomach had toned down due to the breastfeeding, and my hips and ass were on fat. If I knew one thing, I knew Muza would be there. Searching through my closet, my eyes hit some new Gucci items that I had purchased while pregnant specifically for the snap back. I chose the Gucci stamp print silk shirt, a pair of Fashion Nova high waist ripped jeans and the matching pair of Gucci stamp print pumps. I wore my dreads down in the back and a high bun at the top. I topped it off with some gold accessories, and some Fenty lip gloss blessed my lips. Grabbing my coat, I headed downstairs to my nanny and Star.

"You look nice," my nanny Maria said.

"Thank you, Maria, I feel nice also. It's been a minute since I have been able to dress up and just get out," I told her.

“Well you have fun, little Star will be perfectly fine,” she said, easing my heart.

“If you need anything, just call. I won’t be late, and it is plenty breast milk in the fridge,” I told Maria.

“Yes ma’am,” she said. I grabbed my keys and hopped in my Bentley truck Muza got me and headed to The Hamsteads.

Muzaini

I stood in the closet tucking my shirt in. I was ready to get the hell out of here. I almost made that shit solo, but Cru's ass wouldn't stop bitching about her going. This was my aunt's birthday, and Cru wanted to feel like part of the family, so she demanded that she come along. Of course, my aunt wasn't having that shit at first, but she gave in and told me to keep her in her place. I walked out of the closet, and Cru was still doing her makeup.

"If you don't want to get left, I suggest you hurry up. I don't know why you are putting on all that shit anyway. You don't need it," I told her. Cru wasn't ugly at all, but she always caked that damn makeup on.

"I'm almost done, goodness!" she yelled from the bathroom.

I grabbed my coat and headed downstairs. A nigga was nervous because I knew that my aunt invited Nova, and I prayed it wouldn't be no shit tonight. This would be Nova and Cru's first time seeing each other since the ball.

"I'm ready!" Cru sang as she made her way down the steps. I shook my head. She was dressed over the top like she was trying to prove a point tonight.

"You like?" she asked doing a twirl.

"Yeah, if we were going dancing or some shit, but we're going to a dinner at my people's house," I said. We didn't have time so fuck it.

"Come on, we already late," I said, opening the door letting her out.

I was silent most of the ride praying to the Lord above let this night be smooth.

"Why are you so quiet?" she asked.

"No reason, just thinking," I said.

"Is your baby mother going to be here?" she asked. I shrugged my shoulders.

"I don't know. Her and my aunt is really cool, so I'm sure she invited her," I said, hoping she would stop there.

“I’m sure she will be there. Who is watching Star though? She should be home with her kid instead of out on the scene,” Cru said smartly. Jesus, see I was trying to avoid shit like this.

“First of all, our child isn’t your concern, but if you must know, she’s taken care of. You are talking about somebody being on the scene girl when we are going to eat and that’s it. You act like somebody hitting the club. Don’t get here and show your ass. Cru, I swear to God I will turn this car around and drop your ass back off so quick. How you gone speak on somebody’s parenting and you ain’t got no kids nor do you want any,” I said. I knew that hit hard. She crossed her arms and looked forward.

“I can’t believe you just literally bit my head off over that bitch!” Cru spat. I slammed on breaks.

“What the hell did I just say? You can get out right here,” I told her ass.

“I’m not getting out of shit. I’m your woman, and you will respect me and treat me as such,” she said.

"Oh, so now I'm not treating you as such because I spoke up on something that you know nothing about," I said. I started back driving and turned the corner into the subdivision. Pulling into the yard, I got out the car leaving Cru ass sitting there.

Walking into the house, I walked straight in and went straight to the bar. I needed something stiff to drink.

"Well hello to you to, son. Is everything alright?" Malcolm asked. Shaking my head, I let out a huge sigh.

"Man, Cru is gone make me choke the shit out of her. She is always worried about the wrong shit," I said. Unc chuckled.

"You better tell her get her shit together before Elizabeth lets her have it. She already doesn't want her here," Malcolm said. As soon as he said that Cru came waltzing in like ain't shit happen.

"Hey baby," she cooed.

"Where's everybody at?" I asked.

"Sitting in the den waiting on all guests before dinner is served," he said. We all left and headed towards the den.

"Muza, sweetie, it's a pleasure for you to finally join us," my aunt said as we walked in the den. I leaned down and placed a peck on her cheek.

"Hey, Ms. E!" Cru spoke. My aunt gave her a dry look.

"That's Mrs. Hamstead, darling," she said as she took a sip out of her wine glass.

Cru was shocked but laughed it off. I chuckled, took a seat on the other couch, and engaged in conversation with others. Cru took her seat beside me and sat quietly. I knew she had to be uncomfortable, and this was why I told her to stay at home.

"Hey everyone!" I heard Nova's voice. I looked up and my dick started to swell. Nova was looking good and healthy, rocking the fuck out of the Gucci fit she had on, down to the shoes.

"Nova, my baby, you have to show my girls pictures of Star. I've been bragging about her all night," my aunt said. Nova smiled, pulled out her phone, and started showing them photos.

"Chile, if she ain't looking like Muzaini right here. Look Muza," my aunt said. I got up, walked over, and looked.

"I am a fine ass man, so it's only right she took after me," I said cockily.

"Boy, if you don't hush, my child looks like her sexy ass mama," Nova said, pushing me. I laughed.

"Aheem!" I heard Cru clearing her throat. We all turned to look at her like she was crazy.

"Can I see?" she asked. I started to show her the picture and Nova grabbed the phone out of my hand.

"She doesn't need to see nothing pertaining to my child. She will probably try to steal it and sell it to the tabloids or some shit," Nova said.

“Nova,” I said, giving her a look like *please don’t.*

“Nova, grow up. I have a right to see her. I’m involved with her father and will be around for a long time, and I might even be her stepmother. You can’t be childish all your life,” Cru said. I felt like shit standing in the middle.

“Childish is my middle name. You don’t have any rights pertaining to the child that I pushed out of my pussy. You showed me you can’t be trusted, and I can’t wait for the day that Muza see your duck ass for who you really are. I’m sure Muza hasn’t told you this yet, but I’m going to say this and then I’m going to finish enjoying my night with my family, the one you want so desperately to like you. My child is off limits. If you disrespect my child in any way, I will go to jail proudly and serve my time,” Nova said, and she turned to my aunt. “Ms. Elizabeth, I’m sorry I had to go there on your special night. We may continue,” she said.

Everyone exited the room, and I stayed behind so that I could have a talk with Cru.

"You just let her talk to me any kind of way, and it's clear that you love her and need to be with her. You won't even ride for me," she cried.

"Are you serious, Cru? Did you not hear the shit that came out of your mouth? Ain't nobody finna let you sit up and talk crazy to them, especially if it concerns their child. Nova had to go through a lot with that shit Delaunn did, and she swears you had something to do with it, so I can't control how she feel about you. You are going to make it hard for a nigga when it comes time for me to keep my child if you keep on with this bullshit. I will drop you before I let that happen. I'm wanting to keep everyone happy. You because you are my woman, and Nova because I have to co-parent with her. I don't need any extra stress," I told Cru. She wiped her eyes.

"But, do you still love her?" she asked. Damn, why did she have to ask me that shit?

"Not like you think I do. I love her for her giving me the greatest gift and that's my daughter," I told the semi-truth. Now if you thought I was about to tell her that I loved Nova more than anything in this world you tripping. I still had to keep my home happy. Cru leaned in and kissed me.

"I'm going to go to the bathroom and freshen up. I'll be back," she said. I nodded my head and watched her walk away.

Why was I playing these games with Cru and myself? No matter how many times I said out loud that I was with Cru, that didn't change the fact that my heart was with Nova. This girl had stolen my heart and was holding it for ransom. I fucked up big time but how was I supposed to see past the betrayal. What she did wasn't minor. She held a whole escort service from me. I'm a jealous ass nigga so to know that Nova had been with many different men in whatever way she was with them, and that bothered the fuck out of me. I kept Cru around because she was something to do and at first, I was doing it to make Nova mad. I wanted nothing more than to be with my family, but I done got myself in some shit.

Cru

Looking in the mirror, I patted dry the tears that were ruining my makeup, fixed my braids, and gave myself the once over. Muza thought I was stupid, but I knew he loved Nova more than the way he portrayed. I don't know why he thought I was born yesterday. No matter how hard I tried, his ass couldn't resist his precious Nova. Then that bitch kept bringing up the Delaunn situation. I wish she let that little shit go. She had to do more than what she was doing to get me to come out of character. I had to remain the innocent look. I had Muza wrapped around my finger.

I exited the bathroom and went and met back up with Muza. Hand in hand, we both, entered the dining room and took our seats. I played my fake ass role and apologized to Ms. Elizabeth, even though I gave zero fucks about her ass.

"Mrs. Hamstead, I'm sorry for any disrespect I may have caused," I told her. She gave me a half smile.

"It's fine, Cru," she said and took a bite of her food.

I was enjoying Nova squirming in her seat as Muza and I got comfortable as if we weren't just arguing earlier. Nova phone buzzed, and she grabbed it. I noticed her cheesing, and I also notice Muza wouldn't take his eyes off her.

"Who got you cheesing all hard?" he said. I turned my head so fast towards him, pinching his leg.

"Really, why is it any of your concern what's going on with her phone?" I asked him.

"Girl, stop tripping. I figured it was something with the baby," he answered. I dropped my fork on the plate, making a loud clink and pushed my seat back from the table.

"I'm ready to go. You have disrespected me enough tonight," I said. Nova busted out laughing, and I wanted to jump across the table and beat her ass.

"Muza, take this up out of here. My whole damn dinner has been nothing but drama," his aunt said, pointing at me when she said this.

Rolling my eyes, I stormed out of the room. This whole damn family had me all the way fucked up.

I stood outside waiting on Muza who was taking his precious time coming out. All he cares about is Nova and that damn baby. I needed to get into his head and quick. Muza came strolling pass me and hit the lock on the car. I walked to the car and got in not saying shit and I wasn't going to. We drove the whole ride home in silence. Muza hopped out the car all fast and was gone in the house. I slowly walked up the steps and turned the knob to find out the door was locked.

"What the fuck?" I said. I pressed the doorbell and beat on the door.

"Muza, open this fucking door before I cause a scene. You got me fucked up!" I yelled.

He wanted to play these games. I turned around and looked in the yard for a big ass rock. I removed the heels that I had on and walked off the porch, picking up a brick out of the grass. The door opened and Muza stood there filming me.

“I wish the fuck you would with your crazy ass. Take your ass to your house!” he yelled.

“Stop playing, Muza. You can’t keep doing me like this,” I said, walking up to him.

“Cru, ain’t nobody doing shit to you. Your ass is just insecure and making shit out of nothing. You showed you whole ass tonight,” Muza fumed.

“I’m sorry. Let me make it up to you,” I teased. Muza went back in the house.

“I ain’t in the mood, but you can bring your ass in,” he said. I followed behind him and walked into the house.

Walking upstairs to the bedroom, I removed my clothes and headed to take me a shower. I laid my phone on the counter and turned on me some music. It just so happen that my girl Cardi B was paused from earlier. I stay in my damn feelings about Muza. I pressed play, got in the shower, and rapped the lyrics to “Be Careful” as if my life depended on it.

The only man, baby, I adore
I gave you everything, what's mine is yours
I want you to live your life of course
But I hope you get what you dying' for
Be careful with me
Do you know what you doing'?
Whose feelings that you're hurting' and bruising'?
You gon' gain the whole world
But is it worth the girl that you're losing'?
Be careful with me
Yeah, it's not a threat, it's a warning'
Be careful with me
Yeah, my heart is like a package with a fragile label on it
Be careful with me

I felt every ounce of that shit.

"Here you go with the subliminal, indirect, in your feelings shit," Muza said, startling me stepping into the shower.

"Hush, I can't help she is just speaking facts," I said.

"Fuck all that shit you talking and bend over," Muza demanded.

I bit my bottom lip and did as I was told. I felt Muza rub the tip of his dick up and down my slit, and he eased inside of me. I grinded into him while I had one hand on the wall and the other on my leg. If I didn't know any better, I think Muza was trying to punish me because he was beating the fuck out of my pussy.

"Slow down, Muza," I moaned in pleasure and pain.

"Fuck!" he said and pulled out of me. He was irritated and stepped out the shower. Fuck that I wasn't done, nor did I get mine.

"How you go limp like that on me, Muza. That has never happened?" I asked.

"Cru, just forget about it," he said and laid in the bed. I climbed in beside him. I rubbed his back, and he tensed at my touch.

"Baby, what's wrong?" I asked.

"Nothing, I just miss Star," he said, but I knew he was lying. That's when it hit me.

"Baby, why don't you get custody of Star?" I suggested. Muza turned towards me.

"Why the hell would I do that?" he asked.

“I just saying she won’t even let you keep her overnight until she’s six months. If you had custody, you don’t have to deal with that, and you can keep all the money you are dishing out in your pocket,” I told him.

“Cru, it ain’t like she keeps my child from me period. I can see Star whenever I want to. Why would I bring her here overnight and you don’t even like kids, but now all sudden you want to play stepmother of the year? In case you forgot, I’m rich and not hurting for money, so again why would I try and take Star from Nova?” he asked.

“You should just consider it. You’re much more capable of taking care of your daughter. Considering Nova’s past she shouldn’t be raising a daughter,” I let slip out.

“How the hell you know about Nova’s past because I sure as hell ain’t tell you?” Muza asked.

“Huh?” I asked, trying to avoid the question.

“If you can huh you can hear, Cru. How the hell you know about Nova past?” he asked again. I knew I should’ve shut the hell up.

Malcolm

Everyone had left, and I was sitting here enjoying a nice conversation with my daughter.

“I’m shocked you didn’t knock that girl head off tonight. You showed a lot of restraint,” I told Nova as she sat across beside me with her feet in my lap.

“Man, daddy, she kept on trying me. He should’ve kept her ass at home knowing good and well nobody here like her ass. I’m so glad I didn’t bring Star because I probably would’ve had to fight her. He was doing her wrong though,” Nova said.

As a man, I knew all too well the feeling of juggling two women and having feelings for them both. It was the prime example of Mona Lise and Elizabeth.

“Nova, he’s confused as hell and conflicted. He wants to be with you, but he can’t put his pride to the side. I told you that this would happen though. But if you ask me, the both of you are going to get back together. It might not be right now, but when the timing is right, it will happen," I said, hopefully easing her mind a little bit.

"Daddy, I admit I went about things wrong with Muza, but I never thought this would become of us or my life. I was playing with niggas just for the money. My goal was securing the bag by any means. I can't help the feelings, and I can't help I got pregnant, I can't even help that I love him. To me, he gave up to easy. I'm sure it's some things in Muza's past that I wouldn't be fond of, but I wouldn't abandon him nor his heart. He was the first guy that I ever loved. I loved him before I loved you. I just hope he realizes it before it's too late," Nova said. I wish I could take her pain away.

"Well, I need to get home to my baby. I missed my little girl," Nova said, placing her feet on the floor and putting on her shoes.

"Give my grandbaby a kiss for me," I told her as I walked her to the door.

"Be careful, and call me when you make it in!" I yelled as Nova walked to the car.

"I will love you!" she said.

"Love you too!" I said as I watched her pull out of the driveway.

Closing the door, I walked back in the house. First thing tomorrow, I was going to talk to Muza and see what the hell was going on.

Muzaini

I laid awake staring at the ceiling. Sleep was like Nova at the moment, something that I wanted but just couldn't get. When I got in the shower with Cru, I was gone bust this nut quickly and go to sleep. But it's like as soon as she opened her mouth a nigga went limp instantly. I had never had that shit happen to me. I knew exactly what it was. I went in the shower with Nova deep on the brain and so hell the whole time I was hitting Cru, I imagined that it was Nova. Cru just had to open her big ass mouth. But, what was really bothering me was the fact that she brought up something that I know I didn't tell her. Her mentioning Nova's past and how I should take Star away because she shouldn't be raising a daughter made me think about Nova saying Cru was in on that shit with Delaunn. Delaunn knew of Nova past, so how else would she know about that.

I looked over at Cru who just looked like she ain't have a care in the world sleeping peacefully after the night of drama she caused.

Jon Jon

"Her funky ass still ain't answering the damn phone," I said, throwing the phone on the table.

I placed my hands behind my head and closed my eyes growing irritated by the second. The fucking baby was crying and shit. I hopped up and stormed to the bedroom.

"Dammit, Kelly, don't you hear his ass crying?" I yelled.

"Yes Jon Jon, I was getting up," she mumbled.

"Well, you not getting up quick enough. A nigga can't even think with all this hollering," I said, walking over to my son and picking him up. He instantly stopped crying. That little shit touched my heart.

“I know your mama is tripping not doing what she supposed to do. What are we keeping her around for?” I said to my son while Kelly was giving me an evil eye.

It was obvious she ain’t like my ass, and the feeling was mutual. I ain’t never cared for nobody except my sister and now my son. Kelly came back in the room with a bottle, and I handed him to her so that she could feed him.

“I bet not hear him hollering no more,” I told her.

“What did I ever do to you to make you treat me the way you do? I’ve always done everything you asked of me, yet you treat me like I’m nothing,” Kelly asked me.

I thought about if I wanted to tell her the issues that I dealt with, it wasn’t like she was going anywhere. I leaned against the dresser.

“I was only taught to love one woman and one woman only, and that’s my sister. She made me who I am today. We met in the foster system, and she was staying with this family that took me in. She protected me from a lot of shit, and we managed to run away from a fucked up situation," I admitted.

"I never even knew you had a sister," Kelly said.

"We barely see each other. She is doing her own thing, and all I know is what she taught me— robbing niggas and whoever for money. We used to set up so many people together. We have been all over in different states and shit. She's got clout like that so finding a mark is nothing," I told Kelly.

I couldn't believe I had told her all that. The only thing I didn't tell her was why I loved my sister. We weren't blood-related, so this girl took my virginity and did things to me a woman should. I loved her differently, and she always told me I bet not ever love another woman. The only thing was she went off and fell in love with another man.

"Well, I'm sorry I'm not your sister, but when I met you, I thought you were something special. I never knew that I was walking into abuse and other things," Kelly mumbled.

I couldn't break now I couldn't let her see me weak. I turned and walked out the room, closing the door. I stood on the outside of the door and closed my eyes.

"I'm sorry," I whispered.

Muzaini

The next morning, I was out the house and making my rounds. I had a few meetings set up and an interview with 101.1 The Beat radio station. A nigga was drained since I didn't get much sleep, but my job was never done. Walking into my office, I was greeted by my Uncle Malcolm.

"What you doing in here?" I asked, placing my stuff on my desk.

"I went and worked out this morning and decided I needed to come and talk to you about some stuff," he said. I sighed because whenever he needed to talk, it wasn't good.

"I'm sorry about Cru last night," I said, figuring that was what this was about.

"Ain't nobody stutting Cru. I came to talk to you about Nova," he said.

"She ok?" I asked.

"Nova is fine, but we had a talk last night, and this situation between y'all is getting old. I saw a side of Nova last night that I rarely see.

That girl loves you with every breath in her body. Now I know it's hard to overlook the escorting thing, but Muzaini, it was a part of her past. Everybody's got one. Stop letting this cruel world dictate your heart because you are really playing with Cru by using her, and God knows if you ever leave her and go back to Nova, she's not gone make it easy for y'all. That girl is evil, and I'm not saying this because Nova is my daughter, but I know she was working with Delaunn," he said. I snapped my fingers, remembering last night.

"You know something last night she was talking mad crazy when we got home and had the nerve to say I should get custody of Star because of Nova's past, and she shouldn't be raising a daughter. I was like how the hell you know about Nova's past, and I ain't never told you. She never answered the damn question," I told my uncle.

"You know you were the first man Nova loved. She flat out told me she loved you before she loved me," he said.

"Damn, Unc I knocked you out your spot?' I joked.

“Shut the hell up. I’m serious. Your family is over there and not over there. Think about that shit and make shit right,” he said. He stood up from his chair.

“Let me get my ass home and take a shower. Elizabeth will be blowing my ass in a few,” he said, walking out of my office.

“Aite, talk you later, Unc,” I said. He threw me a peace sign and walked out the door.

I leaned back in the chair and looked at the picture of Star on my desk. I needed to stop playing and get my family back.

Nova

I had been writing like crazy since I got up this morning. Star was asleep in her bassinet, so I was getting this word count up. I couldn’t wait to release to this book. This was my life story in a way. That’s why it was taking me so long to write because I was literally writing as shit happened in my life. After finishing up this chapter that I was working on, I was going to get dressed and head to the mall and grab me some things and pamper myself today. Closing my laptop, I paged Maria, asking her to come up.

"Yes, Ms. Nova?" she asked, entering the room.

"I'm going to hop in the shower and run to the mall. Star is in the bassinet sleeping," I told her.

"I got her," she said, walking over to the bassinet.

I stepped into the bathroom and took care of my hygiene. About forty-five minutes later, I was leaving the house and hopping in my truck. I drove to Green Hills and instantly had a flashback of when I met Muza's fine ass. I smiled at the thought of how far we come. Well, I guess it wasn't nothing to smile about since now we weren't on the best terms. I got out my truck and walked towards the entrance of the mall, and my phone rang. I reached into my bag and grabbed it. Looking at the screen, it was my father.

"Wassup, daddy?" I asked, placing the phone on speaker.

"What you got going on, girl? Where you at?" he asked.

“I just got to Green Hills about to run up a check.” I laughed.

“I had a talk with Muza today. I think I might have talked some sense into him,” he said.

I rolled my eyes.

“Daddy, you might as well leave that alone. You know he ain’t leaving Cruella Deville.” I busted out laughing.

I turned the corner and walked into the Louis Vuitton store. I was wrapped up looking at the bags and daddy was going on and on about his convo he had with Muza.

“Hmp, I thought that was you,” I heard from behind.

It was a female voice, and I knew exactly who it was. I looked over my shoulder and gave Cru an up and down look. I turned right back around and continued to listen to my father.

“You know I’m still trying to see what it is that Muza saw in you. I thought for sure that when I called Delaunn and told him that we needed to come up with a way to get rid of you, the video would’ve been enough to send Muza running, but your ass was already pregnant," Cru said.

"You know what you ain't telling me shit I didn't already know. I knew you were in on it all this time. The only thing was getting Muza to see you for the trifling bitch that you are," I told her.

"Don't worry baby girl, I heard the whole thing!" my father yelled. I still had him on speaker phone.

"Well, your little past is going to help Muza get custody of Star. We both feel an escorting whore shouldn't be raising a little girl." She laughed. My mouth dropped.

"Close your mouth, sweetie. I don't have anything for you to put in it," she had the nerve to say. My breathing picked up, and I slowly turned back towards the bags I was looking at.

"It's ok. You should be getting papers soon, bye bye sweetie enjoy your shopping," she said.

I turned around and grabbed her by them long ass braids wrapping them around my hands and flinging her ass on the floor. Once she was down, I climbed on top of her and repeatedly punched Cru in the face. Her bitch ass couldn't fight, but she was scratching the shit out of my face.

"Nova, Nova!" I could hear my father voice yelling through the phone, but I dropped that shit somewhere.

Two employees had run over and tried to pull me off Cru, but my strength was unbearable. Nothing could stop me from continuing to beat this hoe ass. Still holding her hair, I lifted my foot and came down across Cru's face with my Timberland boots. The sight of blood leaking from Cru had turned me the fuck on. I had been waiting for this moment. This bitch had ruined my life.

"Ok, that's enough," I heard the police say, grabbing me and placing my ass in cuffs.

Tears rolled down my face not because I was scared to go to jail, but I started to think of Star. That hoe deserved every damn bit of that ass whooping. I watched as everyone crowded around Cru and they hauled my ass out of the store and into the back of the police car.

Malcolm

I couldn't believe the shit I was listening to on the phone with Nova. Cru was talking all that shit and Nova done laid into her quick. I placed a call to my friend who worked downtown to see what was going on with Nova. Cru was pressing charges, and Nova was being processed and book. Elizabeth was heading to Nova's to pick up Star, and my ass was trying to get in touch with Muza. The word was that Nova did some hellafied damage to Cru, and Cru was in the hospital. The blows to the face were horrible due to the boots Nova had on. When I got to the precinct and checked on everything Nova was being charged with aggravated assault and other pending charges. Nova's ass didn't have a bond, and this shit was pissing me off. Muza walked in.

"Unc, what the fuck happened?" Muza asked. I shook my head and sighed.

"I've been calling your ass. Cru and Nova got into a fight. The shit was wild. I was on the phone with Nova she was in the mall. She had me on speaker phone, so I heard when Cru approached her, she was saying some crazy shit and taunting Nova about you getting custody of Star. She also admitted that she had planned that shit with Delaunn with that video. I heard that shit crystal clear. I guess Nova snapped and started beating her ass. I'm thinking Nova blacked out and started stomping Cru's head in with her Timberland boots. She is looking at aggravated assault with a deadly weapon. She ain't got no bond, so maybe you can use your clout to see what you can do," I told Muza. Muza placed his hands on top of his head like he was defeated.

"Where is Star?" he asked.

"Elizabeth went and picked her up from Maria," I told him. His phone buzzed, and he looked down and showed me his phone.

"This shit done made *TheShadeRoom*," he said as we watched the attack that someone had recorded.

"Go see what you can do, and I'm going to call up Darius and see if he can take Nova's case and possibly get a bond or some shit," I told him. Muza walked off, and I started calling my lawyer friend.

Muzaini

These bastards in the mall wanted to press charges against Nova's ass due to the blood that was left in the store that needed to be cleaned. This shit was sticking, and I needed to get Cru to drop these charges against Nova. My lawyer was going to get the video footage from the store, and I was going to see if I could pay these motherfuckers to drop this shit also. From what Malcolm told me, Cru came in there and started that shit, so maybe I can get them to look at it as self-defense. I was on my way to the hospital now to check on Cru since I was waiting for my lawyer to get back with me.

Walking into the room, a nigga was in shock. Damn Nova. You would've thought that she used a brick instead of a pair of Timberlands and her fist on Cru. Cru turned her head and looked at me. Well, I don't know if she could make out it was me because her eyes were swollen so badly. Cru was looking like Martin when he stepped in the ring with Tommy Hearns.

"It took you long enough," she said.

"In the condition that you're in, you still find time to talk shit. Ain't that what got you into this predicament in the first place?" I asked.

"Correction, your bitch can't take the truth," Cru said.

"And what exactly is the truth? That you walked up to her antagonizing her talking shit. That you admitted to that shit you pulled with Delaunn, or that you lied to her about me getting custody of Star. Ain't nobody finna play with your ass about they kid. You lucky this all you got was an ass whooping. So, what you gone do is drop these charges," I told her, walking up to the bed.

"I ain't dropping shit," she said.

I knew this wasn't gone be easy. My phone started ringing, and I looked down at the unfamiliar number. I stepped out of the room and answered.

"Hello!" I answered.

"You have a collect call from NOVA," the recording stated. I finished listening to the recording and accepted the call.

“Hello!” I said.

“Nigga, you got your motherfucking nerve if you think you about to take my child from me!” Nova yelled into the phone. I looked at the phone.

“Nova, calm down, that shit wasn’t true. You’re so hotheaded when it comes to Cru. You fell for the shit she was telling you. Now your ass getting charged with aggravated assault with a deadly weapon, Louis Vuitton wants to press charges, so I got to find a way to get this shit to disappear because Cru is adamant about not dropping charges,” I told her.

“Deadly weapon? I ain’t use no weapon on her lying ass,” Nova said.

“Nova, that Timberland that you used to stomp the shit out of her was considered a weapon. You could’ve caused some damage if you hadn’t stopped,” I told her.

“Where is my child?” she asked.

“Elizabeth went and got her from Maria, I’ll get her once I leave the hospital,” I told her.

“It figures you up there with that bitch. You bet not have her around my child. Did my daddy tell you she admitted to that shit with Delaunn? I’m gone press charges against her ass next,” Nova said.

“Nova, chill the fuck out. A nigga is tryna get her to drop these charges. I’m trying to get you out and you up here bitching at me. Bye dude,” I said, ending the call. Her ass wasn’t about to stress me out. I placed my phone back in my pocket and walked back in the room.

“Have you thought about what I said? You owe her Cru because she is talking about pressing charges on you for that video,” I told her, hoping she would consider.

“I’m not dropping charges, Muza. Do you love me Muzaini, like for real? Did we ever have any hope of getting to that happy part in our life?” she asked. I thought about my answer.

“Cru, I have feelings for you, but now that the truth has come out about some things that you have done and just over the past couple days you have shown a vindictive side it makes me question your loyalty. You lied to me just like Nova did. I'm not with Nova, so why should I be with you?" I asked her.

"It just feels like that's where you rather be," she whispered.

"Cru, listen and don't take this the wrong way. I was going to marry Nova. Nova gave me something that I always wanted, which was a child and a family. You remember when I use to bring up having a kid with you how you would act like it was the plague or something. You absolutely refused to have a kid no matter how bad I wanted that. At that point, I knew I didn't see a future with you. I was angry when we got back together." I stopped because I needed to be very careful about my next selection of words.

"Things eventually would've got great if you would've stayed in your place, but instead you felt you had to compete with Nova," I said.

"Because I did. I can see the love you have for her. I worked hard within your company and alongside you to deserve the honor of being your wife, not someone that you've only known for a few weeks. How bad do you want me to drop those charges?" she asked.

My ears perked up. Maybe I had gotten through to her.

"What do you want, Cru? I need Nova home so that she can take care of our daughter. She is breastfeeding and shit. Name your price?" I said. I was gone write her ass a check and send her on her way. Cru had an evil grin on her face; at least I think it was a grin. Her face was so fucked up that I couldn't tell.

"I will drop the charges and say that I hit her first whatever you want me to say, only if you be with me," she said.

"Be with you how Cru, ain't we together now?" I asked.

"Don't toy with me, Muza. If you want this to disappear, I will make it happen if you marry me," she said. I started choking and tugging on my ears making sure I heard her right.

"Marry you, Cru, are you for real? This shit ain't no game and marriage isn't something you play with," I said. This hoe was delusional. I was convinced Nova knocked whatever sense she had left out.

"Take it or leave it," she said, crossing her arms.

I needed to think about this shit, and I meant really think about this. I left the room and stood outside of the door. A nigga had to make a few phone calls, especially to my lawyer and look at Nova's options to see if any progress had come along. This shit was starting to get on my damn nerves.

Novanna

When they called my name and told me I could go, I flew the hell up out that hellhole. That little short period of time let me know that I wouldn't be back. More than anything, I just wanted to see my daughter. I missed her so much. I walked out the gates, and there stood my father and Ms. Elizabeth. I ran over to them and hugged them.

"Girl, you were only locked up for three days," my father said.

"It felt like an eternity. What the hell took y'all so long?" I asked looking into the back seat for my baby.

"Maria has her, and they are waiting for you at home," Ms. Elizabeth said. We got in the car and headed to my house.

"Is all this shit over or is Cru still going through with the charges?" I asked because I know I was looking at a good ass charge.

"It's over. Muza was able to get the tape from the store, and after heavy conversation and some funds exchanged, they backed out because, from the video, you were in there minding your business and

Cru came in behind you. As far as Cru, I don't know what Muza did or said, but she backed out also. Luckily Muza's lawyer pulled some strings with the state because even though Cru had dropped the charges, they were going to pick it up and still go through with it," he said.

"He probably had to sell his soul to the devil for her to drop them charges that easy. I'm just glad to be out," I admitted.

"Just stay out of trouble because a lot of money was dished out to make this go away. If you see Cru, don't let her get under your skin," Malcolm told me. I rolled my eyes and looked out the window.

"Did y'all get my truck from the mall?" I asked.

"Yeah, everything is all good. Just go in here and love on your baby because she missed your ass," Malcolm said.

I smiled as we pulled up in my driveway. I exited the car and ran up the steps to my house. Maria met me at the door. I stopped her from handing me Star.

"Oh no, let me shower and get all these jail germs off me, and I'll be ready for her," I told Maria.

"Si," Maria said, and I ran upstairs and removed my clothes hopping in the shower.

While in the shower, I made a mental note to call Muza and thank him for getting me out. I prayed he ain't do nothing stupid for Cru to drop the charges. Stepping out the shower, I threw on some leggings and a t-shirt. I pulled my locs up in a ponytail and headed back downstairs.

"Senorita, I'm making you some steak and shrimp chimichangas, your favorite. Star is in the playpen," Maria said.

"Thank you, Maria," I told her.

I walked over to the playpen, reached down, and picked up Star. I sat down getting comfortable on the couch, and I turned the TV on caught up on my shows I missed while I was gone. Star stirred in my arms. I grabbed my phone and decided to call Muza.

"What's up, Nova? I see your home," he answered.

"Yes, I am. What you up to?" I asked.

"Leaving the hospital with Cru about to head to the crib," he said, I rolled my eyes and sucked my teeth.

"Can you tell her thanks for dropping the charges," I forced out.

"You're welcome, Nova!" I heard her loud and clear.

"Am I on speaker phone?" I asked.

"Yeah!" he said. Muza sounded different like the life that once was in him had been drained.

"Oh well, that's all I wanted," I said.

I really didn't have shit else to say since I was on speaker even though I did want to ask him how he managed to make this happen. But from the happiness in Cru's voice, I could tell it had something to do with the both of them.

"Aite, give Star a kiss for me, I'll try to stop by, and her see her before I leave town," he said.

"Ok, bye," I said, hanging up the phone.

Something wasn't right. I was getting some bad juju from that whole conversation. Maria handed my plate of Chimichangas, I laid Star down and went to work on my plate. I loved Maria cooking. Even though she was the nanny, she went above and beyond when it came to me.

"You ok?" she asked, taking a seat beside me.

"I really don't know. I feel like Muza is keeping something from me. I just got a bad vibe from our conversation," I told her.

"Do you ever think when you finally get the man will everything be worth it?" she asked. I thought about what she said.

"Maria, that is a good question, but now I don't know if I will ever get the man," I admitted.

"Always remember that God don't like ugly, and what's meant to be will be," she said, getting up from the couch.

Cru

"Why didn't you tell her we were getting married?" I asked Muza.

“Because she will find out in due time, and I ain’t want to put all that on her today,” he said. This nigga thought I was stupid.

“Don’t try and play me, Muza. You think because she home that you can renege on this proposal, but I’m ten steps ahead of you. I will have her ass back locked up so fast if you think you are going to get out of this. Invitations have already been sent out, and we are getting married next Saturday,” I told him.

I had been planning this wedding for years, so it was nothing to have everything put in place. I was going to get the last laugh.

“Wait how you just gone set a date for a wedding without discussing it with me?” he asked.

“Oh, you thought we were going to be engaged for a few years.” I laughed.

“Nah, it’s all good, baby. I’ll be there waiting on my beautiful bride to walk down the aisle,” he said leaning in to kiss me on the cheek.

That's what I thought I had him by the balls. If he wasn't going to tell Cru about the wedding, she would find out as soon as she got her invite in the mail. A small grin eased across my face.

"I can't wait to be Mrs. Muhammad," I said excitedly.

"Hopefully your face healed by then," Muza said I cut my eyes at him because he tried it.

"Don't worry about my face it will be perfect for our wedding day," I said. You just worry about Nova's face when she sees this shit.

Jon Jon

I was sitting at the table counting some money from another lick that I had hit. Kelly was in the kitchen fixing a bottle for the baby, and there was a knock at the door. She looked at me, and I looked at her.

"What you looking at? Answer it," I told her.

"I was just making sure because you had all that money sitting out," she said. She walked over to the door and answered.

"Is Jonathan here?" I heard a female voice.

"Who the fuck is it?" I yelled, looking towards the door. Kelly moved out of the way, and my sister was standing there. I stood up

"What you doing here?" I asked. She looked at Kelly up and down, and Kelly did the same.

"Kelly, this is my sister Cru," I told her.

"Oh, nice to meet you. I'll go tend to the baby," she said walking off.

I turned to look at Cru and pushed her back out the door.

"What the fuck you doing popping up over here unannounced?" I asked.

"So that's the little chick you got pregnant. You better not love her. What did I tell you Jonathan?" she asked.

See this is the shit that I was talking about. I was so in love with this woman, and she ain't want me being involved with nobody. To everyone else Cru was my sister, that's how I introduced her, but to me, she was my bitch, and I was her nigga. Been that way since we were teenagers.

"Look, don't be coming over here messing up what I got going on. You out doing you, so I needed help and company. Life gets boring when your gal leaves you for a nigga we were only supposed to hit a lick on," I told her.

"I only came over here to deliver you the news face to face," she said.

"What?" I asked.

"I'm getting married and very soon," she said.

"You marrying that nigga, Cru? Man, you bogus as hell for that," I told her, I felt like my heart was ripped out my chest.

"I'm doing this for us. If I marry him, we won't have to do this shit anymore. What's his is mine, and what's mine is yours. Can't you see that?" she said. I shook my head.

"Nall, what I see is Cru looking out for Cru like she always has. You want to control my life but run yours. I tell you what, you go ahead and marry that nigga, but leave me the fuck alone. You sheisty bitch," I said, turning around to walk back in the house. I slammed the door so hard in her face that my son started crying.

"Everything ok?" Kelly asked. I sat quietly for a minute, and I started to smile because I was gone make Cru pay for this shit. Bitch, you break my heart, and I'm gone break yours.

"I need to tell you the truth about my sister," I told Kelly. She made her way to the couch and sat down beside me. I started to tell her everything, pushing forth with my plans.

Muzaini

A Week Later

So yeah be mad at a nigga for marrying Cru, but I did what I had to do to get Nova out of jail. I was for real deal dodging her right now. I had been in and out a town, so besides the pictures of Star, I haven't seen her physically. I don't think I could look Nova in her face and tell her that I was marrying Cru. This Saturday was the day, and it is what it is. I walked into my aunt and uncle's house calling out to them.

"Auntie, Unc!" I yelled. I walked into the kitchen, and they both were standing there with somber looks on their face.

"What's wrong with y'all looking like somebody died?" I asked placing my keys on the island.

"That's because somebody is about to die, what the hell is this?" Auntie asked, shoving a card in my face. I grabbed the card and read it, and my jaw started to twitch.

“What you think it is, it’s a wedding invitation,” I said nonchalantly.

“Oh, no shit we can see that. Why is it a wedding invitation to you and Cru’s wedding?” Malcolm asked.

“Because we are getting married Saturday, and I need my family there to support me on this journey,” I said.

“You sholl are about to go on a journey to hell, and I will not be there to watch you ride off into the sunset with Lucifer,” Auntie said.

“It’s funny how Nova said when we picked her up from jail that you probably had to sell your soul to the devil and boom there it is,” Malcolm said. Auntie gasped.

“Oh Lord, have you told Nova?” she asked me. I shook my head no.

“Nall, I haven’t got around to it yet,” I said,

“I wouldn’t put it pass, Cru. I bet she mailed Nova an invitation. You better pray she doesn’t get an invitation before you have a chance to tell her. When she knock your ass out, don’t come back here asking us to fix shit because we are out of it," Auntie said. I knew my auntie was pissed, and a nigga felt bad enough as is.

"So y'all gone be there?" I asked.

"Wearing all black!" she said as she walked out of the kitchen.

"I can't believe you, Muza. What the hell is going on inside that head of yours? This is why I didn't want Nova getting involved with you. I didn't want you hurting my daughter, I didn't think you would, but you have proved me wrong," Unc said, and he left the kitchen also.

I hit the counter in anger and grabbed my keys to leave. I needed to go ahead and tell Nova the news before she found out from someone else.

Novanna

“Ms. Nova, don’t cry maybe it’s a cruel joke or something. I don’t think he would do something like this,” Maria said, consoling me. After checking the mail, I end up receiving a motherfucking wedding invitation to Muza and Cru’s wedding.

“No, Maria this isn’t a joke. That’s why his ass ain’t been around. He’s scared to show his damn face. I knew it was something when I talked to him the day I got out. It was all in his voice that he was hiding something, and it was all in her voice the joy that a woman feels when she happy about something,” I cried.

I wonder if my father and Ms. Elizabeth know about this shit and were they keeping it from me. How could he marry her after all the things she has done? I swear something wasn’t right about this. The doorbell rang, but I didn’t bother moving,

“I’ll get the door,” Maria said as she left out of my room and headed downstairs. I picked my laptop back up and started to type. Maria came back in

"Who was it?" I asked. She wore an uneasy look.

"It may not be a good idea to have a visitor right now," she said.

"Maria, who is it?" I asked.

Muza popped his head in, and my mood changed instantly. I sat my laptop and got out of the bed.

"What you want?" I asked. I placed my hand on my hips.

"We need to talk," he spoke calmly. I shook my head no.

"I promise you there is nothing to talk about. I just got your little invitation in the mail. I can't believe this shit, Muza!" I yelled, punching him in his chest.

"I'm sorry you had to find out that way, I should've told you sooner," he said.

"You should've told me sooner? Why the hell are you even marrying her? I know you are not feeling her like that. I know you are lying about something, Muza," I told him.

“I’m not lying about anything. I came here to apologize for keeping this from you, but I knew you weren’t going to take it well. This will not change our co-parent situation. I will continue to respect your wishes about Star being around her,” he said.

“Do you hear yourself? You will respect my wishes about Star being around her. Why in the hell would you even marry someone that your kid can’t be around? This shit is backwards as hell. You have no idea how this has hurt me. You are a hypocrite. You called off my engagement because you thought I cheated on you with Delaunn, but here you go and marry the girl who plotted with him. Am I missing something?” I asked I was confused as hell.

“Nova, Cru and I have history,” he said. I waved him off because I wasn’t trying to hear no more of his whack ass excuses.

“If this has anything to do with her dropping those charges, I will fight my case on my own. I’d rather deal with my own issues than watch you sell your soul to the devil in the white dress,” I told him.

“This hasn’t nothing to do with that, and that case is closed,” he said.

“How come when I pulled it up it said pending investigation?” I asked. Yeah, I had to make sure my name was clear, so something told me to look up case information.

“It shouldn’t even be able to pull up. I need to look into that. But please Nova, I will always care about you. I’m here for you and Star,” he said.

“No, remember I told you I don’t need you for anything. Take care of your child and leave me alone,” I told him.

“You're serious right now?” he asked.

“As a heart attack. You can see your way out or go visit with your daughter I have work to do,” I said, pointing at my bedroom door.

Muza slowly turned to walk away, and I hated to see him leave because I felt like he was walking out of my life. I wanted to run behind him. I wanted him for myself. I still loved this man, and I couldn’t deny that shit if I wanted to.

Muzaini

When Nova said her case was pending, that shit caused my antennas to go up. What the hell was up with that shit. I stayed at Nova's and played with Star for about thirty minutes before I left. I couldn't wait to get in the car and call Cru and my lawyer. As soon as I got in the car, I called her ass.

"Hello, my future husband," she cooed in the phone.

"What's up bae, what you doing?" I asked. I didn't want to jump directly into the question just yet. Her crazy ass would've started thinking something.

"Nothing, I just finished up with the caterer," she said.

"Oh, that's what's up. Aye, Darius called me today and said something about Nova's case was pending investigation. What happened, didn't you drop the charges?" I asked.

"Muza, the charges will officially be dropped after we are married. I told you I had my own connections. If this wedding doesn't happen then Nova's ass will be right back in jail picking up where she left off," Cru said.

"Ain't no need for all that. You gone get your wedding, I was just trying to see what he was talking about. A deal is a deal," I said.

"I love you," Cru said.

"I love you too. I'll see you later," I told her and hung up the phone. I dialed Darius' ass next because this nigga had some explaining to do after he done took my money.

"Wassup, Muzaini?" he answered the phone.

"I thought I paid you money to make this situation with Nova disappear for good, especially with them state motherfuckers," I said.

"I did, and then Cru went above the D.A. to whomever she knew up there and told them to hold it for a while. I didn't even know she had clout like that," Darius said.

“What the hell, aye check this out, I need you to draw me up some paperwork, I’m getting married Saturday,” I told him.

“Damn nigga, you getting married and this is how I got to find out? What you need some prenup papers?” he asked.

“Nall, I’m going to email you all the details and make sure you send them to Pastor Antonio. I will like to request his services to be our officiant,” I told him. There was a slight pause.

“Ok, I gotcha. Send that on through,” Darius said.

“I appreciate that,” I told him and ended the call.

Cru

Wedding Day

I couldn't believe today was my day. The day I was going to marry the man of my dreams. Everyone was giving me such a hard time, but I invested years with this man, so I deserved to be happy. Everything had come together perfectly. We weren't having a huge publicized wedding. We were going to announce to the world on our own time that we had gotten married. That was the thing now in the celebrity world, keeping secrets then boom a baby born or someone got married. Only our family and close friends would be in attendance. Jon Jon was so pissed at me that he hasn't been returning my texts or any of my calls.

Looking in the mirror, I twirled around admiring my Julie Vino dress from the 2018 Venice collection. The sheer and decorative lace that covered the top part of my gown was to die for.

"I can't believe that you are actually about to marry Muza. Is Jon Jon really letting you go through with this?" my ghetto ass cousin Kesha asked. I rolled my eyes. I only invited her ass because her hating didn't work.

"Well believe it. See, you doubted me, but now look at me," I said,

"Yeah, I did doubt you because he had made it clear he didn't want your ass, and I still think you drugged him or something because I can't see to save my soul how you made it happen. Jon Jon ain't came in here shooting up the place either. Yeah, sister, you got the power," Kesha said.

"Jon Jon won't be doing anything. He knows I'm getting married and I told him already," I told her.

"And he ain't trip out on you, Cru? You know how he is about you," she said.

"He hasn't even returned my calls or texts, so I know he is mad, but like I told him, I was looking out for us because he knows whatever I got is his. This marriage will set us for life. Yeah, I know coming into this when I first met Muza was a money scam, but eventually, I grew to love him, and I'm not going to pass up on this opportunity," I told her.

"Well I hope everything works out for you and you don't get a dose of bad Karma," she told me.

"Girl, go take your seat. It's almost time for me to walk out," I told her.

Malcolm

"I don't know why we came to this shit. I feel like I'm betraying my daughter by being here," I looked over and told Elizabeth as we sat out front of the church.

"I don't know why we here either, but we're here, so we are going inside, and as soon as the wedding is over we are heading home. I don't have time to be fake with no damn body," Elizabeth said. I laughed because Elizabeth literally had on all black like she was about to walk up into somebody funeral.

"What's so damn funny?" she asked.

"You dressed in all that damn black," I told her.

"This is just describing my mood. Come on so that we can get this shit over with," Elizabeth said.

For her to be so uppity at times, I loved when the real South Nashville came out of her. I got out the car and walked around to the passenger side and opened the door for Elizabeth. She grabbed my hand, and we walked in the church.

"Do we have to sit in the front?" I asked.

"We are considered his parents since we raised him so yes," she said.

"I thought we walked out with the bridal party?" I asked.

"I don't know, and I'm not walking out with shit. We're about to sit our black asses down right here," Elizabeth said as we took our seats in the front row.

Muzaini

I ran my hand over my fresh fade and slid my shades on my face. Running my hands down my suit jacket, a nigga was looking spiffy.

"I know you're not about to wear them shades down the aisle, my nigga?" Darius came busting through the door.

"Hell yeah, this is a part of my outfit. What you think I shouldn't wear them?" I asked Darius.

"I mean will your wife think it's acceptable? You know how women are about their wedding day. I could see if we were having an outside wedding, but we are in a church," he said.

"Cru's ass won't give two shits about no damn shades as long as I'm standing there so that she can marry my ass," I told him.

"Have you talked to your baby moms anymore? You sure you are going through with this?" he asked me.

"Nah, not since that day I left her house. I don't want to dwell on that. This is supposed to be my big day, right?" I laughed it off. We shook hands.

"Aite, then let's get this show on the road then," he said as we left the room and headed to the altar.

Nova

I was parked in the cut watching everyone walk into the church. I even saw when my father and Ms. Elizabeth walked in. Ms. Elizabeth had me cracking up wearing all black, but hell, I guess great mind think alike because my ass was wearing the same thing. I started not to come, and Maria begged me not to, but what I look like turning down the invite. Cru made it her point to rub it in my face that she was marrying Muza by sending me an invitation, so I was gone give sis what she wanted— my motherfucking presence.

I looked at the time, and the wedding should be starting shortly. I opened the door getting out of my truck and made my way across the street and up the stairs of the church. I walked in and took my seat in the very back. I didn't want to be seen.

The music cued, and the wedding started. I could see that Cru planned this shit to the tee. Everything looked nice. I ain't gone hate. Both parties marched in and took their places at the front of the church. I watched Muza as he stood there behind his shades. I chuckled because this nigga knew he was wrong. He did that shit so he that couldn't be read. I could tell he ain't want to do this. It was supposed to be me walking down that aisle heading towards him. The doors reopened, and the music started playing. Everyone stood up as Cru stood there alone. One of Muza's groomsmen came down and escorted her down the aisle, so I'm assuming she ain't have no daddy. Cru's dress was bad as fuck. I must give it to her ass; she had taste.

Finally, we all took our seats. I noticed my father had seen me because his eyes were glued on me and then Elizabeth turned around also. I smiled and turned my attention back to the wedding. I sat there watching my man, my baby father, the man I loved, standing hand in hand with the devil. My nerves were so torn up that my leg was shaking like a stripper. All I saw were mouths moving. I had tuned out everything so I couldn't hear any words. I had my ears trained to hear what I wanted and needed to hear.

"The bonds this couple has made today are sacred and holy and should not be broken. However, nearly every relationship is tested at one point or another, by conflict, temptation, strife, and change. Will you, their loved ones, family, and friends, agree to help them keep those bonds holy, reminding them of their love for one another, and helping them cross through those stressful periods?" the pastor asked.

"We will!" Everyone in the church answered. I stood up.

"I will not!" I shouted. Everyone turned around in their seats looking at me and whispering. Muza and Cru looked my way.

"Are you really going to do this, Muza?' I asked. My father and Ms. Elizabeth had gotten up and was making their way towards me.

"I don't know what you're doing or why, but this is a huge mistake you're making. You don't love her, and you know it. Your heart is with me and your daughter, and you're willing to walk away from that.

Muza, you wearing shades mean you are hiding something. You can't look your bride in the eyes because it ain't me!" I yelled.

"Nova, come on. You're making a fool out of yourself. You don't need no nigga to be with you. I don't care who the hell it is," my father whispered in my ear.

'No, I'm not making a fool of myself. He is being a hypocrite. Come on y'all know that he doesn't need to be marrying her ass, and y'all up there sitting front and center like some happy ass parents.

"You need to leave," Cru said.

"Now you want me to leave, but that didn't stop your messy ass for mailing me an invite. The preacher asked a question, and since we're in church, I told the truth," I responded. Muza removed his shades and looked at me.

"Nova, I have made my decision, and I know you are hurting, but I'm marrying, Cru. Now can you please leave so that we can continue with the wedding?" he asked.

I didn't want it to, but the tears started pouring. I couldn't believe the words that he let pass out of his lips.

"Really Muza?" I cried. My father and Elizabeth were literally dragging my ass out the church. I gave one last look at Muza as he shook his head and turned to finish marrying Cru.

Elizabeth

Ooh, child the pain that I knew this girl was going through, I could feel her pain. When Malcolm told me that Nova was sitting in the back of the church, I didn't think she was gone cause a scene like she did. Malcolm and I hopped up so quick so that we could get her out of there. I was in shock. We stood outside the church trying to get her to get herself together.

"Nova, what were you thinking?" I laughed.

"Don't be laughing at that shit. That shit wasn't cute at all. Doing all that damn crying and begging over a nigga," Malcolm huffed.

"Hush, Malcolm! You can't control how she feels about him. I probably would've done the same thing had it been me," I told him.

"That's not how you go about it. Leave that nigga alone, and he will come back," Malcolm said.

"I just wanted to get that off my chest and at least try and give him a chance to make it right. He looked so uncomfortable in there. He doesn't want to marry that girl," I said.

"Well, newsflash he is still in there marrying her ass. Go home to your child and focus on you and her," Malcolm said. I don't know why Malcolm was being such an ass about the situation. I hugged Nova and looked at her.

"You did good. Don't worry about what your father says. We all knew that he was making a mistake, and you're the only one that had the balls to call him out on it," Ms. Elizabeth told me.

I looked back at the church and knew I needed to leave before the ceremony was over because I didn't want to see him. I hugged my father and Ms. Elizabeth again before getting in my truck and pulling off.

Muzaini

The rest of the ceremony was a blur. My mind wasn't on what was taking place. All I could think about was the hurt on Nova's face and the pain in her voice. I hated to hurt her like that. Cru was looking like a kid on Christmas morning. She fed off Nova's pain.

After the wedding, we had a small reception, and I was drunk off my ass. A nigga got so drunk that I had to leave I was throwing up everywhere.

"Why in the world would you get this drunk and on my wedding day?" Cru asked as she removed my shoes as I laid across the bed. She had been nagging the whole damn time.

"Well, you better sleep this shit off because I will not miss my honeymoon," Cru huffed.

"Wait, how you gone plan a honeymoon without checking my schedules first. I got shit booked for the next two weeks." I sat up, removing my shirt.

"Really Muza, it's our honeymoon?" Cru looked at me in shock.

"I understand that, but you also have to understand we basically had a shotgun wedding. You demanded to be married asap, but you're going to have to wait for the honeymoon because my money comes first. I don't like missing important things. Once this is all over, we can go anywhere you want to go," I told her.

"Anywhere?" she asked. I knew then she was going to plan something outrageous.

"Anywhere," I told her.

Cru jumped up and down and climbed on the bed, and I shook my head telling her to calm down cause a nigga head was spinning. She leaned over and placed a kiss on my lips.

"It feels so good to be Mrs. Muzaini Muhammad," she said. I closed my eyes and smiled but quickly dozed off.

Two weeks later

Things were started to get back on track and spring was approaching, so I was about to debut my Cognac Spring Collection. Over the past two weeks, after the wedding, I had buried myself in my work, and that was really to keep my mind busy and keep me busy and away from Cru. Call me wrong, but it was the truth. I knew that soon Cru's ass would be asking about the honeymoon, so I had to move quickly in what I was trying to do.

I haven't had the chance to see Nova. She was keeping her distance far away from me. When it came to me seeing Star, she had me deal with Maria all the time, or she would try and leave out whenever I came around. I couldn't blame her, but I wish she would at least talk to me. We couldn't go through life like this period. I was going to give her time to calm down, but soon, and I mean real soon, she will sit down and listen to what I have to say.

I pulled up to my lawyer office. He had some news for me that he said he wanted to deliver in person. I was all for it, so I headed there immediately. Walking in to see Darius, I bypassed his secretary and headed straight to his office.

"Wassup man, what you got for me that's so important?" I asked, taking a seat at his desk. Darius turned around and placed some papers on his desk. I picked them up and glanced over them.

"So, this is legit and for real. This shit can't pop back up?" I asked. Darius nodded his head.

"Yep, my brother. It's gone never to be pulled up again, closed all that," he said.

The biggest smile crossed my face, the feeling I was feeling man I couldn't even explain, I jumped up out of the chair.

"What about them other papers I asked you about? You know once I bring it up, I'm gone need proof," I asked him. Darius reached into the drawer and pulled out a set of other papers and handed them to me. Reading over the other papers, I was satisfied.

"Thanks, bro, you really came through," I told him.

"It was nothing. Hit me up though," he said. I placed the papers in my jacket pocket and walked out the office.

Novanna

I buttoned up my blouse, grabbed Star, and carried her downstairs. I was running late for an interview. Yes, your girl was applying for a damn job. Don't get me wrong I wasn't hurting for any money, but I wanted to do something that I loved alongside writing books. My book was almost finished, and I was looking to release soon, so in the meantime, I was applying for a writing position for a black newspaper. The paper spotlighted many black businesses such as eateries, hair salons, and anything that was black-owned. My father had put in a good word for me and told me about the place, so I was giving it a shot.

When I got downstairs, I placed Star in her swing and grabbed my laptop and a few mock articles that I had done on some businesses that I had already visited.

"Ok Maria, wish me luck," I told her.

Maria had become a close friend to me, besides Elizabeth. She gave me that motherly instinct that I craved and missed so much from my own mother. I think about my mother all the time, especially when I have my spells of missing Muza. Speaking of him, I have reduced all contact with him. I can't see him because he will see a weak form of me. I know just the sight of him will make me weak. I had unanswered questions, but I wasn't ready to face him to get them answered. He did all his visits through Maria, and I made sure to keep busy so that I wouldn't have to deal with him. From the looks of his social media, yeah, I be creeping, he has down nothing but work and work. He had yet to make a post about him and Cru being married. Cru, on the other hand, hasn't made a marriage post, but she be posting his ass all the time acting like she just the happiest.

"Good luck, Senorita. You will do just fine. Stop and have you a drink to celebrate the good news that you will be getting. I know you will get this position," Maria said. I smiled.

"Thanks, Maria," I said.

I walked over to the swing and kissed Star before heading out. Once in the car, I put the address in my GPS and headed to my destination.

About twenty minutes later, I arrived at my destination. When I looked up at the building, I shook my head. I wanted to cuss my father out. I dialed his number and waited until he answered.

"You get the job, baby girl?" he asked not even saying hello.

"I'm about to pull the hell off. Why you ain't tell me this was Muza's company?" I asked.

"Nova, it's a branch of Muza's company. He doesn't even have anything to do with that side. It's what you wanted. Just go inside please," he stated. I rolled my eyes

"If I see him, I am turning the hell around," I said, hanging up the phone before he could contest.

Opening the car door, I grabbed my things and walked into the building. I looked around, and the place was nice. I couldn't believe this was all Muzaini's. I walked up to the security desk

"Yes, I have an interview on the fourth floor," I told the security.

"Name?" he asked.

"Novanna Collier," I answered. He handed me an electronic key card.

"Take this and go to the fourth floor. Once you get off, this will get you in the door," he said.

"Thank you," I replied headed towards the elevator.

I stepped on the elevator and pressed the button for the fourth floor. I was nervous as hell and praying to the Lord above that I didn't run into Muza. The elevator stopped, and the doors opened. The hallway was empty, so I walked towards the double doors and used the card the security gave me to unlock it. When I stepped through the double doors, my mouth hit the floor. The neon sign that read *Star Editorials* like to take me out. I looked around because this shit had to be a joke. I walked further into the office space and spotted many cubicles that had laptops and all the works. I continued down the hall until I came to a door with a gold plate on it, it read Novanna Muhammad. I opened the door, and Muza was standing against the desk, looking like a slab of ribs.

"Muza, what the hell is all of this?" I asked.

“Is that how you come in an interview?” he asked.

“Muza, I am in no mood for no damn games. What is all this?” I asked again, pointing to everything including the nameplate.

“This is your job. The paper exists, but you got to make that happen. We gone have our own *Flava* magazine going on, but for the black culture. I feel you can do this, take your writing to another level, and put out your dope ass books,” he said. I placed my hands on my head and took in everything.

“Wait a minute. What is your wife going to say about all this and why the hell does this plate says Nova Muhammad?” I asked. Muza sat down and pulled me between his legs. I was hesitant, but the cologne he wore was raping my nostrils, and I was falling weak.

“You know and should’ve known this whole time that I have never stopped loving you. This was all fake. I did what I had to do for her to drop your charges. She was the one that had your case pending to see that I went through with the wedding. She finally had that shit closed, and Darius pulled some strings with the state also to make this shit disappear for good," he said. I hauled off and punched him in the arm.

"Dude, I was at the wedding. You had a whole service, preacher, and everything, so what you mean this shit was fake?" I asked.

"That shit was fake. Well, I knew it was fake. Cru thinks that shit was real. My homie Antonio pretended to be a pastor. He did a good ass job for somebody who only attends church for funerals. Everything was fake down to the marriage certificate," he said. I couldn't believe he did some shit like this.

"Cru is going to kick your ass. Does she know yet?" I asked him.

"Nope, I'm going to tell her. She is waiting on a nigga to go on a honeymoon and shit, but that's why I been prolonging it so that I can get my ducks in a row. I know I'm gone have to get a restraining order against her, and you may have to do the same. But look, I don't care about none of that. This whole time that we've been apart from each other has been nothing but pain for me. A nigga was tired of faking, but I had to do it. I hope that you can see I would do anything for you,

I couldn't even have sex with her because a nigga stayed on limp and that shit was getting hella embarrassing. I've wanted nothing more to make you my wife and for us to raise our daughter together. So, Nova will you give me another chance and let's take this new company by storm?" he asked. This was all I wanted, and this shit was finally happening.

"The only way I will accept any of this is when you get all that mess you created with her fixed. I know this shit is going to bring a lot of drama, and I don't want Star around it. So, do what you need to do by getting that shit in order, and then I will marry your fine, black ass," I told him.

Muza smiled and bit that bottom lip. He reached into his pocket and pulled out the same ring that he used to propose the first time, which last time I checked he threw in the trash.

"Umm, I thought you threw that away?" I asked.

"You remember my stylist, Tammara, right. Well, she held on to it. I never knew that when she told me that I would be using it again for you that she was telling the truth. I feel bad for ever doubting us," he said.

"It's ok. Once we get back on track, nobody will ever be able to break us," I told him.

"Let's go have a drink!" he said.

"I guess we can go somewhere and have one drink," I said. Muza lifted me up off the ground and spun me around. I had my man back.

We decided to stop at Bar Louie since it was in the area. I prayed that nobody paid attention to us. We took our seats at a table.

"You want to grab something to eat while we here, or just do the drink?" he asked.

"A drink would be nice. I got to get back to Star," I told him.

"Thank you for doing an amazing job with our daughter. I know you're all headstrong and stayed telling a nigga that you didn't want shit from me, but I was gone take care of your ass regardless," he said.

"Just hardheaded, but I appreciate how even with your hectic schedule that you still make time to be a father," I told him.

"Welcome to Bar Louie. I'll be your server," the waitress said. I looked up and wanted to smack fire from Kelly.

"Hmp, the tables have turned. You back to bussing tables, huh?" I asked. I felt Muza kick me under the table.

Kelly

I had just started my shift at Bar Louie and had picked the section I was going to work tonight. Things for me was slowly, and I mean slowly, getting back to the Kelly I used to be. After Jon Jon confided in me about the truth behind him and his sister, I felt bad for him. He had been practically used, and now he was out for payback. Jon Jon still had issues with being controlling towards me, but at least the hitting has ceased for a moment. He loved our son, and I think that the love he had for Cru was no longer there. Call me stupid for staying, but this was the father of my child. He even paid for me to get back in school so that I could finish out my last year.

I grabbed the menus and walked over to the table.

"Welcome to Bar Louie, I'll be your server tonight," I said. When the couple looked up, I was looking at Nova and Muza. I could've sworn he was married to Cru.

"Hmm, looks like you back to bussing tables," Nova said.

I knew her ass was gone say something slick out the mouth. That's just how she was built, and I knew I deserved all the backlash. I could tell Muza kicked her under the table because she looked at him right crazy.

"I can get you guys another server if you would like," I said. Muza spoke up

"No, it's fine. We're just getting drinks anyway," he said. I leaned down and pretended to show them the menu because I knew my boss was looking at me, so I had to look busy.

"I really need to talk to you guys, but my boss is a bitch, it's something that I know you would want to know about your wife," I told Muza. He looked at me with a side eye.

"I know the owner. Tell him you're taking a ten-minute break and that I requested it," he told me. I stood up from the table and walked off to find my boss.

Mr. Perkins, Mr. Muhammad is in my section, and he has requested that I take a ten-minute break so that we can discuss some business," I told my boss, pointing to the section. He looked over my shoulder to makes sure I was telling the truth.

"Go ahead," he said.

I turned around and walked back to the table where Nova and Muza were sitting. I stood there, and Muza cleared his throat looking at Nova. She sucked her teeth and scooted over so that I could sit down beside her.

"So, what do you need to tell me about my wife?" Muza asked.

"Sometime before the wedding, Jon Jon had told me he had a foster sister. He left it at that because I had never known he had a sister. So, one day his sister decided to visit, and when I opened the door, it was none other than Cru. She was rude as shit, so they stepped outside. When Jon Jon came back in he was pissed about her getting married, and I found that weird. That's when he said he needed to tell me the whole truth about Cru. Jon Jon would tell everyone that he and Cru were brother and sister because they were foster wise, but it got to a point where they ran away and started messing around with each other on a romantic level. He was in love with Cru, and she was in love with him.

They started hitting licks on folks, and that was their way of making money. Jon Jon said they hit many different states. When she first met you, that's what you were. She told Jon Jon that by marrying you, he was going to benefit also. Jon Jon wasn't trying to hear that though. I don't know what type of hold she had on him, but that nigga ain't been right since," I told Muza. Muza's whole demeanor changed, and he looked like he was ready to kill somebody.

"Why the hell should he believe you after all the bullshit you did? This is right up your alley being messy as hell," Nova said.

"I understand what you're saying, but I don't know what made me do the things I did, but I'm starting to get my life back on track, and when I told you guys that Jon Jon was hurt about this, I meant that shit. He wanted me to tell somebody. This nigga wants Cru to hurt like she hurt him," I told Nova.

"Thanks for telling me this, but this doesn't make up for the shit that you and your lil boyfriend have done. Y'all some fucked up individuals, and he's really fucked up. But, you guys should remember that Karma lays ahead somewhere, so I don't even have to lift a finger," Muza said.

He stood up from the table and looked at Nova. Nova looked at me, and I slid out of the seat and let her get up. They started to walk off, and I called out to Nova.

"Nova, I hope you finally get the happiness you deserve and congrats on your baby," I told her.

I felt like that was going to be my last time seeing her and I genuinely was sorry for everything I did. I hated that I messed up our friendship for Jon Jon.

"Take care Kelly," she said then her and Muza left.

Muzaini

I really wasn't expecting Kelly to tell me that shit she told me. I wanted to roll up on Cru and have Nova whoop her ass again, but I wasn't tripping at all because I was gone have the last laugh anyway. I walked Nova to her car, and we stood there in silence.

"So much for our drink," I said. Shaking her head, she looked at me.

"It wasn't meant to be. I mean in a way it was because we wouldn't have come here if it wasn't, but good thing we did. I can't believe this shit though. Like this whole time, they've been playing. What you gone do?" Nova asked.

"I'm gone go home like ain't shit happened, then just tell her ass about Jon Jon first, then I'll spring the shit on her about the wedding last," I told her.

"Well, be careful, and I'm a phone call away, so if you need me to come through, you better hit me." She laughed.

"Oh, Mayweather, I know your ass gone come off the wam," I said, causing us both to bust out laughing. I leaned in and kissed Nova.

"I love you, girl," I told her.

"I've always loved you," she said. I opened the truck door for her and helped her inside. I watched as she pulled off.

Walking to my car, I ran down what I was going to say so that I hit everything on the head when I confronted her about this shit. This bitch has been a shyster all her life. That explains the no parents or the past she barely talked about. Cru put on this front like she came from money, but it was really another nigga's money. This bitch wasn't gone see a red cent from me ever again. I started up my car and drove home.

During the drive to my crib, all I could think about was finally be able to start my life with Nova and my beautiful daughter. See, Cru outsmarted me once, but what I was about to tell her I know for sure will be the get back that she deserved. I didn't find no wrong in what I did. Look at all the shit she did to me. She's been playing me the entire time. I hit the steering wheel because the more I thought about it, the more I found myself seething.

I pulled into the driveway, making sure not to block Cru car in because she was leaving tonight. Getting out, I stormed into the house. When I entered the house, the lights were dim, and there were candles lit everywhere. I rolled my eyes at the slow music playing in the background. When I walked into the kitchen, I ain't gone front. Cru was standing there in a nice little lingerie piece.

"Hey, my love," she said in her sexy little voice. I flicked on the lights and started blowing the candles out.

"What you doing trying to set the place on fire then collect some insurance money off of me?" I asked.

"No, I was trying to set the mood and be romantic with my husband. Why you come in here messing up shit?" she asked.

I sat down and pulled out my phone and the paperwork I had gotten earlier from Darius.

"I need to plan this honeymoon," I said. Cru pulled up a chair.

"About time, where we going?" she asked. I laughed and looked at her.

“We are not going anywhere. This is for Nova and me,” I said nonchalantly. Cru stood up

“Excuse me, what the fuck is going on?” she asked with her neck rolling and in her pure ratchet form.

“That’s the Cru I was waiting to talk to. That’s that foster child, set niggas up Cru, ain’t it?” I asked. Cru started fidgeting.

“What are you talking about, Muza?” she asked still playing dumb.

‘You know exactly what I’m talking about. Your brother /lover Jon Jon ratted you out. So, this whole time you really been playing a nigga,” I said.

“No, I don’t know what you are talking about. I love you Muza,” she said, walking towards me.

“Don’t come over here. Why the fuck you keep on lying, Cru? Your time is up, and I know everything. I even know about your most recent visit to him and the conversation y’all had. You told him you were gone be set once you married me and for him not to be mad. I was a lick to you at first, and I guess that's why he robbed me awhile back. You sent that nigga here along with Kelly," I said.

"Who the fuck is Kelly?" she asked.

"Don't worry about all that. Your time is up," I told her.

"My time is up? You can't get rid of me that easy. Did you forget we are married? I will take you for everything," she really had the nerve to say. I couldn't contain my laughter.

"Did you ever think about why I didn't get you to sign a prenup? Did you really think I loved you that much to just up and marry you without securing my money?" I asked. The look of fear on Cru face was priceless.

"What the hell are you trying to say?" she asked.

"We are not married, my girl. You really thought I would marry you after all that shit happen. Girl, that didn't make no type of sense. My homie Antonio, I paid that nigga to be the preacher. He wasn't no real pastor. The wedding certificate we signed wasn't real, I had my homie scan and make up some shit. Girl, you thought you played me, but you were getting hella played," I told her. Cru came towards me swinging

"You petty son of a bitch!" she yelled. I grabbed her by her hands.

"As much as I want to beat your ass right now, I am not a woman beater, but your ass is getting dragged out of here today," I told her, pulling her ass towards the door. She was kicking and screaming, and I kept on pulling until I got her on the porch.

"Muza, you can't do this!" she yelled. I looked down at her and turned to walk back in.

I grabbed her keys and her bag off the door side table and walked back outside where she was standing and trying to make her way back in the house.

"Cru, don't make me call the police on you. Take your shit and get the fuck off my property. I bet not see you back on my property or better yet around me period!" I yelled. Slamming the door, I locked it and walked into the kitchen to fix me a drink.

Cru

I stood there on the porch still trying to process what had happened. How the hell did this happen? I wasn't really married to this man? All these questions started to torment me. I slowly picked up my keys and purse and walked to my car still dressed in the lingerie that I had put on. I couldn't believe he threw me out like that. My mind instantly went to Jon Jon, and I got livid. I couldn't believe that he would do this to me. I reached in my purse, got my keys out, and hopped into my car. Starting the car, I looked at Muza's house one last time before pulling off.

It wasn't like I didn't have nothing because I had made a pretty good living off licks and saving money, but I didn't want to go back to that life. That wasn't who I was anymore, and I had to go see why in the hell Jon Jon did what he did.

Pulling up to his place, I parked my car and got out walking up to the door, I didn't care what the hell I looked like and his bitch better not say shit to me. With my hand formed in a fist, I beat on the door like I was the damn police.

"Jon Jon, open this damn door!" I yelled. I heard the door unlock.

"Bitch, what the fuck are you doing here?" Jon Jon asked with a mug on his face.

"Why did you tell Muza all that bullshit?" I asked.

"You walk around here like a nigga ain't got no feelings all the shit I did for you. Bitch, you're just as scandalous as any other bitch out here. Now that you done got found out, you want to come back here questioning me. Hurt people hurt people, right?" he had the audacity to say. I launched towards him trying to fight.

"Man, get your ass off me, and I ain't the one that told your little dude anyways," he said.

"Well, if you didn't tell him, how the hell does he know everything?" I asked.

"Oh, I told my girl. I guess she ran into them. You know she used to be cool with Nova," he said, crossing his arms.

"So, you let that little bitch come and just mess up what we had?" I asked. Jon Jon started laughing.

"Mess up what we had? Cru, you messed up what we had when you fell in love with a lick then tried to push me away like I wasn't shit. I got a kid now, so I don't need your type of negativity around me," he said. To know that he no longer cared bothered me.

"I hate you, Jon Jon!" I yelled, and I smacked his ass with all my might. Jon Jon grabbed me around my neck, and I didn't see that shit coming.

"You of all people should know to keep your hands to your damn self," he said through gritted teeth as his grip got tighter.

"Jon Jon, let her go!" I heard the girl that was holding a baby come in behind him.

"Nah, fuck that. She wants to come in here and put her hands on a motherfucker. I done hurt people for way less," he told the girl.

I had scratched up his arms trying to get his hand from around my neck, but his strength was unbearable. I felt myself getting weak, and I could no longer put up the fight.

"Jon Jon, she is turning blue. Oh my god, let her go!" she screamed.

Kelly

I was in the room trying to put my son to sleep. I was tired as hell. I had literally just got off work. It hadn't even been ten minutes, and I was still in my work clothes. The loud beating at the door startled me at first, but when I heard a female yelling Jon Jon's name, I knew then that it was Cru. Word must've gotten back to her about what had happened.

I smirked a little. All I heard was her and Jon Jon going back and forth in the living room. I wasn't going to step out, but when I heard her hitting him, I decided to look. Jon Jon was choking the shit out the girl, and I can't say I was surprised. That nigga was crazy and didn't give a shit. I know, my ass has been beaten plenty of times by the hands of that nigga. It was started to look ugly, so I had called out to him to stop, but he was in a trance, and he wasn't trying to hear nothing I had to say. I could tell Cru was getting weak because she had stopped fighting. Her strength was becoming weak. I had to do something and something fast because Jon Jon was on the verge of killing this girl. I walked out of the room and placed my son in the car seat.

"Mommy will be right back," I told him even though I knew he didn't understand shit I was saying.

Walking back into the room, Jon Jon was still choking Cru, and she looked to be lifeless. I looked around, grabbed the statue off the shelf, and hit Jon Jon over the back of the head, causing him to drop Cru and fall beside her.

"Shit!" I whispered and ran to Cru's side and checked her pulse. There was nothing, and she laid there lifeless. I looked over at Jon Jon, and he was out cold. He was still breathing. I was not about to go down for any of this. I grabbed my cell phone and called the police.

"Yes, there has been an incident at my home, and I need the police here right away. I think one person is dead," I told the operator.

"Ma'am, can you tell us what happened?" the operator asked.

"I came home from work, and my boyfriend was arguing with his ex-girlfriend. Things got heated, and he started choking her and never stopped. I hit him over the head to break them a loose. He's still breathing, but she has no pulse," I told the operator.

"Ok, ma'am stay put. Someone should be pulling up shortly," the operator said.

Hanging up the phone, I just prayed that Jon Jon didn't wake up. I took that chance to go in the bedroom and clean out every red cent he had in the damn safe. He was always so damn mean that I made sure to watch everything he did and paid plenty attention when he didn't think I was. I placed all the money in a few duffle bags and a baby bag. Once the police came to get his ass, I was going to make a run for it.

After packing the bags, I walked back into the living room and made my way to the door that was still slightly ajar from when they came in the house. I heard the sirens outside, so I opened the door wide and waited for the cops to enter.

The cops came in and started processing the shit, and sure enough, Cru was dead. This man had really killed her. About time the officers got to Jon Jon, he was stirring and coming to after being knocked the hell out. When he noticed Cru laid out, this nigga started going crazy and crying.

"Oh my god, what did I do?" he cried. He looked at me, and I shook my head.

"I'm sorry Kelly, please do right by my son," he said.

This nigga was ugly crying, and I ain't ever seen no supposed to be hard ass nigga break down like this. I knew he had blacked out when it came to him choking Cru, and that's why I did what I did. He loved Cru, but he was just a man scorn.

When they placed him in the back of the police car, he looked so pitiful, especially when they brought Cru out in the body bag. The police remained at the scene for what felt like forever. No soon as they left, I grabbed my bags and all the money and placed my son in the car and we were getting the fuck out of Nashville for a while. I would just have to finish school somewhere else. My time here was done.

Novanna

My ass was happy and in a good place since Muza left here earlier, and I was writing my ass off. I was literally about to finish up this book and send it off for editing. I was waiting to hear back from Muza too, and his ass still hadn't called. I know one thing his ass bet not be over their kissing Cru's ass. There was a knock on my bedroom door.

"Come in!" I yelled. Maria walked in with a frightened look on her face.

"What's up, Maria?" I asked.

'Do you know the name of the young woman that Mr. Muhammad married?" she asked, which I wasn't expecting.

"Cru, what about her?" I asked.

"Do you know her real name? she asked, reaching for the remote to my TV.

"No, what girl you are scaring me," I said, looking at the TV Maria had turned it on News Channel 5 it was a breaking news story. The headline read: *1 dead and 1 arrested*

"Turn it up!" I yelled at Maria, causing her to jump.

"We are on the scene of a murder, details are still being handled. We don't know the motive behind this, but one man has been taken into custody," the reporter said. My heart started racing. Oh Lord, what did Muza do?

"Arrested was Jonathan Boyd, he has been taking to the jail. The victim was Crumari Noble. We are unaware of what took place, but officers said Ms. Noble appeared to be strangled and that it was a scuffle involved. We will have more details later as we get them in," she said, and the news went to a commercial.

I sat there with a blank stare. I couldn't move I couldn't do nothing.

"Nova, you need to call Mr. Muhammad. This is serious," Maria said, giving me a shake. I shook my head.

"I'm sorry. This is just so crazy. Oh Lord, yes I need to call Muza," I said, grabbing my phone and calling him.

The phone just rang and rang, and I was starting to get worried. I jumped out of bed and threw my sweats on. My phone rang, and I jumped to answer it.

"Hello, Muza?" I asked.

"No, this is your daddy. Did you see the news?" he asked.

"Yes, daddy I did, and I'm trying to get in contact with Muza. This shit is crazy. He was supposed to tell her about us and this fake wedding shit," I said.

"What fake wedding shit?" he asked. I didn't have time to go into details right now.

"Daddy, I promise I will tell you everything. Let me call Muza again," I told him

"Ok, baby girl," he said. As soon as I hung up, I dialed Muza again, this time he picked up.

"Hello," he answered groggily.

"Muza, where the hell you at?" I asked.

"I'm at the crib. A nigga got on that drink and passed out," he said. I rolled my eyes.

"So, I assume you don't know what happened tonight?" I asked.

"No, what's up?" he asked.

"Crumari aka Cru is dead, your boy Jon Jon killed her ass, and that shit all on the news," I told him.

"You are kidding, right?" he asked.

"Hell no, did you ever talk to her?" I asked, wondering if he told her the news.

"Yeah, I dragged her ass out of here and told her she better stay away from me. I told her about that Jon Jon shit, and that's probably why she was over there trying to confront that crazy ass nigga. Damn, that's fucked up. Cru did some fucked up shit and hell I wanted to beat her ass, but I would never want no shit like this to happen. Did they say how she died?" he asked.

"They said she appeared to be strangled. Look, I'm going to pack Star and me a bag, and we are coming over to stay the night with you," I told him.

"Nah, it's too late to bring her out. Let me make some calls first then I'll come to your crib," Muza said.

"Ok, be careful. Love you," I told him.

"Love you too," he said.

I took that time to call my father back and fill him in on everything that had transpired. Apparently, he was out of the loop.

"What's up, baby girl? Did you get in touch with Muza?" he asked.

"Yes, his ass was knocked out drunk. He's on his way to stay the night with Star and me," I told him.

“Y’all couldn’t wait for that girl to die so that y’all could be together, huh?” he asked me. I didn’t want to laugh, but I swear sometimes this man had no filter.

“Daddy no, don’t say that. I may not have liked the girl, but I don’t wish death on no one. So, I take it you knew all about this fake ass interview with Muza, right?” I asked.

“I didn’t know the details. He just asked me to get you there, so I had a part in that. Why what he do?” Malcolm inquired.

“Daddy, this man gave me a whole floor for a business to run. It’s called Star Editorials. He wants me to do a magazine or paper something like that show *Living Single* where she had that magazine *FLAVA*, do you remember?” I asked.

“Yeah, boy that nigga got moves. His little slick ass.” Malcolm laughed.

“Yeah, he’s slick alright. So, I walked into the office and saw my name on the door, peep this it said, Nova Muhammad. I’m like what the hell is going on? This nigga tells me that his marriage to Cru was fake down to the preacher and the marriage certificate. The only reason he married her was so she would drop the charges on my case." I sighed, letting out relief as I thought about everything.

"Well damn, I knew it had to be something as to why he was marrying that girl. Well, thank God it was fake. I guess I got to apologize for calling him a dumb ass nigga," Malcolm said.

"Daddy!" I laughed.

"What? That was the dumbest shit ever. I was like this boy done threw his life away. Well, I'm glad that things will finally be good for y'all," Malcolm said.

"Yeah, I hope that we can move forward, and it's been a long time coming. I just want to be a wife, publish this book, and run this company. I'm claiming it now," I told my father with a smile on my face. The door to my bedroom opened, and Muza walked in.

"Hey daddy, I got to go. My man is home," I said excitedly.

"Bye girl," he said. I placed the phone on the night table and watched as Muza came and sat at the edge of the bed.

"You ok?" I asked him. I knew he probably was harboring a lot.

"Yeah, it's a lot to process. You know it's death, and I've never been the one to process death well. I don't know how this may sit with you, and I don't want to start our relationship back with keeping things away from you or just starting out on the wrong foot period, but I need to pay for her funeral arrangements. It's only right. The media is about to eat this shit up. I have to make a press release somewhat about her past but also not giving up too many details," he told me. I lifted the covers and crawled over to where he sat, placing my arms around his neck.

"I'm gone be here every step of the way, and we will get through this together," I told him, placing a kiss on his lips.

Muzaini

When I rolled over, seeing Nova knocked out with Star on her chest, it made a nigga feel like a king. This was all I ever wanted. Damn, who would've thought Nova and I would even get here. I hated the way I treated her after finding out about her past, but that was something that I promised I would never bring up. I wanted to uplift my woman and give her everything she needed to prosper and follow her dreams. I wasn't going to be that nigga that kept reminding her of all that I did for her. We were gone get this money together. Star Editorials was hers, and I trusted she would give it the love that it needed to grow into the next big thing.

I agreed to do one interview today addressing the situation with Cru, and I wasn't gone speak on it again. I was waiting on Darius to get back with me. He had gone and spoke with Jon Jon. I just wanted to hear his side of everything so that I could know exactly what happened. Knowing Darius' ass, he'd probably come from down there and be this nigga lawyer. That nigga was all about a dollar, but shit, I don't blame him.

I eased out of bed and headed to the bathroom to handle my hygiene. I stepped into the shower and turned the shower on letting the water just run over my head. I know I didn't move for about ten minutes. The last two days had my mind on overload. It was like being on a high and not being able to come down. I was tired of being high.

"So, you thought you were gone be able to get naked around me and I not do nothing?" I heard Nova's voice.

I looked up, and she stood outside the shower, pulling her t-shirt over her head. My dick instantly started rising. Man, a nigga ain't felt the inside of Nova body in so long, shit. I opened the door, and she stepped in.

"Girl, your ass was gone get this dick sooner or later. I didn't want to wake Star," I told her. I moved one of her locs out of her face and kissed the tip of her nose.

"Where she at anyway?" I asked.

"Still sleeping. I put her in her bed and turned the monitor on," she said, pointing to the sink where the baby monitor was sitting.

"Oh well in that case," I said, dropping down to my knees.

I pushed Nova on the wall in the back of the shower. Before I devoured her, I just looked at my pussy. Yes, this was mine and was gone forever be mine. That shit was pretty and fat. Nova was tantalizing. Shit, just being in her presence I was ready to eat her ass like a biscuit. I placed my tongue on her center and sucked out her soul. Nova had one hand on the wall, and the other was on top of my head, burying me further in her pussy.

"Shit, Muza!" she moaned.

"You miss this?" I asked because God knows I missed every inch of her.

"Yes," she answered.

I stopped licking and turned her around. I grabbed the both of her hands and placed them on the wall like I was the police and was about to frisk her ass. I found my way to her ass and gave her a deep licking.

All I wanted to do was please Nova in the worse way. This felt like I had to prove myself all over again. It's been so long since we've been intimate. I was ready to feel inside now, grabbing her hands

"Touch the floor," I demanded.

Nova bent all the way over and touched the shower floor. I massaged her clit before easing inside of her. *Lord, don't let a nigga bust in three seconds,* I thought. Nova's shit was tight as fuck. I started out with slow easy thrusts so that I wouldn't hurt her.

"Muza, you know how to fuck me, and I need you to do that," she had the nerve to say.

Well damn, a nigga was trying to be gentle and shit, but if it was the dick she wanted, I was gone give it to her. I started beating the shit out of her pussy. Nova was a freak, and she took the dick well. She was matching my thrusts by throwing that ass back and bouncing on the dick while bent over.

I smacked her on the ass as I continued to slide in and out of her pussy. A nigga didn't know how much longer I could go because she was about to feel a nigga's nut. I slowed down and pulled out, and Nova turned around and got on her knees, taking me in her mouth. I couldn't do shit but throw my head back because Nova had that damn tornado mouth. Her head game was stupid, and she had a nigga's knees weak. I wanted to grab her hair, but I had to hold on to something. You know what made that shit ten times better. She never took her eyes off me when she sucked. She wanted to look me dead in my eyes and see that she took my soul because that's exactly what she was doing. Using her hand to jack me off and that vacuum mouth of hers, I was nutting in seconds. Nova smiled as she continued to suck, and I wanted to pop her ass on top of her head. She sucked a nigga dry and swallowed my kids.

"Damn, girl," I huffed, trying to regain my composure.

Nova smiled and wiped her mouth. Grabbing the soap, she started to wash off her body. Just looking at her body, I wanted to go another round, but I had to get the hell out of here. I followed suit and washed my body also before getting out the shower.

While getting dressed, my cell rang. Looking at the screen, it was Darius.

"Wassup, nigga? It took you long enough," I answered.

"Man that shit was depressing as hell. That boy for real deal snapped all because he loved her, and she played him. I've never seen no dude stressed about no gal like that. Shit, all we do is move on to another one. But considering their history, and how they only had each other while they were in the foster system, Cru was all he knew. I wish the shit would've come out that y'all wasn't really married first before he fucked his life up over that girl. He got a whole son out here that may never see his ass again, and they said old girl left town immediately," Darius said, filling me in.

"I see where you are coming from, but Cru had issues. Her issues were beyond the shit that happened to her. She put that man through all that shit feeding into his head that she was his and they were gone be together and live off my money, and he snapped," I told Darius.

"He just kept apologizing and shit. I hope he doesn't do nothing to hurt himself while he up in there," Darius said.

"He'll be aite. Let me get my ass dressed and get to the office because this camera crew will be there for the interview," I told Darius.

'Aite man, keep yo head up," he said. Hanging up the phone, I started to get dressed.

"You want me to go with you?" Nova asked as she came into the room.

"If you want to. I'm just going to the office," I told her.

"I'll let you handle that, but I am going to my office so that I can get things running. I'm eager to get this off the ground," she said. We both continued to get dressed and got ready to go our separate ways.

* * *

Arriving at the office once Nova got off on her floor, I kissed her and continued up to my floor. The news crew was already there and waiting.

"Thank you guys for being patient with me this morning. I had a hard time getting here," I said, fixing my jacket.

"No problem, we are just thankful that you are giving us and only us this interview. I'm Lacy Taylor, and I will be conducting the interview," she said. Thank God they sent a sister maybe she will have some sympathy for a brother.

"Have a seat," I told her. Lacy sat down. Her camera crew was working the room.

"They're just going to start setting up, and we can have an off the record conversation.

"Ok, that's fine," I told her.

"Anything you want us to know off the record that I may ask during the interview that you don't want anyone to know?" she asked. I knew I shouldn't tell this lady, but maybe it would get her to see where I was coming from.

"Well, everyone knows that Cru and I had history and that she was in the spotlight with me. Eventually, we did break up, and some things came about that I never knew Cru was behind. I was going to get engaged to the woman I'm with now, but Cru was behind some things that stopped that. She and the woman I'm marrying had got into a big fight, and I sort of told Cru I would do anything if she dropped the charges. Cru asked us to get married, so we had a ceremony and all that, but it was private. Once the charges were dropped, I told her that the marriage was fake, as well as the pastor and the certificate. So, if you can avoid that or similar questioning that would be perfect. I'd just rather say we broke up," I told her. Lacy was stunned. I could tell by the look on her face.

"Wow, so you really had a fake wedding? Who thinks to do something like that?" she asked me. I smiled.

"You would do just about anything to protect the one you love, "I told her. A mic was placed on my suit jacket, and the lighting was turned on.

"Ok, so I'm just gone to ask you a little bit about your background. You can tell what you want us to know about you and Cru and anything you know about what took place last night. You ready?" she asked.

"Yep," I said. I watched as the man counted down on his fingers, and we were live.

"Hi, Lacy Taylor here and I'm sitting with the one and only Muzaini Muhammad with an exclusive interview that you will only hear from us about the late Crumari Noble. How are you doing, Mr. Muhammad?" she asked.

"I'm doing ok, considering the circumstances," I said.

"I'd just like to say that we are sorry for your loss. Can you give us a little background about you and Crumari?" she asked.

"Sure. Well, I met Cru about four years ago, and we instantly clicked. Our relationship was up and down, but that's normal now. I always spoke on wanting a family, and that was something that she just didn't want. I never knew the history of why she didn't want kids, and I later found out that she was a foster kid. I end up meeting Nova, and we instantly hit it off. Cru wasn't happy at all, Nova had gotten pregnant with our daughter Star, and I was preparing to propose to her, but something happened that caused us to split up," I said.

"That was the video of Nova and ex NFL running back Delaunn Fleming who at the time played for the Tennessee Titans, right? I saw that he was suspended from the team after the revenge porn?" she asked. Now this hoe knew exactly what it was.

"Yeah that's it, I don't keep up with him but anyways, Cru and I got back together. Nova and I continued to co-parent, and it put a strain on my and Cru's relationship. Long story short, I had found out that Cru was involved with the Jonathan man since they were teenagers, and when he found out about us, he snapped and hurt her. In no way what he did was ok, but I also can't speak on how he felt being lied to and played by someone he loved. I realize Cru didn't have any family, so I will take care of the funeral cost, and my family and I ask for privacy during this time," I said ready to get this shit over with because ain't no telling what else she wanted to ask a nigga.

"Was it true that Crumari had planned on taking money from you, and that's really how you met? She had teamed up with Jonathan, but she ended up falling in love with you. We spoke with him this morning," Lacy asked. I didn't even know she knew about this shit, but that's her job to put a nigga on the spot.

"Yeah that's true, and that's why I broke up with her. I have a meeting to get to, but I hope I was able to answer all the questions you needed," I said, removing my mic. She signaled for the cameraman to turn the camera off.

"Did I say something you didn't like?" she asked.

"It's all good, but I wasn't aware that you had spoken to him, and I wasn't comfortable with that information being disclosed. When you gave me an opportunity to tell you what I didn't want the world to know, you should've told me that you were going to ask me that. But you got your interview, and I'm done talking. I have work to do so my assistant will see you guys out," I told her and excused myself

Novanna

"I can't believe you guys got back together, but I'm happy for it all girl. And I'm so happy to see you're taking charge in here," Tammara said. I had gotten her number out of Muza's phone and invited her to the office to help a sister out.

"I'm just blessed. You know at times it still feels unreal, like any moment, I feel like somebody is gone pop up and cause some more damn drama. I swear every time Muza and I are back on good terms it happens," I told Tam.

"I think everything will be fine as long as neither of you has any more skeletons in the closet. Have you guys decided on a date yet?" Tam asked.

"Nah, I don't even need a date, and I don't want no huge ass wedding. I want a destination wedding with just us, my father, and Ms. Elizabeth," I admitted. It was something that I had been thinking about for a long time.

"Oh, hell no. I have to be in attendance because you will not find the perfect wedding dress without me," Tam joked.

"I was gone have you do that anyway, and of course you can come. My ass doesn't have any friends," I said and felt a little sad as I thought about Kelly.

"Why the sad look when you said that?" Tam asked me.

"I thought about my old roommate Kelly. She was the only person I ever considered a real friend. That girl was like my sister. When she started dating Cru's boyfriend/brother, she changed," I said. Tam busted out laughing

"Bitch, you stupid! Boyfriend/brother?" she asked me.

"Yeah, they were brother and sister because the same foster family took them in, but that shit turned into a relationship. But yeah, she changed. He turned her into a weak bitch. She did so much stuff that I don't think I could forgive her for, especially between Muza and I. We're both mothers now, and that was something I always envisioned us doing together. Now she's got to raise her kid alone because Jon Jon killed Cru," I told Tam. She let out a huge sigh.

"Boy, I swear you guys' lives are so juicy. It sounds like it's made for TV," Tam said. The door to my office opened, and Muza walked in.

"Hey, baby, how did the interview go?" I asked.

"Sup Tam, and man it was just an interview. I rushed through that shit. Ain't too much they're gone get from it but Cru and our past, how she lied, and how we broke up. They brought up that tape shit about you and that jerk ass nigga," Muza said. I rolled my eyes. I thought that shit was behind me.

"Oh," was all I said.

'What y'all got going on?" he asked.

"Girl talk nothing major. We're talking about this destination wedding that I wanted to have," I threw out there so that he could catch it.

"Destination wedding, huh?" he replied.

"It would be nice. I really don't want a huge wedding. Plus, I want to hurry up and marry you before you change your mind," I joked.

"As long as you ain't got no more secrets, I ain't going nowhere," Muza said. I wanted to smack the hell out of him, and Tam was over there cracking up.

"Don't entertain this fool, girl. Get out. I have work to do. I have some people coming in for interviews. I've got to get some folks in this office because it sholl ain't gone run itself," I told Muza. Muza came around to my side of the desk and kissed me.

"I'm going to pick up Star and go over Malcolm's, so stop by when you finish up," he said.

"Ok love," I told him. I watched as he walked out of the office.

"Bitch, help me plan a wedding!" I yelled excitedly. I stood up and started twerking at the desk. I couldn't believe I was for real deal securing the bag and his heart now.

* * *

After five interviews, I had hired a crew and was doing more interviews tomorrow. I was looking to bring on ten people to help me run Star Editorials. After finishing up, I grabbed my things so that I could get to my father's house. I really wanted to go to bed because I was tired. I had to get used to this working lifestyle, but I couldn't complain. I locked up everything and got on the elevator. When I stepped into the lobby, I asked the valet to bring my car around. I was ready to get out of these damn heels.

When my car came around, I removed my shoes and threw them bitches in the back seat. I looked at the time, and it was going on eight p.m., but it felt later than that. Before I pulled off, I texted Muza letting him know that I was on the way. I turned on the radio and jammed to the sounds of Toni Romiti and DC Young Fly new song "Never Thought" .

Never thought that I would give my all like this, but now I'm all in
Never thought I'd be sprung like this
Never thought I'd wanna have your kids
I never thought you could have my heart
Every night you got it, hope these feelings never fade
You touch my body, boy, in all the right places
We switch positions now we making' our bed shake

And now we're kissing' while we're making love faces

I was so into the sound and singing to the top of my lungs because I was feeling this shit; whoever thought that DC Young Fly's crazy ass could sing.

After a nice twenty-minute drive, I pulled into my father driveway. I turned the car off and sat there for a while. I remember the day I first stepped foot here coming to visit my mother. Man, I missed my mommy so bad. In a way, I'm glad Malcolm was my dad because sometimes it felt like she was still here when I was around him. I knew that he really loved my mother, but he also loved Ms. Elizabeth. She was a sweet lady, and I was happy to have her in my life also. I came a long way. I could've still been escorting trying to make a quick buck if I hadn't of went to the Burberry store that day. I smiled and grabbed my purse. Excuse the ratchet moment I was about to have, but I left my shoes in the back seat and walked inside the house barefoot. When I walked in the house, all I heard was Surprise!!

Muzaini

We all stood in the living room waiting for Nova to arrive. I know that I had asked her to marry me before Cru had died that day in the office, but I wanted to do it right, and in front of our family because she did say once everything was taken care of, she would marry me. When she brought up the destination wedding, I looked at Tammara because I was hoping she didn't tell her about the surprise that I had set up.

I had the steps lit up with candles and white roses lining the steps. Everyone was dressed in white, including Star. She wasn't expecting a thing. When she walked into the house, everyone yelled surprise. I laughed because she jumped and looked around taking everything in. I think she was in a state a shock because it took her a long time to say something. The next thing I know she started crying. I walked over to her and closed the door.

"Baby, where your shoes at?" I asked while wiping the tears from her face.

"In the car. My damn feet were hurting. What is all of this, Muza?" she asked. My Uncle Malcolm and Aunt Elizabeth were standing over there along with Star, Darius, and Tammara.

"Come here," I said, taking her to the bottom step and sitting her down.

I grabbed her hand and removed the ring she had on her ring finger that I had already given her. Tammara walked over and handed me another box, taking the ring that I had. I got down on one knee.

"Nova, I know that I already gave you a ring, but I felt you deserved a new ring because we have been through so much, and I felt like that old ring was a thing of the past. I want to create new memories with you. I want everything to start off fresh as if we just met. Remember when we were playing life was a little easy then, but now, we are parents to a beautiful baby girl, and we must set the perfect example for her. You know I think God knew what he was doing keeping us apart. He knew then we might have kept saying we were ready for marriage, but we really weren't. You make me the happiest man on earth, well besides Star, she comes first. But, I can't wait to make you my wife, so again, I ask you Novanna Collier will you do me the honor of becoming Ms. Muhammad?" I asked her.

Man, Nova was crying her ass off. I ain't seen her cry this much ever.

"Muzaini, I would do anything you ask me to, and I most definitely will be your wife," she said. I slid the ring on her finger, and she wrapped her arms around me and continued to cry.

"Come on Nova with all this damn crying, girl," I said, and she started fanning her face.

"I can't help it. These last few days have just been overwhelming and exciting," she said.

"Well, I got another surprise," I told her, handing her an envelope. Nova opened the envelope.

"This can't be?" Nova asked, jumping up and down.

"Hell, when are we leaving? I'm ready to get y'all asses married!" Uncle Malcolm said. Everyone laughed.

"I have to call up my homie Fiyah that owns Cole Funeral Home. He's going to handle Cru's arrangements for me. I was really considering having her cremated since she doesn't have any family," I said.

"What you gone do with the ashes? I don't want that bad Juju around me," Nova said.

"She's got one cousin that I know of. I don't know if they blood related, but I can have my people reach out and see if she wants the ashes. I can have Cru cremated, and we hop on the next thing smoking out of here so that I can make you my wife," Muza said, looking at me.

"Make your calls then," Nova said, looking at her ring. I stepped out of the room, but not before stopping at Tammara.

"Can you try and get in touch with Cru's cousin Kesha?" I asked.

"Sure," she said.

Continuing out of the room, I called Fiyah. I knew he was still probably at work. That nigga lived for burning motherfuckers. Don't get me wrong he has a legit business. Matter of fact he and his wife, Desire, got two funeral homes. Besides the undertaker business, that nigga is an undertaker for the streets and some more illegal shit, but I try to stay away from all that.

"Yo Fiyah!" I yelled into the phone.

"Hold on," he said, turning the radio down.

"What's up, stranger? You big time now don't have time for motherfuckers that grew up with you," he said.

"Aw hell, here you go. Don't do me like that. I'm calling now," I said.

"Yeah nigga, probably because your ass needs something. So, what you want?" he asked.

"I need to make funeral arrangements for Cru. I really want something simple. Cremation and placed in an urn, well that's if her cousin says she wants her remains," I told him.

"Cool, I'll get Desire to contact the coroner and get her body," he said.

"Let me know the damage, and I got you. I'll stop by in the morning," I told him.

"That's what's up, nigga," Fiyah said.

I looked back in the room at my family. They all wore smiles on their faces and was enjoying the moment. I guess that was the code to life. Live every day and moment like it's your last because tomorrow is never promised.

Anguilla

Nova

When I stepped off the jet in Anguilla, I was in awe. Everything was so beautiful. I don't know what made Muza pick Anguilla for our destination wedding, but I was glad he did. It was hot. I looked at my phone, and it said it was 87 degrees. I wanted to get to the beach as soon as possible. We took a limo to the Four Seasons resort we were staying in.

"This place is so beautiful, baby," I told Muza.

"I knew you would like it. You know when we get to the hotel we have to go our separate way until tomorrow," he told me. I pouted

"Yes, I know. I can't wait to marry you tomorrow," I whispered into his ear.

"Lord, I wish you guys cut that out. You will have plenty of time for all that later," Ms. Elizabeth joked.

"I swear all y'all just a bunch of haters." I laughed. We arrived at the hotel, and that was another beauty. I swear this island was so beautiful. We entered the hotel, and Tammara walked off.

'Where is she going?" Ms. Elizabeth asked.

"She's making sure everything is situated for the wedding. She had a person she was working with to plan everything. I wanted a nice simple wedding, and I can't wait until you see what I'm wearing," I told Ms. Elizabeth.

"Oh Lord," Muza said, coming up behind us.

"Well ladies, this is our stop. You girls behave yourselves, and I'll see you tomorrow to make you my wife," he said, leaning in and kissing me passionately. I hated to see him leave, and I wanted to be up under his ass 24/7, but I knew the rules of the wedding. I watched as him, Darius, and my father headed towards their suite.

"Don't get any ideas. You know you don't have to worry about him doing anything crazy," Elizabeth said.

"I guess you're right," I told her.

We received our keys to the suite and headed upstairs. Once settled inside the room we popped open a bottle of champagne and sat around engaged in conversation.

“What did Muza end up doing to Cru?” Ms. Elizabeth asked. Cru was the last person I wanted to talk about the night before my wedding.

“His friend cremated her, and I don’t know what he did with the remains because the girl that he asked if she wanted didn’t want them,” I told Elizabeth. Tammara walked in and plopped down on the couch.

“Ok, can I see my dress now, what if I don’t like it?” I asked. Tammara said she had special something made for me since our wedding was on the beach, and I have yet to see or hear about the dress.

“I swear you are getting on my nerves about this damn dress,” she said, walking over to a bag that was hanging up.

“Now this is from Israeli designer Alon Livne,” she said unzipping the bag. Once she pulled the dress from the bag, a smile graced my face.

“Where is the rest of it?” Ms. Elizabeth asked.

“I love it, Tam!” I said, standing up and grabbing the dress.

“It’s gone look even better once it’s on. Go try it on,” Tam said.

I headed to the bedroom and started to remove my clothes. Tam and Elizabeth came into the room to assist me. I stepped in the gown, and Tam zipped me up.

Lord I thought this was two pieces. The dress was called “Heaven” and it looked like heaven on my body. It really wasn’t a dress. It was a flesh tone bodysuit/swimsuit that was jeweled out in the crotch, breasts, shoulders, and butt area. It had a white long flowing silk overskirt connected at the hips, which flowed behind me. This shit was off the chain. It was different. It was beach and wedding ready. I looked at myself in the mirror, and I watched as a single tear rolled down my face.

Wedding Day

I stood there looking at Muza in his white linen short set. A single tear rolled down my face. I was extremely happy that this was finally about to take place. I was about to become this man's wife. My father stood beside me looking dapper as well. Holding my bouquet tight as hell, I knew it was time. Once the saxophone player started blowing in the saxophone, we took off down the aisle. I felt like I was walking in molasses, and the butterflies in my stomach weren't letting up. This mixed emotion shit I was going through was for the birds. A mixture of excitement, being impatient and scared all in one was a bit much. Then to see Muza crying, that shit took me out. It was a moment that I would forever remember and use against him. He looked nothing like this at he and Cru's "wedding". And you know what here we were on the beach with the sun shining, and he didn't have on no shades.

Muza stepped up and took my hand, placing it in his and giving my father a head nod. He leaned over and kissed my cheek.

"Ok, you can wait on the kisses," the officiant said.

Everyone laughed. As the officiant started the wedding, I got lost in Muzaini's eyes. I saw the first time we met, our first date, our first time, which conceived our daughter, I saw deep in his soul the love that he had for me and only me. We had overcome hell and high water to get to this point in our lives. I know once we are married we will face some more obstacles as we know relationships aren't perfect, but it's nothing that we couldn't handle together.

I heard Muza say, "I Do", snapping out of my trance. The officiant was now talking to me.

"I Do," I answered with a wide smile.

"You may now kiss your bride," he told Muza

Muza leaned in, grabbed my face, and we kissed. We held our kiss for I know five minutes— I ain't seen my boo all night. I was officially Mrs. Muzaini Muhamad.

We walked back down the aisle as the photographer took our pictures. I looked at the purple bouquet that I was holding and held it to the sky showing my mommy, who I wish was here sharing this moment. It was over, and I end up doing all that I set out to do, SECURING THE BAG AND HIS HEART TOO!!!

To whom this may concern.

The day I met Muzaini, of course, we all know the intentions weren't good. Along with meeting him, my own life changed in so many ways. Dealing with the illness of my mother was hard for me, but finding out about my father was even worse. Through those hardships, the changes that came about were challenging. I had to deal with heartbreak, betrayal, becoming a mother, and trying to get my life together.

So much has happened and changed since Muzaini and I exchanged vows. We enjoyed our honeymoon for two whole weeks. It was much needed because when we got back to the city, it was go mode for me, and of course, Muza never stops his grind. We are thinking about more children, but that might come at a different time. Star has all our love for the time being.

I finally launched *Star Editorials,* and it is doing great. We have a physical magazine and online site. You guys probably want to know about the book I was working on, well you're reading it. Thank you, guys, so much for letting me share my journey because every happy ending wasn't perfect getting there.

Love,

Novanna Muhammad

Made in the USA
Monee, IL
11 May 2024